'Horrifying and be...
lifelike in their all-too-human co...
emotionally compulsi... I loved it'
Harriet Tyce, author of *Blood Orange*

powerful and thought-provoking page turner. The definition
of unputdownable'
Katerina Diamond, author of *The Heatwave*

...ttled through *Call Me Mummy*, biting my nails the entire time.
... and gripping, these characters will stay with me for a long time'
Alice Clark-Platts, author of *The Flower Girls*

...'sychologically twisty and utterly gripping – a novel to make
you question the way things appear at first sight'
Lisa Hall, author of *The Perfect Couple*

...turbing, distinctive and peppered with black humour, this is a
...couldn't put down. If you like your fiction dark and compelling,
you'll love *Call Me Mummy*'
Amanda Jennings, author of *The Storm*

...n astonishing debut. Beautifully written, but also raw and
uncompromising, this is a gut-punch of a novel'
David Jackson, author of *The Resident*

...eak but totally compelling and peppered with dark humour.
...e, twisted and totally unputdownable. Shocking and brilliant'
S.J.I. Holliday, author of *Violet*

...lessly original thriller, pushing at the sore edges of motherhood
...ildlessness. I read it with my free hand over my mouth and my
heart in knots. Spectacular'
Kate Simants, author of *A Ruined Girl*

CALL ME MUMMY

TINA BAKER

VIPER

This paperback edition first published in 2021

First published in Great Britain in 2021 by
VIPER, part of Serpent's Tail,
an imprint of Profile Books Ltd
29 Cloth Fair
London
ECIA 7JQ
www.serpentstail.com

1 3 5 7 9 10 8 6 4 2

Printed and bound in Great Britain by
CPI Group (UK) Ltd, Croydon, CR0 4YY

The moral right of the author has been asserted.

A CIP catalogue record for this book is available from the British Library.

ISBN 978 1 78816 524 2
Export ISBN 978 1 78816 523 5
eISBN 978 1 78283 703 9

MIX
Paper from
responsible sources
FSC® C020471

For Jean Mary Baker.
And anyone who yearns to be called Mummy.

Mummy

Christmas kills me.

I vowed I wouldn't do this again, but I'm already inside the shop. When did I decide this?

No idea.

Disturbing.

It's not good for me. I know. But, too late.

I find myself touching hems of tiny pink dresses. Small, smaller, smallest. The baby size guide has nothing for the unborn.

Stop. You can't think of that.

I stroke the snout of a Peppa Pig and drift around the pastel aisles. I'm dizzy with the humid fug but lack the energy to remove my hood. I catch sight of myself in the window's reflection – a giant penguin in my black padded coat. I do not look at my face.

I watch the glad tidings and joy bestowed so carelessly on others. A Polish mother and pregnant daughter, laughing together, talking fast, mirroring each other. A minuscule butterfly T-shirt, miniature lilac socks in their basket. The soft singsong, 'I know, I know,' of a mother hushing a grizzling child. A father whistles, pushing his double-buggy like a chariot, triumphant with his purchases.

Carols clot the store.

A sharper voice: 'Will you give it a bloody rest, Tonya. I've told you, no. You're doing my head in.'

These lucky ones, gifted with the luxury of impatience.

'Tonya. Stop going on. For fuck's sake!' This hissed.

The little girl is gorgeous, if grubby. Her mother, a feral-faced slattern.

I see you: bags from Iceland lazily looped round pushchair handles; tawdry butterfly tattoo on the wrist; giant 'gold' earrings; crude blonde streaks; the parka designed for fashion not function, flapping open. Slovenly.

She drags her daughter by the hand, wrenches off the child's tatty coat. Distracted, distant. Disgraceful.

The girl pirouettes away, as her brother, an angular toddler in a baggy Spider-Man costume, rebels in the pushchair. An older, darker boy trails behind, glowering. Different father. Blended families, they say. I say, lax knicker elastic.

No matter. Her brood, a blessing.

And this shoddy woman has no idea how favoured she is. One of the chosen people – a parent.

She turns to snap at the toddler, 'Just shut your mouth, Darryl,' and there, a final insult. Perched proud above skinny legs clad in gaudy Lycra leggings – her magnificent pregnant belly.

Clenched by hatred.

I.

Can't.

Breathe.

I am wringing a plush bunny in my hands. I force myself to relax my grip and let it go.

The little girl, Tonya, is now trying to get her mother's attention, but the woman is talking into her phone, batting her away. Selfish *bitch*. What could be more important than a precious little one?

Bored, the discarded child wanders over towards the Peppa Pig pyjamas. A pearl before swine.

The notion that I might still make a joke surprises me.

'Silly Daddy,' she babbles.

She looks at me shyly. Children mistrust sunglasses; they like to see your eyes.

I'm holding my breath again.

Then I risk it. 'Silly Daddy,' I reply, and oink at her. She laughs and her face transforms.

I feel something unravel inside. Yet my mouth seems to be smiling. I hope I'm not baring my teeth.

I see my hand reach out to touch her hair. It feels scraggly. If she were mine I would brush it gently every night. I smooth it a little and crouch down next to her. I raise my glasses and she gazes at me. A few wonderful seconds of connection.

Bliss.

She skips over to the miniature boots. I trail behind, entranced. She is the golden goose; if I touch her once more I will not be able to tear my hand away.

She points, 'George!'

'Yes, that's right, darling.'

The wellingtons are for boys, featuring Peppa's little brother, George, and a dinosaur.

She grabs for the rail, then stretches up, offering me one boot. A love token.

'Thank you, sweetheart.'

The low winter sun suddenly floods the store, framing her in light. An angel!

Then I notice it. And I stumble in shock.

A huge bruise.

An oval of teeth-marks around her tender upper arm.

An adult-sized bite.

Freefall.

Nothing is planned. My thoughts fracture. God help me.

I must save her—

But—

Protect her—

Hide—

Quick—

I take her hand and whisper puppies, kittens, promises of mermaids.

She squeezes my fingers.
Then I walk with her.
Out of the shop.
Out of my known life.

Kim

Kim's desperate for a fag.

Darryl's screaming his head off and she really needs a wee as the new baby batters her bladder. Billy Bloody Big Bollocks, booting her night and day. Typical boy. Steve's already bought the latest Arsenal strip 'as an early Christmas present' even though the kid's not due until mid-January.

'Yeah, yeah—'

She props the phone between her shoulder and ear, rooting for her purse, only half-listening to Steve as he goes on about why she needs to pick up grout, as he's still round at Skid's. Lazy fucktard. Like she's got nothing better to do two and a bit weeks before sodding Christmas. And she just knows he's not at Skid's. He'll be in the bloody pub as usual.

Faisal's playing up as he always does when she looks after him. Tough luck, mardy arse. Give your mum a break. Give your dad some peace so he can study and earn a bit more after he graduates. Keep you kitted out in Nikes when you're a stroppy teen, which, by the looks of it, is just around the corner.

She assumes Tonya's singing 'Let It bloody Go' again next to the Princess Elsa headbands. She's not having one – five quid for a bit of plastic. Rip-off bastard Disney.

She pauses, checking off the shopping list in her mind, putting off the moment she'll have to wrestle the shopping home and start bollocking Steve into pulling his finger out to help with the present wrapping for once in his life, because, after all, this is the season of fucking miracles. She can't face a row. She's too tired for a row.

She looks round for Tonya.

Mummy

I hurry her along as fast as I can, her small hand clammy in mine. My shoulders are cringing against a shout that will impale me: 'Stop! Stop, thief!'

Is this what I've become?

I have to go at the child's pace, making agonisingly slow progress. We need to get away, but she sings to herself, skipping and pulling me towards shop windows, stopping to poke some broken piece of shiny earring in the litter by a sickly tree. I push down an urge to pull her along and rush on as fast as my heels will allow.

She has no coat. People will think I am a terrible mother.

I lift her. She is heavier than I thought. I wrap my scarf around her shoulders. I wind her body to mine with my cashmere scarf and tell her all sorts of nonsense in a sing-song voice I've never heard come from my mouth before, rushing towards the corner, to the car.

No!

Somehow I manage to keep walking, albeit unsteadily. We will be captured on car park cameras. Please, God – what should I do?

My legs move as my thoughts swirl. I need to get out of the country. But ports and airlines will be notified, won't they? Some sort of alert goes out. Stephen Fry said so. Do you need a passport for a child this age on the Eurostar? How long does it take police to get CCTV footage? Should I walk home, so they can't trace my car? But if I leave it in the car park would that be suspicious?

'Where's the puppy?'

For a second I don't understand. Then I realise what she's asking. 'At home. The puppy's at my house.'

'Can Mum see it?'

'She'll be along in a minute, sweetheart. She asked me to take you with me.'

'Can Mo come play with it?'

I don't understand what she is asking me. 'Yes, darling. Soon. Yes.'

I have no idea what I'm promising her – sweets, stories. A new life. With me.

Kim

'Tonya!' Kim shouts again and again, louder each time, the edge to her voice catching her throat. People turn to stare, hearing the note of urgency. Two shop assistants are searching messy back rooms because there's nowhere on the shop floor the child can be. They've looked.

'When did you last see her?' asks the security guard, surprised out of his daydreams by an actual incident.

'She was just here. A minute or two, max.'

Was it more? Her belly lurches. She holds her bump.

'Are you sure you didn't see where Tonya went? Faisal?' The lad stares right through her with dark, dopey eyes, so she asks slowly, like a Brit abroad, 'Did. You. See. Where. Tonya. Went?' No reaction. She grasps his shoulders, shakes him roughly, shouts in his face, 'Faisal!'

This is noted by customers, soon to be re-categorised as eyewitnesses.

'Did you see where your sister went?' asks the guard. Faisal shakes his head.

'She's not his sister,' snaps Kim, jiggling her leg, itching for a cigarette. 'Can't you look on the CCTV?' That's what they do on the telly.

She'll bloody skin Tonya's hide when she finds her.

The security bloke stalls, trying to remember what to do next. Suddenly, there's a beat of absolute nothingness. Kim feels the edge of an abyss, dizzies for a moment, then she's frantic, shouting at the shop girls, 'Find her! Just fucking find her!' which she knows will do no good. Pacing, she lunges to yank at Faisal's arm when he starts to wander off, no doubt towards the SportsDirect across the road. She wishes she'd not offered to take him for

8

Ayesha – sure, her mate's got a shitstorm on her own plate, but she doesn't have to do Christmas on top of everything else.

Darryl starts whining, a noise that goes through Kim like cheese wire through a windpipe and she yawps, 'Shut up! Just shut the fuck up!'

And suddenly she knows.

Tonya isn't hiding. She's not playing. She's not lying ill or injured somewhere, which would be bad enough, but right now Kim would take that, because deep in her gut she knows – Tonya's gone.

She bolts on a surge of adrenaline, running into the street to grab coats, shout in the faces of passers-by, 'Where is she? Tonya! Tonya! Have you seen my girl?' The security guard rushes after her, grasps her arm, pulls her back, asks her to stay put, says the police are on their way.

Kim half-listens. Wracking her brain for clues. Where would she go? Did someone take her? Did anyone see? Can they find her before anything terrible happens?

What if it already has?

She hears sirens.

One of the shop girls soothes Darryl as Kim backs away from the terrifying sound and plonks herself on the floor, hugging her knees towards her giant belly. She freezes, straining, stretching beyond physical senses, trying to connect with her daughter. She concentrates hard, unmoving, stony-faced.

Darryl wails along with the sirens.

Mummy

I am pushing through a crowd, which all of a sudden is churning. I hear a shout, a scream, and feel faint.

'What's happening?' – a startled female voice. Several shoppers rush round the corner towards us. I brace.

Sirens.

I battle my instinct to run.

I hear panicked fragments: 'outside the mosque—', 'Terry, quick—', a babble of unintelligible languages into mobile phones.

What's happening? A group of three young men hurtle towards us, swerving at the last minute. Two police officers chase the other way. One shouts into his radio. The other barges by me, jostling my shoulder.

More people running in different directions. A herd mentality grips them, infects me, threatening to sweep us away. I hear a helicopter.

Fear. Sudden, sharp, all around me.

People are always afraid in cities these days. It could be anything: a madman with a gun, a bomb; a madman aiming a lorry as a weapon of mass destruction; a madman with a sword, a knife, a screwdriver.

And I could weep, because in a flash I realise this chaos makes me invisible.

Few fear the mad woman.

I make a snap decision and push my way onto a bus just as the doors close. We move away from the melee.

I keep my head down and hug her close to me, holding her towards my neck because I know there are cameras on buses.

It's hard to grab the rail and support a child, but a woman with a trolley makes space for us as the bus pulls off. I sit heavily and turn away from her eager face to avoid a conversation.

I take off my sunglasses, which would make me look suspicious as darkness swallows us. I rub the bus window with the sleeve of my free arm and the surface reflects my eyes a moment (I need to reapply more concealer) before steaming up again. I can't stop smiling.

I have a child!

She seems to be getting tired. Her head leans heavier against me. I cannot hear what she is saying, mumbling into my chest. She slackens as the rhythm of the bus soothes us. I'll come back for the car later.

I cover her head with my scarf as we get off, a few streets away from my house, although I don't think there are CCTV cameras here. My head darts round, even though this may appear suspicious. Am I being watched?

I walk slowly so I don't disturb her. She has been through enough. My arms and shoulders ache from carrying her. Perhaps she has never been lulled to sleep like this before: held and cherished, safe in someone's arms. I cut through the back way, open the lock with one hand, leaning against the cold stone wall to support her.

As I step through and close my door on the outside world, I breathe a prayer of relief.

Kim

Darryl's forgotten his tears and he's now bouncing up and down, making delighted cheeping noises. Faisal's just as excited, although he's trying to play it cool because he's, like, almost eleven; almost a man. He thinks this must be better than a ride at Disney, not that they've ever been, not even to the French place where it always pisses down. But this! Sirens and lights and driving fast! Uniforms and radios! It's brilliant.

He holds on to Darryl's hand. One of the coppers turns in the front seat and smiles at them, so Faisal hides his grin fast. But, as they brake round a corner, he can't help it and both boys laugh.

Kim heaves. Too much movement. Too much Lynx wafting from the plod who looks like a reject from One Direction. Someone hands her a bottle of water. The taste of sick in her mouth makes her retch again.

As she wipes her lips on her sleeve, leaning her head against the cool condensation of the car window, her other arm cradles her bump.

She can't think. She's all instinct, fighting her rising nausea, urging the driver onwards – to what, she's not sure.

At the station, they pile out of the police car into a blast of icy air, then Kim's engulfed in a flurry of uniforms and questions and Ayesha's there to pick up Faisal, so she must have called her at some point, although she can't remember doing it, and there's sharp voices and bustle and the bitter taste of profound fear and vile coffee. Ask her, and she doesn't remember much of what happens next.

Mummy

Her eyes open as I carry her into the house. She stares through me, groggy, before focusing. Then she starts wriggling and pushing against my arms, so I set her down on the sofa. She scoots to a corner and draws her skinny legs under her. I swallow the urge to tell her to remove her boots from the furniture – pink, scuffed, with a glittery pattern up the sides.

'Would you like a drink, darling? Something to eat?'

She shows no sign of hearing me.

I stand looking down at her, realising I have no idea what to do next.

I leave her to take off my coat, straighten the crucifix in the hall, then decide to make myself a cup of herbal tea. My hands shake.

I keep looking round the door, checking that she's still there – a child, here in my home! I catch myself holding my breath. She hasn't moved. Water boils swiftly in the Bosch kettle. As I pour it over my teabag, she is suddenly at the doorway, which makes me jump. And it's like she has been uncorked.

'Where's the puppy? When's Mum coming? I want a wee. What's that?'

She points at my rack of coloured knives. I realise I am tongue-tied. It feels like a first date.

'Shall I show you where the loo is?'

'Where's the puppy?' She says it louder this time, her chin set, perhaps sensing my deception.

'The puppy is having a little rest because he's very tired.' A white lie. 'Let's pop to the loo, shall we?'

She refuses to take my hand as I climb the stairs. She follows behind me kicking at each step.

'Please stop that.'

She looks up at me and scowls. My heart skitters. I feel so unsure.

I show her to the bathroom and stand outside. There is no lock, so she should be safe. I got rid of Michael's razors a long time ago and lasers see to my needs.

I find my mind is racing, yet towards no clear destination. I need to work out some plan of what to do next. Rather than leaving the country, perhaps I should hide her here for a while – although the Christmas travel chaos might work to our advantage.

I realise I have not heard a sound for some seconds. She is taking so long I push the door open a little to check on her.

She shouts, 'No!'

I pull back. 'It's okay, sweetheart, I just wanted to make sure you were all right in there.' I try a jokey tone, 'Make sure you'd not fallen down the hole.'

She does not react. Or wash her hands, or flush the toilet. She flounces out, squeezing past me to jump down the stairs one by one. Before I dash after her, I see she has left the seat wet, which makes me feel slightly sick.

For the next half an hour or so, questions spill out one after the other, mostly about the puppy. Then, abruptly, she seems to give up. We watch each other warily.

I think of offering her biscuits, but of course I have nothing of the sort in the house. I make my voice light and say, 'Would you like one of these, darling?' She regards the apple as if she has never seen one before. Poor little mite – probably one of those modern urchins malnourished on empty calories.

What a terrible start to her childhood she must have had. But I will care for her. I will love her better.

Later, I will learn the 'Seven Sisters Road Bomb Scare' aided our escape. All eyes and cameras were on a van, abandoned near the mosque, disguised as a broken-down vehicle. It *was* in fact a broken-down vehicle. The driver called the RAC then waited in a local branch of Costa. He emerged to a pandemonium of armed police, bomb squad officers and yapping sniffer dogs.

I send the driver's stupid, startled face my thanks and prayers.
That is the second item on the news.
The first is the abduction of a five-year-old child.

Kim

Hours become confused. Each minute stretches too long. Impatience builds like a heroin itch. Then, with a vicious lurch, it seems to be the middle of the night, or at least teatime and they're somehow back in the flat and Steve sits on the sofa looking crumpled and gormless, like a hollowed-out, rotting pumpkin, and Faisal's gone home with his mum, Ayesha's face tense with shock, and the place is a mess, total chaos, and the bastard police are everywhere and Darryl's in bed and

And Tonya's still missing.

Where is she? Where the fuck is she?

Mummy

I watch her sleep on top of my duvet for a while. Then I carry her to the bathroom and start to unwrap her like a Christmas gift.

I peel off one sock. Her foot looks so fragile. My Cinderella.

I slide the dress from her narrow shoulders, slipping it down her body. The inside of her elbow beckons. I place my thumb there. Can I feel a pulse?

As I gently turn her onto her stomach, I marvel at how pale she is, almost translucent. Hardly a bottom, not even a plump curve of thigh. I run my hand down her bony back, the pads of my fingers feeling her warmth.

She's flawless. Her body so tiny, compared with mine.

She stirs, her cheek squashed against the fluffy, pale pink bath mat from Heal's. I told Michael I bought it in the sale. Another white lie. Not a practical colour, as he pointed out.

Good at sneering, weren't you, Michael?

Yet now, what I would give to hear his jibes.

I lull her back to sleep, the flat of my hand caressing her spine in a lazy circle, my breathing following the pattern. The rhythm, a trance, a spell.

Whispering, "There, there. Hush now."

I should put her into the bed, but I can't bear the thought of the grime on my sheets. The filth she wallowed in – my sweet Peppa Pig. Her nails, a horror. A rind of black underneath. A scab on the knuckles. I bend to sniff her. Something . . . off. Underneath, though, a perfect angel.

Except – I count more bruises. A thumbprint on her thigh, a shadow on her side.

Suffer the little children. What has the poor thing been through?

I kiss the inside of her scrawny wrist but she startles awake and kicks at me. When I reach for her arm, her eyes widen and she wriggles away, flattening herself against the wall tiles. I put my hand out to calm her, but she tries to bite my finger.

The shock destabilises me and I shout, though I don't mean to, 'Stop that!'

I mustn't shout. It will scare her. It scares me. I take a breath.

'Come along, sweetheart.'

'No.'

'But you must.'

'No!'

She fights me because she doesn't understand. I need to take off her clothes to check her body for more injuries.

'We have to get you clean.'

'Go away, you!'

She glowers at me. Children are so funny when they are angry. They exaggerate the frown and the clenched eyebrows and the pout, like a panto dame.

When I used to annoy my sister, Margaret, she'd scowl at me like this. It made me sad to see her pretty face made so ugly.

'Don't you want to get in the bath with these lovely bubbles?'

She shakes her head.

I reach out to remove her other sock and she kicks at me, which makes my heart pound.

I once fostered a feral cat for the local animal charity, SNIP – the Society for Neutering Islington's Pussies. I named her Miss Holly Berry, because she was so prickly. She reminded me of an autistic child, sitting rigid, looking at me with undisguised venom. I sat for hours hunched inside the vast cage provided by the organisation, a piece of cat food on the palm of my hand, willing her to take it.

Eventually, she'd snatch the titbit, then squash herself as far away from me as she could while gobbling it down, radiating hatred as she did so.

If I put my hand on her fur, every muscle would tense and she'd hiss in warning.

I couldn't bear it. They came to collect her after a week.

It wasn't my fault. No one could tame her. I phoned for updates. She went to a special outdoor centre for rescued ferals.

I never visited.

She wasn't like this on the bus.

'Come along, darling.'

She screams and both her legs snap rigid, bucking her body. I manage to grab her foot and she starts shrieking at a pitch that makes me withdraw.

'Be quiet now!' The tone is snappish because I'm rattled. I calm my voice with a deliberate pause. 'It's all right.'

I try to soothe her with words, but she flails her arms at me whenever I get near.

'I'm not going to hurt you, sweetheart.'

I imagine even her hopeless mother might have mentioned Stranger Danger to her. Perhaps that's what this is about.

'Do you want to get undressed yourself? I promise I won't look.' I smile at her.

She wails louder. It hurts my ears.

'This is not acceptable behaviour.'

I cannot say I'm surprised though, given the sort of upbringing she must have endured. She will have to learn some manners. Self-control.

'Come along now.'

I do not want to say her name – so common – but perhaps, just for tonight, as it's something familiar to her.

'Tonya, darling, we must wash before going to bed.'

Goodness knows if she even had a proper bedtime routine with that awful woman; she was probably a crack whore.

Eventually, she lets me peel off the other sock and wraps her arms around her skinny chest. At least she's stopped asking about the puppy.

I reach for her pants and her foot catches me hard in the stomach. I pull at her ankle, perhaps a little more forcefully than I should, but she cannot be allowed to be violent, and then she's screaming and I have to do something to stop her, so I grab her shoulder and wrestle her to me until I'm holding her arms next to her sides and I lift her struggling body off the floor and half lower, half drop her into the bathwater.

The shock quietens her for a moment. The floor and her clothes are sodden with the slosh of water, but they will have to go – I must get rid of the evidence – so no harm done. I can burn them at the bottom of the garden in the fire-pit Michael made, not that we hosted many barbecues.

She sits in the water, looking stunned, and starts a different, quieter crying. More like grizzling. There's something about the tone that cuts through me.

I need a moment.

Down in the kitchen I make myself a calming peppermint tea. I shrug off my damp blouse, pop it into the machine and pull on my favourite Jaeger cardigan from the coat rack in the hall, quickly checking my face in the mirror. Flushed, but in a good way. Upstairs, she is silent at last and I allow myself a small smile of relief.

It is only as I am adding a tiny spoonful of agave syrup to my cup that I think, how stupid! God, forgive me! You should never leave a child unattended in water! They can drown in a saucer of liquid, let alone a deep clawfoot tub.

I scald my hand as I accidentally knock the cup against the chopping board and I run back up to her, taking a deep, steadying breath before I push open the bathroom door, afraid of what I might see.

She sits in the water, glaring up at me.

Kim

Kim feels nothing for long minutes. The next second, she thinks she might die before she takes another breath.

All the strangers around her, so many faces gawping at her like she's in a bastard aquarium, throwing the same questions her way, again and again, as she bats back the same non-answers.

Those in uniform mill about in a space that's too small even without them clogging it up, getting in her way but telling her absolutely fuck all. She wants Ayesha, but her friend had to leave to give Faisal his tea and see to Mo. Cock-head Khalid wouldn't do it. Not for one night. Not even a night like this. Mo's a real handful, but you'd think Khalid could step up for once.

She looks to Steve and is shocked to see him quietly crying, which is almost as disturbing as the police crawling all over the flat. She's never seen him like this in public, apart from that time he was totally kaylied and Arsenal were so appalling she almost understood.

She doesn't think he's been drinking today, but Christ, she wants one. If she did have one though, she might never fucking stop.

And she yearns to smoke, craving a fag to punish her lungs, otherwise she might get the scissors and stab herself in the leg.

She hauls herself up from the sofa. In the kitchen, she rummages in the bits and bobs drawer, rootling out the pack of 'emergency' cigarettes she's hidden in an empty Tampax box.

She catches a pinch-faced woman officer watching her. Hair in the tightest bun she's ever seen. Judging her. And she'd given up entirely before this. Almost.

She spits, 'Want one?' stabbing the cigarette in her direction. Marlboro Lights – hardly worth inhaling.

The copper looks away, thin lips biting back some comment, registering another black mark against her: the slack mother who loses one kid and poisons another.

Questions keep coming at her through air that's become weird, almost liquid. The words make little sense, but she catches some of the hard edges.

She clutches the fag like it's a life raft.

She lists Tonya's friends and their addresses, as many as she can remember. Scrolls through her phone to get numbers she has for some of the mums from her school and Darryl's playgroup, although she's already called all of them. Steve hasn't got a clue. He holds his head in his huge, dusty paws, glancing up at her with his washed-out blue eyes. Trying to catch hers. Like she can help.

Her knowledge of Tonya's small social circle should make her feel useful, but doesn't.

She's not sure which is worse, the professional sympathy from the police liaison woman, or the clinical frostiness from the one poking round the flat. Others are upstairs, going through Tonya's things.

'If I knew you were coming I'd have hoovered.'

The pathetic attempt to lighten the mood dies in her mouth and she feels a slither of shame. She sees the look the stony one gives her and agrees with it.

Steve gathers himself and offers to make her a coffee, but she can't keep still as it is, like she's speeding. Her lips are quivering, making her look like a nervous dog, both snarling and smiling, and they won't let her roam the streets because they have more stupid questions and why the fuck haven't they found her girl yet?

When, after more of this shit, Liaison Woman says she should try and get some rest, she laughs with a sharp bark that makes her cough. Steve parrots, 'Try and get some shuteye, hey, babe?' and she says, 'Don't be so fucking stupid, Steve,' and he snaps, 'Don't call me fucking stupid,' and she sees the police watching them argue, as if that's got anything to do with any of it.

She catches the glance one of the uniforms sends Steve's way – a whisper of a suspicion. But she knows this doesn't have anything to do with him.

It pisses her off. Every bit of this fucked-up scenario. She's raging inside, *Stop wasting time here! Do something! Just fucking do something! Go and find her!*

She goes upstairs for a wazz – to get away from the coppers more than anything – and sits, slumped forward as much as she can over her belly, frowning, promising Tonya she'll find her and bring her home soon. Telling her it'll all be okay. Whispering, to her daughter and to herself, 'Hold on. Just hold on!' like a mantra from that free meditation course at The Stress Project.

She must be in there for longer than she thought because Steve taps on the door and whispers, 'You all right, babe?' like she could ever be anything close to all right.

She washes her hands over and over before she comes out. Glances in the mirror – can't see herself.

When she opens the bog door, she notices some kid playing dress-up in a police uniform, rifling through Tonya's plastic jewellery box, and she roars, 'DON''T TOUCH THAT!' and she'd have punched the cunt, only Steve grabs her as she lunges for the officer and pins her arms as she screams some other stuff that she doesn't exactly understand, but it's good to struggle against Steve's bulk and kick his shins, although the knock-off Uggs don't connect with any satisfying force, and she tries to head-butt Liaison Woman because she's so fucking calm and whispering stuff right up in her face, which is a dangerous place to be just now.

Mummy

The smell of her now she's clean and dried!

I rinsed away the grime, which seemed to be ingrained in her pores, and a faint scent of what might have been chicken fat. I scrubbed the black from under her nails. The ablutions, a battle. I have not been able to comb out her hair yet.

Her breathing is faster than mine, but she seems calm enough now she's sleeping.

I made her hot chocolate from the hidden cache I keep for emergencies, and popped in some Rescue Remedy. Only a teensy, tiny drop. I've run out of the real thing, so brandy had to do. It is basically the same, though. I read that all homeopathic tinctures are rubbish, no matter what Prince Charles says, although I do agree with him about organic. I had to do something to stop those shrill cries, and, somehow worse, the whimpering.

Now I curl myself around the curve of her back. I wish I could wiggle out of my nightdress and press my skin to hers. But I daren't move. I hardly breathe in case I wake her.

I wish Michael were here to share this.

I am too excited to sleep.

From the moment I clasped my sister's doll to my chest, I yearned for a child of my own. I knew it would take a miracle. And here she is!

*

In the morning I know the precise moment she wakes. I force my sticky eyelids apart. I forgot to remove my mascara last night, but then I had so much else on my mind.

She looks at me, blonde lashes framing her grey eyes. It wasn't a dream! I feel the sting of tears and thank our Lord. I am so grateful that she's here. I'd like nothing more than to take her in my arms and hug her. But she observes me from across the bed – cautious, confused.

In slow motion she places the sole of her foot against my side. I feel its coolness. The first contact she's initiated. I smile at her. Then she pushes against me, as if to roll me away from her to the other side of the bed.

Cruel.

But she isn't used to me yet. She's probably disorientated.

'Would you like some breakfast, darling?'

She shakes her head but her face says otherwise.

I leave her beneath the covers as I rush down to the kitchen. Do I have anything suitable for a little one?

I decide on an egg. Free-range. Nutritious. Hands wobbling, I set the pan on a low heat to poach it, and dash back to the bedroom. When I try to scoop her up, she braces against me, so I have to set her down and attempt to shepherd her towards her breakfast. After she uses the bathroom, she comes down the stairs on her bottom. Bump, bump, bump. My T-shirt swamps her.

I herd her towards the kitchen table, saying, 'Sit here, please, sweetheart.'

I have to put on another egg. It's taken so long to get her down here, the yolk has congealed like an alien eyeball and my saucepan has almost boiled dry, leaving a metallic tang in the air. I must be more careful.

When I finally put the egg and sourdough toast in front of her, she regards it as if I have given her toad spawn and hemlock. She looks at me, her face somewhat pinched, and reaches out in slow motion to poke the egg white. She pulls a face as she squishes the yolk between her fingers.

'Yucky, yuk, yuk!'

'Stop that! It's disgusting!'

She freezes. Then tucks in her chin, glowering up at me, and mumbles, 'Don't like egg.'

I feel a rush of rage from my past, when Daddy pasted me for not eating every single morsel of my dinner. Those hellish mealtimes, with Margaret on one side of the table, me the other. Never a harsh word for her. But then, she would cut up her food into small, neat mouthfuls, clean her plate and lay the cutlery quietly against it. My sister's table manners were exemplary.

Perfect, beautiful Margaret.

How I hated her.

I snatch the plate away from the child, swallowing back bitter memories. 'Please yourself.'

I try to wipe her hand with kitchen towel, but she wriggles and starts to pull her arm away from me.

'No! You need to be clean.'

'Gerroff! Gerroff me!'

'Stop that right now, young lady!'

'Where's my mum?'

I ignore her.

Her voice becomes louder, 'I want my mum!'

'That's enough now!'

We have a small tug of war with her fingers, then—

'Fuck off, you!'

I am so shocked I can neither speak, nor move.

Seeing my appalled face, she laughs – a nasty sound.

To hear a child shout such profanity, one so young, is beyond me. What sort of people has she come from? How could they corrupt her innocence like that?

I prayed for a child for so long, but in some dusty nook of my mind, I hear Mammy's voice saying, 'Be careful what you wish for.'

That afternoon, I leave her sleeping on the sofa, close and latch the shutters at the front windows and hurry away to collect the car. I drive back in heavy, school-run traffic, my arms trembling as I grip the wheel.

I'm so preoccupied, I forget to signal and a blast of a vengeful horn makes my heart race. Then I almost miss a turning. Parking near the house is even more cut-throat than usual and I have to drive around the block twice before I find a space I can squeeze into on the third attempt. Reversing is not my forte. Relieved, I walk briskly round the corner and hurry up the garden path.

I halt, sensing something amiss.

Movement. There—

My letterbox opens a little, then snaps back shut. It widens again. One wary eyeball peeks out, then disappears with a clunk.

When I open my door, I find her in the hall, hiding her naughty fingers behind her back, slouched against the wall.

Looking out, clattering the letterbox, trying to attract attention, or escape! And I've only been gone for thirty-seven minutes.

There will have to be some changes.

Kim

Outside the window, scabby pigeons rustle in their sleep. Three photographers sip drinks from containers one of the reporters brought back from her coffee run. A police officer stamps his feet to get the feeling back in his toes.

Inside the flat, Kim can't breathe. There's a crushing heaviness on her chest. Like that time she fell asleep, pissed, naturally, in a Wonderbra that was too tight.

She needs oxygen. She tries again. Two tiny sips of air.

Steve's mum, before she conked it, reckoned Kim had asthma. Two-packets-of-fags-a-day asthma at her worst. She quits every time she falls pregnant. But then—

Kim clenches her muscles to force a little more air into her lungs. Not nearly enough. She panics and flails, but can't move her arms, which are pinned tight. She tries to open her eyes, but the awful realisation hits her.

Her eyelids have been sewn shut.

Something straddles her chest. She feels a rush of terror for the baby – he'll be crushed. Above her, a malformed bird of prey's body and some kind of sneering female form. A smile slimes across what might be its face.

And she fights to get it off her, thrashing and twisting this way and that and—

She gasps awake, drenched, mouth wide in terror, arms caught beneath the duvet. She drags herself up to sitting, realises where she is and looks in all the corners to make certain she's alone in the bedroom. Then she hears Steve downstairs and Darryl's nonsense chatter. And she takes a deep breath, drawing air into her chest, muscles relaxing, almost sobbing in relief.

Then she remembers.

And that punch in the gut is worse than the nightmare.

Tonya.

Later, she watches the fuzzy images of her girl on the TV, leaving Peacocks with that terrible dark shape – you can't even tell if it's a man or a woman. The footage plays on the news, between the seasonal glee of schmaltzy adverts and trailers for a rerun of *Elf*.

The same images replay in Kim's mind in an endless, accusing loop.

Mummy

My house is detached. My garden wall is high and the wisteria, now gnarled and bare, even higher. Plus, London is such a noisy cauldron at the best of times, at my insistence we installed triple-glazing. Michael grumbled about the cost, but I paid with my own money.

No one can hear her.

Except I can. Her constant whingeing pummels my ears until I feel raw. What is she crying for? I have rescued her.

Yet on and on it goes. She wailed for most of the night. I was forced to get up and come downstairs, leaving her alone in the bed for a few hours. I simply could not take any more.

This morning she was hiccupping, her pale face streaked with unpleasant secretions.

They adapt quickly though, little ones, don't they? By the time she's settled, she won't remember the traumas in her past, the poor thing, or this period of shock, finding herself so suddenly in this strange new sanctuary.

If only I could take some of those refugee kiddies too, I could be like Mia Farrow, or Angelina Jolie. Although things didn't turn out so well for them in the end, did they. As for Madonna, she is more an attention-seeking Magdalene than the self-appointed Saviour of the African Orphans, in my humble opinion.

I don't understand why people mock these celebrities. If you have a lot of love to give, like them, like me, it's your God-given duty to help in any way you can. Save as many as you can. Perhaps people think they are being greedy with so many rainbow urchins clinging to their designer skirts. Or perhaps they are too pretty. Too thin.

Other women do not forgive you that.

I was deemed too thin.

That judgement killed my hopes, my dreams. As if I should turn into a wallowing, blubbery sow. As if the fat I sloughed off and fought, tooth and nail, to keep at bay could make me a mother.

I did everything the medical experts advised and demanded. I gave up so much: smoking; drinking; much of my inheritance; my dignity. I just could not seem to put on enough weight to satisfy the draconian doctors. But I could not risk a return to the maggoty, bloated body of my youth.

The miracle procedures were a hormonal hell. And for what? Mine was a hopeless quest. The promise of my own child dangled in front of me by the great gods of science, and then denied me by cruel Mother Nature. Life snatched from me, clawed from my womb. Again and again. Hope dying on the bathroom floor, in an ambulance, in a hospital bed.

I was never to be a mother.

I would read about the enchanted lives of the famous uber-mummies, in their magical, expensive bubbles, and weep. Unfair that they should have so many when I ached for just one. Although I didn't begrudge them those children. Not at all. Unlike some – female journalists who snit and snark and snipe, with their perfectly procreated babies wrapped snug in their smug beds.

But celebrities don't do much of the actual mothering themselves, do they. An army of nannies and assistants at their disposal. But surely the point is to prepare a child's food, wipe their smeared faces and clean up after them. To be there with them, rather than far away on some film set. A good mother keeps her children safe without the help of bodyguards. Your job as a mother is to nurture and guide and offer advice. To give them a moral compass.

I vow to be here for Tonya, although I must never call her that again.

Tonight I will pray for a new name to come forward for her.

Kim

She feels untethered.

Once she'd thought, briefly, before she realised what a useless, though likeable lump he was, that Steve could be her rock. But really, that turned out to be Tonya's role. Being a mum was the thing that grounded her, stopped her from being so self-absorbed. Stopped her from being such a monumental fuck-up.

She knows that's the wrong way round. She's supposed to be the grown-up. She's the mother. But what kind of mother? There were a few precious moments since her kids were born when she actually believed she was doing a fair enough job. Had that faint glimmer of confidence – like letting yourself believe England can win the World Cup.

Stupid cow.

Now Kim's aware of a room full of dead air. She sees faces, lots of them, although she can't focus on any one. She registers a grim-set mouth here, a pair of glasses there, a bright blonde hairdo moving to her right, but her attention's gripped by the lenses, all pointing towards her. Like she's facing a firing squad.

She hated smiling for school photos, not that her mum ever bought one. She cringes when anyone snaps at her with their phones, loathes images of herself on Facebook. The only time she doesn't feel achingly self-conscious being photographed is when she's with the kids. Holiday pictures show her looking towards Tonya or Darryl. One or two rare images show her laughing up at the lens, perhaps when Steve's said something daft.

She's superstitious, almost like those primitive tribes who believe cameras can capture their souls.

Tonya's inherited her mother's distrust of lenses. The only good pictures of her are sideways on. Recently, if the little sod knew you were trying to take a photo, she'd pull a face or run away. The image the police use is a recent one of her laughing, taken at an angle, so her snaggle tooth shows as an 'identifying characteristic'.

Kim can't make out the words the copper's saying. Police babble. She switched off after half an hour of Liaison Woman and some press officer droning on before they were brought through to the media room. The briefing meant little to her.

Now she knows she's not asleep, but she wishes she could wake up. She hears her name, Tonya's, Steve's. The shock numbs her to everything and the lack of sleep makes her slow and stupid.

Kim's mistake in this strange scenario is to sit, arms crossed, and stare back at the lenses. Like she's hypnotised, or drugged. But she refused the Valium they offered, even though, because of her pregnancy, it was a low dose.

Ayesha came round early to help her get ready and look after Darryl during the press conference. He likes playing with her youngest, Faisal. Tonya has an epic crush on her eldest, Mo, who's only twelve but already has a fuzz on his top lip.

Ayesha agreed about the Valium.

'Slippery slope, innit.'

Kim can't afford to be anywhere near that particular slope.

She sits rigid in front of the cameras, saying nothing. Tears do not fall, which is a known requirement in these situations.

Only Kim didn't get the memo.

Gathered journalists will have to spin a different tale to the one starring a tragic, preferably attractive, wholesome mother. She has failed to play her part. It's the mother's despair cameras crave at this stage.

Steve, though, sitting forward, desperately eager and puppyish next to her, is a natural: weeping on cue, reading the statement, begging anyone who knows anything about 'our little girl' to get in touch.

Liaison Woman seems well chuffed with his performance, although news outlets, the public, the police themselves – none of them trust a man so much at this stage. The father is always smudged with a scent of mistrust when things like this kick off.

Back at the flat, Ayesha says, 'You should've got your roots done, hun.'

For a second, Kim fears she'll smash her knuckles into her friend's pretty nose. But she surprises herself with a single 'Ha!' It sounds weird and tastes sour. She reaches in her bag for her fags. Remembers she's not smoking.

On the table, her phone buzzes. She holds her breath. Desperate for news. Dreading news. She daren't pick it up. Ayesha can't stand it any more and answers, handing the phone to her.

It's only one of the mums from the estate asking if she needs anything.

She wants to scream, 'I need my fucking daughter back! Get off the line, you dozy fucking cow!'

When her breathing calms, as she bites the skin around her nails, she asks Ayesha, 'How do you think the press thing went?'

Ayesha tells it like it is. 'Could've been better.'

'Do you think it'll get her back?'

Ayesha mutters a prayer in her own clipped language, then adds, 'If Allah pulls his finger out.'

She sips her coffee, then puts a hand on Kim's arm, gives it a squeeze. 'Could've been worse, hun.'

Her mate's tone tells Kim this is yet another thing she's fucked up.

Mummy

Thanks to a fractured night, I'm antsy with nerves, so I have taken a little medicine, just a sip, because I must be calm now, to think, to plan. Now I am thinking for two.

I also need an afternoon nap, so I take her with me to bed. The idea is not a success.

I didn't expect this constant weeping. It slices through me, hour after hour. Sleep is impossible.

Are a child's cries calibrated to cause maximum irritation? If you give birth to your own baby, are you attuned and therefore immune? Is it only the cries of other people's children that hurt so?

It's torture. How do you not dash their brains against the wall?

But then, as I start awake yet again, I wonder if this might be a test. I need to prove myself worthy of being a mother.

I pray, but the pains in my head bloom blacker with the lack of sleep.

It's not how I imagined it would be. And I can't ask for help. Partners, friends, grandparents, sisters – no one left in my life any longer. There will be no respite care.

There is no milk in the fridge either.

This fatigue makes me useless. I need to order an Ocado delivery as soon as I can see straight and assemble my thoughts clearly. Then I remember, I can't – the driver might hear her screams. I need to think this through.

The other thing I'm not prepared for is the constant terror. Will she stop breathing in the night? Will she snap her neck as she thrashes in a tantrum?

Will we be discovered?

When I was afraid as a child, Mammy would instruct, 'If I listen to Our Lord I will dwell secure, at ease, without the dread of disaster.'

But I never dwelled secure. I was never at ease.

In daylight, her whining continues to wear on me, so I try to distract her. I attempt to engage her in conversation, but receive only single-word answers. I read to her, which seems to soothe her a little. I offer her food, which she refuses to eat and pushes away. Then she throws herself on the floor and screeches. It assaults me. I can't abide waste.

I put on music to drown out the cries and leave her with a plate of fruit on the table. I have to calm myself. I can't be around this maelstrom. Or the temptation of grapes. Her anger makes her lovely face so ugly. Her sharp cheekbones I would die for, but in her fury, I see a glimpse of her mother. A ferret-like hardness.

But this is my calling.

No one said it would be easy.

Kim

The dream is more a feeling than a story. Bad things happening to Tonya. There's no way she can let herself slide back into that.

For the next hour, the clench of anxiety in her belly keeps her awake, turning and fidgeting and nervy. She could kick out at Steve's heavy leg, but she suspects there's as much trauma beneath his resting muscles as there is in her own taut body.

Losing her girl has shaken something at her core. She asks herself what could be worse than losing Tonya.

Nothing.

Except losing everything else. Darryl. The baby. Steve. Losing her fucking mind.

And there's something that frightens her as much as that.

She's to blame for Tonya's disappearance, everyone knows that. But what if awful things happen to the other kids, because there's something bad inside her?

What sort of mother does that make her?

She sighs like a balloon deflating, and there's an echo from Steve's side of the bed. She tries to lie still, knowing that if she gets out of bed Darryl will wake up, and it's hard to deal with his demands when she's so shattered, running on fucking empty.

What effect is this having on the poor little sod? Will he be scarred for life by all the disruption and her snapping at him for every last little thing and their preoccupation with 'the investigation'?

Tonya's always been good at getting more attention than her brother.

Perhaps Darryl's young enough that this will slide off him. Perhaps he won't remember any of it. But Kim remembers things she'd rather not from when she was a kid, so she's not optimistic.

As if her thoughts have been too loud, right on cue, Darryl starts grizzling. Steve sleeps on as she swings her legs out of the warmth and pads next door to see to her lad.

His face looks blurry and a little snotty. She sits on the side of the bed. They're going to get bunk beds when the baby's old enough, so the brothers can share. She strokes Darryl's head. But he wants more, so she budges up and lies against him. Her giant belly makes it impossible to curl around him snugly, but she does her best.

That's all she can do.

Mummy

The sobbing jags at night continue.

After three days of this nightmare, she finally eats. Oatcakes. Then she vomits. One of my T-shirts ruined – annoyingly, the pastel pink Kenzo. And she wails again. She is making herself ill.

In desperation, I rummage through drawers until I find the keys Michael and I never had use for and I lock her in the spare room. She screams louder. I switch on the radio, but her noise still disturbs me. As I apply my make-up – disguising the dark circles, covering the old scars, making myself presentable for the outside world – my hands are unsteady and I am disappointed with the result. I have always found my reflection difficult.

I turn up the music and close the front door on her nonsense, stepping out into the damp chill. Taking a long, refreshing breath.

But I mustn't dawdle.

I hurry to the bus stop on the main road. The W7 passes from leafy Crouch Hill to the uninspiring north London buildings and uninspiring north London locals of shabby Stroud Green Road. I get off at Finsbury Park station (beyond vile) and walk around to the hideous Lidl supermarket I've never visited before, buy everything I can think of to childproof the house, and rush around grasping foods that she might be used to. By the time I reach the till I'm sweaty. I discreetly check my make-up in my hand mirror, then pay for cereals with lurid cartoon characters on the packs. She refused my organic artichoke puree.

*

I return sticky, my chest tight.

When I walk up to her room, I see the key wiggle in the lock. I remove it, bend and put my eye to the hole. Her bony finger jabs towards me.

I busy myself shoving plastic into plugholes as she sits at the kitchen table, gulping down a bowl of Frosties with full-fat milk – the first time I've had such things in the house. I remember liking the cereal as a child.

I've also bought a soft toy rabbit for her to play with.

After this topsy-turvy breakfast, when we should really be having afternoon tea, she falls asleep on the sofa, clutching the bunny. I stroke the softness of her cheek. She seems to flinch.

When it's dark, I lock her into the spare room once more, hoping I will finally get some rest. But the night is a bad one. Each time I wake hearing her sobs, I feel so jangled I have to get out of bed and pace until my breathing calms.

I do not go in to her. I can't let bad habits take hold.

In the morning, the toy is wet with either tears, mucus or sweat. I put on my rubber gloves to pick it up and wash it.

To amuse her, I offer paper and crayons. A puzzle book from the supermarket. She ignores both.

I will not provide electronic devices. They ruin children.

Michael used to mock me as 'a technophobe'. But I showed him, learning to order online being my most satisfying breakthrough. So, on days I can't face the outside world, I can still shop.

I try to talk to the child, or pray with her, but when I attempt to engage her, she shouts, 'No!' or, 'Shut up!' or, 'Leave me alone, you!'

This too shall pass. One of Mammy's maxims.

My lack of sleep brings on the inevitable migraine. In the afternoon, I lock her door and go to my room, pushing in the newly purchased silicone earplugs, and I try to sleep it off.

The stress of sleep deprivation produces cortisol, which is very ageing.

'Love must be patient and kind.' This child tests me on that.

How – after less than a week, as I hear her shrieks build once more, making any rest impossible – just how does it come to this?

I ached for, yearned for a child.

But now, what I crave more than anything else, is sleep.

Mumsnet

How long does it take for an adopted child to settle into a new home? Mine won't stop crying. (8 posts)

JJames

Adopted and foster children will have experienced more trauma in their lives than others and this reflects in their acting out. These days they don't just give out perfect babies.

Candycane3

It's never plain sailing settling in an adopted child. But it's worth it!!!

YumMum96

Most of these youngsters have moderate to severe issues. A child psychologist said so.

BabySummer

I have one who cries all the time too and I'm gonna be honest I just leave him to it. Don't feel bad. He'll get over it.

JudithfromSwansea

I'm glad I was adopted. I love my adopted parents more than words can tell.

KB332

You must expect some behavioural problems. But there are many agencies to offer support and advice. It's also good to talk to others who are adopting children of a similar age.

LittleBags

Message deleted by MNHQ. Here's a link to our Talk Guidelines.

Sunnysmiles

After a few months, there'll be no difference between them and your biological children. Sending you love and hugs.

Kim

Kim's sister, Heather, fucked off to Sydney as soon as she bagged herself 'a gorgeous, filthy Aussie barman'. They keep in touch via email and WhatsApp. Just texts. No Skype or Zoom or FaceTime. If Kim sees her sister's face it unsettles her, but words are okay.

In any light, Heather looks like their brother, bastard Dave. She's got that hardness about the eyes, although Heather's are a paler grey, and, same as Kim, she rocks the 'don't fuck with me' jawline. Kim's skinniness feminises the overall impression a little, whereas her sister's width – jaw, brow, general girth – means she could pass for a bad drag queen.

Kim doesn't want to see anything or anyone that reminds her where she's from, what she and Heather went through.

Heather was shocked out of sleep on the other side of the world by some journalist before Kim got her act together to phone her. She called to ask, 'Do you want me to fly over?' It was an easy answer, even before they addressed who the actual fuck might pay for the trip.

'No. There's nothing you can do this end.'

'Are you sure? I could help with Darryl. You'll need an extra pair of hands when the baby comes.'

Does she think this bastard mess will still be carrying on when the baby comes? That Tonya won't be home safe by then?

Kim says, 'No, you've got enough on. I'm sure. Thanks.'

She's not sure of anything any more, but she hears Heather's relief on the line. She's got her own concerns, her own kids. The jolly barman isn't so jolly after years of hard partying, despite the sunshine and beaches.

And even though Heather irritates the buggery out of Kim, she's always felt protective of her younger sister. She hasn't got the energy for that at the moment.

Heather's voice wobbles thousands of miles away. 'I'm so sorry, Kay-Kay.' The old, tender nickname that never had much of an airing.

'So am I,' says Kim. 'So am I.'

She almost regrets biffing away her sister's offer when some Facebook cunt spills the beans about the drug dealing – not that's she's done any of that for months and in any case it was just a bit of weed for mates, or sometimes when cash was shorter than usual, mates of mates, and yes, sometimes it was more than just a bit.

Saint fucking Steve's name is nowhere to be seen on the post and it was his idea as much as hers.

The police are on it like pit bulls on a puggle. Steve and Kim are summoned to the station. The 'lead detective' talks about it like he's delivering a sermon. Liaison Woman looks sad and disappointed in her. Uniformed bitch-features looks pained, but that might be because her bun's pulled as tight as Botox. What is it with these copper cows and their Croydon facelifts?

Kim hisses at the main guy, 'What the fuck's any of this got to do with Tonya? Why haven't you found her yet?'

He eyeballs her with disdain. She stares him down.

'Initially this was taken as an opportunist abduction. But we need to take this new information into consideration – some form of retaliation, or threat over territory, or an unpaid debt, perhaps?'

'Like I'm fucking Scarface now?' snorts Kim. 'This is the Andover Estate, not *Breaking Bad* country.'

'Kim. Leave it.'

It's the way Steve says her name now that drives her frigging insane. It sounds like a warning. Either that, or he's wheedling and creeping round her. He shakes his head. Every time he talks to her it's with a kind of exasperation – a heavy disappointment in everything she's ever done, or failed to do, something she's said, or not said, or just who she fucking is.

After the police dismiss them, she gives in and reaches for a fag on the short walk back to the flat, and catches another look from Steve.

'Just one.'

And it is just one. In the circumstances that's a fucking miracle.

The freelance photographer who trails behind them, who seems to have set up shop on the estate, catches a nice snap of the fag and the pregnancy bump.

Steve's face kills her.

She knows he thinks all this is her fault. It is. She's a crap mother – so sue her. It happened while she was supposed to be looking out for Tonya. She can't take that back.

Steve's always been better with Tonya. Daddy's girl. Made Kim jealous sometimes.

And when he thinks she's tuned out again, as Kim's prone to do right now, she'll turn her head and catch him looking at her as if he's never, ever seen her before.

It's worse if they're on their own, so they don't go to bed at the same time. That's an easy lie – to 'take a nap' in shifts and let the other one 'watch for news'. Steve spends hours talking to the coppers. More hours on Facebook, updating posts, appealing for information, like the police advised. Reading out a few good wishes to her, like she cares a toss about anyone's wishes. Wish in one hand, shit in the other – see what fills up first.

She jumps every time she hears the ping of an alert, or the vibration of the phone against the table. That helpless, horrible pause before she or Steve lunges for it.

Their unspoken fear – what if they've found a body?

Unless someone's calling to say, 'She's safe. We've got her. We're bringing her to you right now,' they should all just fuck right off and leave her be.

And Steve can fuck even further off.

That night in bed, when he says, 'What do you reckon we should do for Christmas?' she wants to stab him in the eye.

The trolls are all over the drug story. Steve shakes his head when she asks, 'How bad is it?' He doesn't read them out to her, the vile words of the haters: those who judge as a hobby; those who judge as a calling. Nearly all women. A few cockless cowards.

And the newspapers are all over it, stirring the bile. If Kim had given an interview, an Exclusive, they'd have portrayed her steeliness as 'Mother Courage', 'Brave Kim'. Even better that she's pregnant, about to pop.

Instead, there are snide whispers. Quotes from people who claim they know her. Some twat from school she can hardly remember. People saying all sorts on forums. Sticks and stones, slurs and slanders.

A headline that catches and hooks the public's imagination, from some-one's quote – 'SCUMMY MUMMY'.

Blame by different names, blame in different shades. She knows this. Even though she doesn't read any of it herself, Kim can't not know. She reckons she deserves it.

She hangs her head out the bathroom window and breathes in the glo-rious night air of north London.

She also knows – although she tries not to, spends most of her remain-ing energy pushing away the knowledge – that with every hour that passes, there's less likelihood of Tonya being found alive. She's seen police shows, the news. She knows how this story goes.

Yet—

She believes she'd know if her daughter was dead. There'd be some sort of . . . disconnect. There was when her cunt of a brother died. A weird sort of relief even before her mother called with the news.

She pokes her head round to check on Darryl, has yet another wee, goes back to bed.

But Tonya's death isn't her worst fear. As she lies cold, curled tight under the duvet, with Steve playing the Xbox downstairs to avoid being in the same room as her, she imagines her child being kept alive, tortured by some bastard maniac. If that's the case, she wishes her a swift death, although she could never admit as much to Steve.

The drug rumour isn't the only problem, although they find nothing in the flat, so there's a stay of execution on that front. There's also the 'issue' that Kim had been drinking when Tonya disappeared. A shop assistant smelt it on her breath. Punters in the pub saw her, even though it was only one or two sodding Baileys at the Wetherspoons round the corner from Peacocks. Like she didn't deserve it. A celebration, a treat. She'd just packed in her cleaning job, ready for the baby. Had to, really – could hardly bend over to wring out the mop with her belly. And it's nearly fucking Christmas. But police say the bad press doesn't help. They need to get the public 'on side'.

Kim wonders if they think she's on side.

Facebook and Twitter

Cindy-Lou Watkins
@CindyLou29

I can't dredge up much empathy for a woman who smokes
and drinks in charge of children. #ScummyMummy
#KimSearle

♡ 1   ⟲ 1   ♡ 11   ⇪

Eran Bright will eat you
@Metalhead666

@kimsearle1985 YOU IS NASTY CUNT. YOU DINT DESERVE
THAT CHILE. YOU DESERVE TO DIE
YOU BICH LIKE SHE DIE.

♡ 3   ⟲ 0   ♡ 1   ⇪

Hayley Smith
@MrsVanDiesel

Why wasn't she watching that kid?
#ScummyMummy #Family #Fam4Ever #fastandfurious
#RIPPaulWalker

♡ 3   ⟲ 0   ♡ 0   ⇪

S-J Bounds
2 hrs 💰

Can you remember her from Year Eight? She used to give blowjobs round the back of the Co-op. She was smoking weed even then.

Frankie Billingham Didn't she knock around with that lad who ended up in Pentonville?
Sharon Tatling Billy G. Yeah, I think so. Another fuckin druggie.
Amy P She disappeared to London dint she.
Sharon Tatling Gd riddance.
Maz Brown The whole family were a nasty bunch.

👍 10

👍 Like   💬 Comment   ➤ Share

Mandy Richards
@Prinze_4ever9

There's something the police aren't saying. Hard faced bitch. #FindTonya

💬 3   🔁 0   🤍 3   ⬆️

Lilian Edwards
4 hrs 💰

You evil woman. That poor defenceless girl left to roam the streets with a stranger while you pursued your carnal desires. It's the other wee ones I pity, that unborn one you carry inside you. God will be your judge—

👍 Like   💬 Comment   ➤ Share

Louise G
@LouiseGeddingshops

Someone should take those boys off her as well.
#ScummyMummy #justsayin

$\heartsuit$ 4   ⟲ 2   ♡ 6   ⬆

Ricky Lakke
@JUSTHANGIN_22

That flat had wasters round at all hours. #KimSearle
#nosmokewithoutfire

$\heartsuit$ 1   ⟲ 1   ♡ 2   ⬆

Mummy

I find the online forums exhausting. I was up most of the night trawling through the inane comments, confusing threads on fostering, adoption, settling in new children. So many opinions. So many horror stories. And I had to submit my email address. But needs must.

Michael would probably have come up with a way to disguise it.

I miss him. The absence on his side of the bed gnaws at me. I do wish it hadn't come to this.

Thankfully, there has been some shift in the child's behaviour today. I find her dancing around my kitchen like some native from a primitive tribe, flailing her arms and kicking her legs high so anyone could see right up her nice new skirt, then galloping around, shouting, 'Whoop, whoop!'

'Sweetheart! What on earth are you doing?'

She yells, 'Whoop, whoop – Gangnam style!'

I often have no idea what she's chattering about and I'm amazed that, for one so slender, she makes such a racket. Her footfall, a stomp.

The dance is followed by 'Quack-quack, oink-oink, woof-woof-WOOF!'

She skips around and barks louder. I sip my black coffee, attempting to let it wash over me.

I'm afraid she is singularly clumsy, knocking items off surfaces with sickening regularity. One of my favourite Diptyque candles was smashed when she careered around the lounge, shouting nonsense words, as if she were playing with her own shadow.

I tell her, 'Be careful!' a dozen or more times, but she pays no heed.

She is laughing like a reeling drunk. I'm not keen on the rowdy laughter

– it exposes her unfortunate, uneven teeth. But if she smiles keeping her lips together, she can look so pretty.

I've ordered such lovely things for her online. So many skirts and dresses in gorgeous hues of pink for a girl, because I am old-fashioned like that, and the PC Brigade can keep their beaks out of my business, thank you very much. Amazon Prime and NET A PORTER Kidswear is a Godsend when you need an entire new wardrobe at short notice.

I have them leave it in my Safe Place, in one of my recycling bins, to avoid them coming to the door.

Then I panic, wondering if they can somehow flag up a warning if someone who has never bought a single item of children's clothing before suddenly orders so much.

For these sprees, I raid the nest egg Michael and I built up. And I am grateful for Aunty Kathleen's money and my daddy's will affording me the luxury of not having to work. Mammy fought against it, but whatever she said, I had as much right to my inheritance as my sister.

Many new mothers are not so fortunate.

She could be so dainty in these nice new clothes, but she does not carry herself well.

Ungainly.

Plus, there is a nasty scab on the side of her mouth.

She continues marauding around my lounge and then moos like a cow. That noise unearths a terror—

I bury the memory.

Once the relentless wailing stopped, I brought her back into my room. I now sleep in fitful episodes, yearning for just one long, uninterrupted night. But catnaps have to do. The child's elbow catches me in the side as she tosses and turns. She moans in her dreams and sometimes snores like a baby piglet. She stretches out diagonally, taking up most of the mattress, stealing most of the duvet. While this is charming, in parts, the new, enforced intimacy hurts my head.

It doesn't help that I'm keeping a new rabbit-shaped nightlight switched on, so she won't be fearful when she wakes in the small hours, as she often does. After I've had my fill of gazing at her, I put on my eye-mask to try and block out the light. Pure silk, so as not to damage the delicate skin around my eyes, although the elastic pulls at my temples.

I feel a pulse wincing there.

I have to get up. I take more medicine. A few sips. I know, it's not ideal. But the memory, the lowing of cattle, always makes my skin crawl.

I wake at three. And the old thoughts, the old torments, refuse to let me slide back into any sort of relief.

Thou shalt not fail to breed.

But I didn't breed. Couldn't.

In the long, confused night hours my fears grow tendrils, which creep and knot themselves around the well-worn despairs.

I could never fulfil my heart's desire to be a mother. What sort of woman does that make me?

Hail Mary. You mock me, blessed Virgin.

I am no longer a virgin and never a mother. What am I left with? My only other career option as a Catholic – if not a nun, if not a mother – *whore*.

And what sort of deity decrees you go forth and multiply, but makes that impossible? Yet gives a child to a vile, abusive drug dealer? Isn't that plain cruel? Like childhood cancer – just not fair.

I kick away the duvet and get up so quickly I feel dizzy and have to lie down a moment more.

Alongside me, she whimpers in her sleep.

Is she my most treasured gift? My angel? My miracle?

Or is she just a consolation prize?

Tonya

I have a coleslaw. The woman says not to put my tongue on it. Fuck off, woman. You ain't my mum.

Kim

Kim does not want to face reporters again. Ever. But she must.

This time the press officer tells her she will be 'required to answer a few questions', to keep the investigation 'fresh in people's minds'. Fragments of these instructions connect with some level of understanding, only Kim can't compute how Tonya could not be at the front of people's minds every waking second of every single hour.

Liaison Woman also cautions her not to swear because it's going out live. So how's she supposed to do that, while she's also told she must 'try to relax' and 'give more information'? It's her natural language. For Kim, swearing's like breathing – you don't notice until someone says you can't do it.

Kim and Steve are told that they'll be asked to describe Tonya. Not just what she looks like and what she was wearing when she went missing, because that's been everywhere, on all the bulletins, day after day. They're supposed to say what Tonya is like. As a person. As a little human.

This is supposed to be a direct appeal to whoever may have her. Or someone who might know who has her. Someone who's covering for them out of some warped love and loyalty, although they might be another sick fuck like Myra Hindley.

The morning starts badly when Steve tells her to change her top.

'Why?'

'That blouse makes you look – better.'

'Better? How?'

He shrugs his meaty shoulders in that useless way that makes her want to punch him in the mush.

'What the fuck does it matter what I wear? It's not a cocking fashion show.'

'He's right,' says the liaison bitch, simpering up to Steve again. 'The blouse is . . . nicer.'

Steve opens his mouth, but before he can spout any more Trinny-Tranny stylist crap, Kim snaps, 'Fuck right off, Steve.'

She's had enough of his comments and the looks he gives her. And she guesses he's telling the police stuff about her past that she doesn't want them to know. She doesn't want anyone to know.

Her mind's jetlagged and the scrambled thoughts are getting her nowhere fast.

She ignores the advice and wears the top she picked, mainly because it's already on and it would require effort to take it off, although she doesn't like it better than any other. Another mistake. Low cut, and her tits are like a ship's prow now, bracing on full alert for the new baby. But choosing what she wears is a way of grasping a tiny bit of control in a world that's got totally away from her. In the mirror, she sees the state she's in – stringy hair, sunken cheeks and bruised shadows beneath her eyes. Like the bad old days.

The press room is stuffy. She notices some of the camera blokes are sweating through their shirts, even though it's achingly cold outside. God knows how the female reporters manage to look like shop dummies, all groomed and perfect despite the fug. They must go to the same school as Barbie air hostesses.

Some of the young journalists seem to have a glimmer of sympathy about them, but most look suspicious. Hard. Worn down by all the crap they have to report. All are waiting on Kim to dish her innards.

Hers is the worst sort of fame. No recompense, no glory, just the gusset of your drawers spread out for the mob to sniff.

Daniel Wilson, Sky News

It's a bloody good story. This is often a dead time, these last few days in the lead-up to Christmas, and he's sick of the corny old 'feel-good' seasonal shite they tend to pump out. Either that or he's posted to Gatwick to cover 'Travel carnage as the festive getaway gets underway' for the zillionth time.

He wonders what the traffic will be like on the way back to Isleworth.

The couple are led in.

The father, Steve, looks towards them and attempts a grim smile. Exhaustion suits him. Dan has the same blue Gap shirt at home. But, Jesus – what is the woman wearing? She looks like she's on a Blackpool hen do. The top's so low it almost cries out for pixelation. A great shot. The comments will be mental. He catches the eye of Trevor, the reporter from *Good Morning Britain*, and they both suppress a twitch of the lips.

Sophie Cooper from BBC News kicks things off, asking, 'Kim, would Tonya have willingly gone off with anyone she didn't know?'

And the mother sits there, thinking about it, which everyone knows you must never do with a camera in your face. It makes you look stupid or shifty. You must start a sentence immediately, even if you don't know where it might take you. Often it's a sentence that has little relation to the question. Politician-speak.

But the poor cow's missed out on the media training.

When the silence becomes uncomfortable, Steve answers for her, 'No. She'd never go off with—'

'Of course she bloody would,' interrupts Kim. All eyes are back on her and she's sweating through the powder they put on her face for the camera lights.

Police bods look at each other, not knowing how this is going to play out.

'You think she'd have walked away with a stranger?' pushes Sophie, a good, solid journalist underneath all that Oxbridge-bluestocking-clever-yet-you'd-do-her BBC sheen.

'Yeah. Tell her there's a fucking kitten round the corner. She'd go. They all would.'

Police discomfort and journalists' adrenaline cranks up with her language. Dan's anchor back in the studio will be apologising for airing the expletive. But it all adds a little spice. Good for publicity. Swearing clips do well on YouTube.

Dan senses he can push this, and interjects, 'Didn't you warn her?'

'Of course I fucking warned her,' spits Kim, eyes bulging.

Steve puts his hand on Kim's arm and she pushes it off with more force than necessary.

'Why do you think she might ignore you?' continues Dan.

Kim half stands, bracing her arms against the desk. 'Because she's five fucking years old!' A plod starts to apologise for the language, but she shouts over him to Dan, 'Have you got kids?'

'Yes,' says Dan. He sees his lad every other weekend. His mum's turn for Christmas this year. Unfortunate.

'Then you know.' She flumps down again, glaring.

When you watch this bit back, she looks more than a little barmy.

Before anyone else can ask another question, he needles further, 'What do you have to say to the accusations that you were drunk when she was taken?'

And they hear something about the press conference being over, but Dan sees it's personal between him and the mother now and even though Steve tries to hold her back, when he turns to his camerawoman next to him, asking her to focus in tight, Kim lunges towards him and that's the shot they all use:

Kim, mouth twisted into another, 'Fucking—'

Kim, eyes wide, deranged—

Kim, neck muscles straining, teeth bared, as if to rip out the reporter's throat – a crazed animal trying to kill the middle-class cunt who's called her out; an actual enemy in front of her at last.

A woman who, at that precise, preserved moment, doesn't look anything like a media-friendly mummy should look.

Unless it's a mother lion defending its cubs and most viewers will be too busy judging to clock that.

TV gold! Dan is bloody delighted. Herograms and G&Ts all round back at base.

Within a couple of days, Kim's a meme.

Mummy

I take the knife, the one that feels satisfyingly heavy in my hand, and sharpen it on the gizmo Michael bought me the Christmas before last. He must have known I would have preferred Jo Malone rather than anything related to food preparation. The edge catches the ceiling spotlights. I keep my blades in tip-top, Gordon Ramsay condition, not that I approve of his language. I am no slattern in the kitchen. Or anywhere else, come to that.

She shrieks. It goes right through me, but I manage to keep my voice level: 'Be quiet, please.'

The red stains my marble kitchen top. I'll have to scrub it with bleach spray after I finish this. I stand and watch the liquid spread until it fades to pink at the edges. When I catch myself drifting, I give myself a talking to. No more medicine tonight. I need a steady hand.

I cut again, slicing through more smoothly now, making smaller chunks.
'NO! Nooooo!'
'Stop that noise!'

Everything I do for her is unappreciated. In my most despairing moments I wonder why I managed to end up with this peculiar child. One who neither loves nor likes me. One so disobedient.

As Mammy always said, 'These things are sent to try us.' It is interesting how many of her sayings keep popping into my head now that I am finally mothering a child myself.

I chop more than cut now, cubing the beetroot, then the ginger and apple. I never liked cooking. So much mess.

'Don't want none.'

The same belligerent protest we've had for days on end after I decided Frosties were off the menu.

The website said she might be tetchy. This is what addiction does to you. She's craving the sugar that makes my angel into such a whiny wretch. But her system must be cleansed. Sugar is a poison.

I don't like the word 'detox'. It brings back all sorts of bad memories – loud, unpleasant, circular discussions with Michael about rehab, more insistent after each drunken incident staggered into its downward, shameful spiral, as they tended to.

'Detox' also has the blemish of a fad about it. As if it's something new, tainted with Gwyneth Paltrow's pixie dust and snake oil. Yet many gurus and saints cleanse themselves. Purge, taking little or no food for days on end, sipping only water. Only then, purified, can they focus on spiritual things.

Tonya perches on the chair, watching my hands intently. I can see she is focused on the apple. Perhaps I'm being too soft-hearted, but I cut her a small piece and hold it out to her. She snatches it without so much as a thank you.

I need apple and beetroot as a sweet disguise, for no matter what astounding nutritional qualities it possesses, no one would ever eat kale by choice. I also add some coconut water and place the ingredients in the NutriBullet. I cried when Michael gave me that for my birthday, feeling sure it was a nasty hint aimed at my waistline.

The noise judders through me.

The beetroot has made the drink pink, which I'm hoping will entice her to try it. She eyes the glass with suspicion. I must buy some plastic beakers.

She curls both her small hands around it and sniffs like some woodland creature.

I turn for a second, to clear away the mush of vegetable off-cuts, which already jangles at me. I aspire to have my kitchen as spic and span as Mammy's. Everything scrubbed clean and polished there.

The explosion of the shattering glass makes me jump. Pink gloop spreads across the floor I cleaned only this morning. I have to battle an urge to scream at her.

Did she deliberately dash it to the floor? Or did she simply knock it over? She watches me with lizard eyes.

Kim

Her dreams are jumbled: she's fighting a Nazi; she's fighting her brother; she's screaming at a man hitting a dog; she's throwing a bottle of Lucozade Sport after the deaf old cunt who hurtles round corners on her mobility scooter – a danger to everyone on the estate.

That last one's a rerun of something she actually did, although it was only a small bottle.

The fury's still in her as she wakes. She rolls to her side of the bed, otherwise she might lash out at Steve, who's too near and too hot, despite the cold air. That sweaty, muscled back is so exposed. Vulnerable. Asking for it. She hates that phrase.

This man has never done anything bad to her. Not deliberately. Yet if she could reach her bedside cabinet, and if there was a knife hidden there, as there used to be, she feels she could stab it between his shoulder blades.

She itches with irritation, which only intensifies as she comes round from a sleep that was more like a coma. A whole twenty minutes of it.

Her leg starts jiggling as she thinks of Liaison Woman. What sort of fucking job is that? Paid to simper and suck up to her, telling them lie after lie about what the police are doing, when they're just floundering around, waiting for some shred of evidence to emerge and fall into their stupid, lazy laps because they've got no fucking idea.

The team is currently 'sifting through hours of CCTV images' according to the liaison bitch. 'Impulsive abductors make mistakes' they're told, as if that's any reassurance.

There's no comfort in anything she says.

Kim knows from police dramas that they always look to the families themselves for suspects. In most cases kids are taken by someone close. The husband, step-dad, partner; the shady uncle, or family friend, who might have fiddled with Tonya and whisked her away to fiddle some more. Or worse, to shut her up.

And she wants to scream at the police: 'Don't you think I'd fucking *know*?'

This, after all, is her area of expertise. No one has ever fiddled with Tonya. She's sure of it. If anyone did, her girl would kick and scratch and bite and scream and run home to tell her. She's trained her well for that.

And she also knows, without a shadow of a doubt, that Steve would murder anyone who so much as thought a bad thing about his girl. How he'd top himself if he ever harboured any shade of wrong urge towards her himself.

She dares to turn and look at him again. His back's scarred and craggy and lived-in – totally unlike the smooth skin of male models in magazines and the chiselled, plucked twats on reality shows, who do absolutely fuck all for her. He's got a few hairs sprouting on his shoulders, which used to make her smile, in the days when smiling was possible.

His beefy arms are capable of holding tiny new bodies and swooping Tonya high in the air to make her squeal with a giddy delight. They're considerate enough to take his weight as he plunges into Kim to make her sigh with a different kind of giddiness, both of them keeping in the noises so they don't wake the kids.

Those arms have held her close when she's freaked out – afterwards, or, in the early days of their romance, during those sweaty sessions. That happened a lot at first, without anything to dull the edges. He'd rock her like she was a kid again. He'd murmur stuff into her hair until she stopped fighting, and until, much later, she stopped shaking.

Of all the arms that have ever held her, his are the kindest. Steve's body is the one she trusts.

But ever since Tonya disappeared, she just wants to fucking kill him.

Later, she's getting ready to go out on her own. The first time . . . since. And Steve wants to come with her and she tells him to 'Do one' and it escalates pretty quickly as it's been tending to lately, and without warning he flips from narked to totally nuclear, shouting – not that she's to blame for losing Tonya, although that's what he's been thinking ever since it happened and what he wants to shout. Instead he says the thing that's simmered beneath the surface, for years—

'You never even wanted her!'

But, oh, she did.

As she wept, terrified – weeing on the pregnancy test in the stinky public bogs by Morrisons, because she couldn't wait until she got home – she wanted her. When she told Ayesha she couldn't possibly have a baby, she was such a mess she could never, ever be a mother – she wanted her. When, after a week of worry, going round and round in her mind, she booked the abortion – still, she wanted her. When she screamed at Ayesha for telling Steve what she'd planned, although her friend had never actually promised to keep her secret, and when she fought Steve, after he tracked her down in Lidl's, hitting a security guard who tried to get between them as they aired all their mess in the cut price cold meat aisle. When she groaned as they had that fantastic make-up sex back at Skid's place. And when she roared as she gave birth to the skinny little girl who made her life into *something* – she always, always wanted Tonya.

She just never felt she deserved her.

And now she's been proved right.

She has to leave the flat and face the outside for the antenatal appointment. There's only a couple of snappers left on the estate now. She flicks them the V and turns her head away from them, semi-jogging, half waddling away, which is a fucking achievement given the size of her.

Anyone in the waiting room considering offering the pregnant lady a seat turns away quickly when they catch the look on her face.

The midwife doesn't bother telling her to avoid stress, although she shakes her head when she takes her blood pressure. She tells her they might have to think about bringing the birth forward if she develops pre-eclampsia, like she did with Darryl.

Kim hasn't got patience for this sort of planning, someone else interfering with her life, her body; probably so some knob of a doctor can crack off to the golf club in time for an afternoon round. The baby will come when it bloody comes.

She stands outside the surgery to get her breath, watching eyes trying to pretend they're not watching her. A couple of women she doesn't know approach to say hello and how they're sorry and to ask if she's 'coping with it all'. She clocks them as a weird type of star-fucker, drawn to her notoriety. She's been on TV after all. They've seen her knackered face in newspapers. She should sign bastard autographs.

She glances back as she walks away and notices the line of their lips. In the raw air and watery sun, she catches a prickle of their judgements. She picks up her pace. But she doesn't blame them.

Losing a child for five seconds, five long minutes. It happens to most mums. But the rest can't happen. Losing a child forever . . . the worst fear.

And if this terrible thing has happened to her, she must have done something to deserve it. A mother has a sixth sense about her babies, doesn't she – a good mother. She can't simply be unlucky, can she?

Kim reckons those old bear-baiting shows like *Jeremy Kyle* and *Jerry Springer* were so popular because they kindled this particular brand of judgement. There's a gap in the market for another show like those. Viewers still want blood. They want the chavs, the scum, lost souls like her, to rip each other apart in the name of entertainment, so observers can sit on their high fucking horses, looking down on their godforsaken misfortunes. Because the audience is so much better than those up on stage, hung out to dry, like she is now. Those not cursed, not pilloried, have more manners. And teeth.

Mummy

A little over a week and I've given in and switched on the television. We sat through an episode of *Peppa Pig* together, which made me smile, and when she leaned against me on the sofa, I almost cried.

Now she's sitting on the floor, too close to the screen, watching more inane cartoons and the endless sleigh bell 'ching-ching-chinging' of seasonal adverts, promising us happiness and joy if only we buy more disposable rubbish.

While she is preoccupied, I have a moment's peace at last. I lie back on the sofa, snuggling against its pleasing hugeness, feeling like a child again myself, and close my eyes.

Just a couple of days to go before our first Christmas together!

I wake drenched, my heart trying to escape my ribcage like a fish fighting a net. My fists still clenched, as if to ward off the blow.

The memory grips my body even as I try and shake it off by getting up, rigorously cleaning my teeth, which feel furry, my mouth suddenly putrid.

The screams and shouts and lunges feel as real as my pasty face reflected in the bathroom cabinet. I shake my head to dislodge the pain and reapply my smudged mascara.

I sit on the loo and the images wash over me once more. Memories stored in my muscles and bones. I feel a momentary light-headedness, hearing him shouting.

The panic as I came to, bruised and aching, cold against the floor. Michael standing over me, screaming.

I put my head between my knees to stop myself fainting.

Post-traumatic stress. I googled it. Mine is a domestic version – just as pernicious as battle fatigue. Worse, I suspect, because I don't need to see sand dunes, or hear the clatter of a helicopter, the retort of a machine gun, to send me scurrying back into my nightmare. A glance at a kitchen tile can set me off. Every mealtime I see the ghost of old blood on the draining board, the bathroom floor—

I hear the awful words, 'Fucking bitch! Slut!' Worse.

And I vowed I'd never end up like Mammy, cowering from Daddy's fists, as she shouted at me, 'Go to your room!' so I wouldn't have to see.

Hearing was worse.

I promised myself I would never marry a drinker, a Russian, or an Irishman come to that, so deep is that vice in their cultures.

And I blame myself for all that came after, for how I forgot my good intentions the moment Michael, a Dubliner if you may, smiled his slow, sexy smile and my insides turned to liquid, like some whore's.

So I got my 'just deserves' as Mammy liked to say. Although how such a fervent judgemental streak fit in with her bleeding-heart Catholicism was never clear to me. Her God was pure unconditional love – until it came to judging others. Judging me. Then she breathed His fire and brimstone.

I leave Tonya mesmerised by the TV set and go to the pantry, reaching to the high shelf, where, like a good parent, I have hidden the bottle well out of the reach of tiny hands.

I sit in the kitchen, gathering myself. Even after I pour twice as much as usual, my hands still shake as I relive those terrible times with Michael.

Since the child has been here I've not had so many of these 'bad episodes'. And, with a shock, I realise I haven't thought of her for a good five minutes. Wallowing in the past, not organising our future, or tending to her current needs. That's what bad memories do – they ruin your chance of present and future happiness.

I swing my feet onto the deep bedroom carpet. I'd not realised that I'd come back to bed. I must have needed to rest my eyes for a moment. I will try to stand once the room stops shifting. The television blares and booms a world away downstairs.

My migraine throbs with a lethal insistence and I wince at each beat. Another memory clutches me in rhythm with the pain, beating out the refrain, 'Cunt. Cunt. Cunt.'

How I hate that word. Yet it was unleashed when we argued about the drink. Harsh words flung in all directions. Threats and punches. Michael's fury. Shame and guilt and disgust and screams destroying our beautiful home.

I am not blameless in these scenes. I admit I also lost control, slapping at him, trying to escape his awful, violent embrace. But I can forgive myself for striking out in self-defence. I vowed I would never be like Mammy or Aunty Kathleen.

I was fighting for my life.

Kim

Kim's lulled by the instantly forgettable chirps of pop music and the cheery chat of Scott and Chris, which mark the passing of her dark afternoons. Sometimes those hours are worse than the nights, because then at least Steve's there, both of them pretending to be asleep, stiff and awake in the bed, like those figures on tombs inside ancient churches, lying next to each other with their hands pointing up to heaven in prayer. Steve and Kim don't clasp their hands, but in their own way they're praying.

When Steve gets back from work, she hurries to switch off the radio. It seems wrong to have music on, not that she really takes it in, but she needs the programmes to keep track, so that she remembers to feed Darryl. She can't eat much herself, forgets to put fuel in her body, then gets dizzy with low blood sugar and feels guilty about the baby, so she grabs something Steve's brought back – usually a pasty, or pie, or a sandwich (he likes any food wrapped in another food, does Steve) and stuffs it into her dry mouth.

She watches Darryl eat his little plate of pasta, and picks up a bit with her fingers to keep her going. Illuminated dots flicker in her peripheral vision, like sperm under a microscope.

She forces a smile for the lad. Darryl grins back up at her, losing half a mouthful, which spills and dribbles down his chops, so she gets the tea towel and gently wipes the sauce away, making him laugh and pull his head away from her, intent on shovelling in the next spoonful.

If she's alive, is Tonya eating something?

Kim's vision dissolves and she can't see Darryl any more.

Steve nags her to eat. He seems able to function on this biological level, fuelling himself, no matter what he feels, needing the energy to hump and carry bricks and scaffold poles and his hulking great work bag full of tools. He doesn't feel, like she does, that it's some sort of betrayal of Tonya – eating, living, when she might not be.

He even managed a slice of pizza immediately after the reconstruction aired. Seeing the kid – Liaison Woman told them it was a girl from the Sylvia Young Theatre School, wearing a blonde wig and similar clothes to those Tonya was wearing when she was taken – Kim had to turn away from the telly. And she wondered what sort of stage school mum would let a kid so little perform in something like that. Wouldn't it tempt fate?

In the days since Tonya's disappearance, Kim's not sure whether the pangs that grip her are a hunger for food, or for her daughter – both are an aching, clawing feeling deep in her belly. But she still can't eat.

So it's lucky that Steve's at home, the current job being rained off for the afternoon, when her knees buckle and she grabs for the drawer handle and feels the tea towel slip through her hand and then the hard, sickening bash on the side of her head.

And the next thing she knows he's asking her, 'You okay, babe?' over and over, and she wants to tell him to shut the fuck up, but finds she can't, and when she manages to open her eyes he's kneeling next to her.

Her first thought, finding herself confused and horizontal on the floor, is that she's used again. But that feeling passes. Then, as he sits her up she fights a slew of nausea and her head throbs and she's back in the present.

The next awful thought is that she might have hurt the baby, although by the time he's helped her onto the sofa and made her a cup of tea, she instinctively knows it's fine, she'll just have a comedy egg-shaped bump on her bonce.

And when he tells her to eat, she does her best.

And in two days it will be Christmas.

A Christmas without her girl.

Tonya

Santa's been. He's been! And I've got a real princess dress with a crown and some sweets and some books and, and some puzzle stuff and a cushion with a heart done in sequins on it and it goes all silver this way and, and all pink when you stroke it the other way like this and The Woman is laughing and we have hot chocolate with marshmallows in for *breakfast*!

I wonder what Mo's got and if Darryl's got more presents than me, but when I ask her she don't know.

Kim

Christmas Day. Life, apparently, goes on.

It surprises her that it's here, as if it's a normal year. But it's just like any other dead day.

Steve supervises Darryl's plastic tat-fest downstairs, while Kim lies in the bath. Water so hot she almost feels something. Fuck the gas bill.

Her immense belly rises from the water like an island. Her hand circles the top of it. Soothing the baby. Thinking the word 'sorry' over and over.

Steam curls to the ceiling like cigarette smoke. She's giving up for good, she tells herself, for sure this time, promising herself, promising the baby. She will not start again when this one's born. She barters with the universe – give me back my girl and I'll give up the fags. She'd give up anything.

She strokes her butterfly tattoo. The symbol for rebirth. The Eye of Horus is etched low on her back – for protection. When she was younger, and even more stupid, she considered a four-leaf clover, or Celtic cross on her upper arm – like her gran's horseshoe on the fireplace, or her manky rabbit foot brooch – hokey nonsense to ward off evil. But Kim clings to the old superstitions. She needs to cling to something.

She rubs the healed track marks, not for luck, stares at the faded silvery scars across her wrists. If only she could have slipped away then – before kids, before this.

She's not wanted to use for years. Not since Steve arrived on the scene, the one good thing in her shitty life at the time. Her white knight for about five minutes – until she realised his shining armour was only tinfoil and underneath the beef and bravado he was as needy as a little kid.

They were her real saviours, Tonya, then Darryl. Now she's a mum, there are lots of good things. A reason to get up in the morning. Now her fucking brother's deep in the earth, where he can't hurt her or her sister any more, she doesn't feel the need to use.

Didn't.

But she'd shoot up in a second to take away this pain, worse than any withdrawal.

Kim can't imagine the blame over losing Tonya ever easing. She tries to numb it out, the way she learnt to numb out other bad things. But she won't let herself think of that. Can't, because she's at her fucking limit. One more thing and she'll blow like a leviathan, breaching the water, rising and tearing apart the bathroom, the whole fucking flat, with her bare hands.

Steve's switched on the telly and a carol wafts upstairs. She hears Darryl's chatter. She should be glad he's having a good time but his giggles are like sandpaper. And she should give Steve a hand. Try and make today easier for him. Like her, he doesn't have a great big store of jolly Christmas memories to draw on, although his mum and dad were simply hopeless, rather than a vicious fuck-bag like her mother.

Steve's parents, Sherry and Bill, visited when Tonya was born. And after Darryl arrived, Kim would troop round to their cluttered Camden flat with Steve to display the kids, until she was excused, on account of both sides not giving too much of a fuck and Steve took them on his own.

Sherry (not Sherrie – Steve's granddad ran a pub; they also have an Aunty Stella) lost her fight with cancer just over a year ago. It was a one-sided battle. His dad came by himself last Christmas. This year Steve will take his present round – a Val Doonican-style jumper she bought from Peacocks in the sale – if he can be arsed.

Steve's told her stories from when he was a kid. As an only child he was left to his own devices more often than not, until (the poor, lonely little sod) he suggested going to a few home games with his dad. He only went once or twice because it cost a fucking fortune, but then him and his dad started bonding, at least over tactics and substitutions.

Kim doesn't think his parents were bad people. Pig-shit thick, but not evil.

So Kim and Steve promised each other they'd make new, happy memories together. Babes in the wood. Keeping each other warm and safe against the darkness. Hollow promises.

She's not even bought him a card.

She's not sure if the wet on her face is water, steam or tears.

She'll get out the bath in a minute.

Mummy

How I love Christmas Day!

But I do not agree with the gaudy commercialisation of the season. We have lost sight of what we celebrate. Apologise, so as not to cause offence to other faiths – those who make no such apologies for their own festivals – and call it not the holy day, but the 'holidays'.

I wanted to make it special for the girl. I wanted so much for our first Christmas together to be a happy memory – one she might share with her own daughter in the future.

I am not sure how the day disintegrated. Perhaps too many sweets made her cranky. Wrapping paper now lies discarded, along with the pink ballet slippers – too small for her feet – and the mother of pearl rosary I bought her from the Nazareth Store online. She threw a tantrum when I tried to turn off the television. We exchanged words and I shocked myself by bursting into hot, angry tears.

Some time in the dusky afternoon, leaving her watching more nonsense on the TV, the only way to calm her, I take out my journal and read the words I wrote a few years ago – a poem about a bauble on the Christmas tree, so fragile it might implode with the hairline cracks. No small hand to reach up for it.

> *Every day, a Christmas denied*
> *As shame, self-pity, hatred*
> *Ooze like blood through every pore,*
> *While her womb remains as empty as—*

Fragile as—
Red as—
The shiny bauble.

Michael cried when I showed that to him.
I have to lie down for a little while.

The following hours blur as I celebrate the birth of Our Lord alone now she is finally asleep.

This is the child my Lord gave me. And I receive another gift in the night – her new name finally comes to me.

For I am Sarah.

Of course! It is obvious to me now. This child is as longed for, as beloved as Abraham and Sarah's precious son, Isaac. Sarah's ancient, barren womb blossoming in a miracle.

Isaac was shackled to the pyre as a sacrifice, just as I was displayed for the medics on their cold hospital gurneys.

I subjected myself to all their invasive cruelties and violations. And I have always hated examinations I cannot revise for. Ha ha.

I need another drink.

If Michael thought my mood swings were bad before we sought treatment, he had seen nothing. Our life became a hormonal horror show.

But enough of that.

Now I have my miracle. This child is my Isaac.

I watch her clutch the toy rabbit to her bony chest. She is so loveable when asleep.

I shall call her Isabel. Izzy for Isaac.

She will call me Mummy.

Cheers, Michael!

Tonya

She wakes me up and makes me pray with her.
It's like wishes.
I wish really hard the rotten woman would drop down dead.

Kim

A wave of cramping, a tsunami of sweat running down her face, soaking her back. She curls around herself, holding her innards tightly, staggering to the bathroom. Her body wrenching poison out of her guts. She slumps forward; spots fly in front of her vision.

She's on the floor, cold in her sodden nightdress, hunched in the foetal position. Then she's on fire.

Shouting for Steve is too hard.

It wasn't the turkey. They all had that. Must have been the prawn cocktail he bought her as a treat. Steve doesn't do fish, or 'any shit without a proper face'.

In a panic she tries to hoick herself up as another wave grips her. Shaking, she uses the side of the bath and sits heavily on the bog as another violent eruption wracks her. But the slick on the back of her thighs makes her slip forward. Shamed, she lies like an animal, soiled, wrung out, helpless.

She thinks she might die here, boiling in her own juices, and doesn't really care.

As she slips in and out of awareness she seems to call out to her daughter, 'Stay alive. Stay safe. Come back. Please.' And when she prays, 'Keep her safe. Let her go,' it's not directed at the sick fuck who took her, but at some universal energy, the same source to which everyone turns in times of crisis – 'God help me!' ringing out in different languages, to deities with different names and faces and special powers. The old God from school hymns? Where's that old bastard when you need him?

She's no clear idea who she calls to. She could never imagine some old bloke on a cloud. But she strives to see some light, some hope, somewhere in the bleakness.

Round the corner, Ayesha's praying up a storm, even though it's not her Christmas. Some of the other ladies on the women's side of the mosque are praying too, even though they don't know Kim and have never met Tonya and they're not *sisters*.

Steve tries to pray, open-mouthed, snotty, like a little kid asking God for a new bike. And he says sorry, because he thinks this must be some sort of punishment for something he did wrong along the way.

Kind strangers in churches up and down the land write Tonya's name on prayer lists and light candles. Their good wishes are emailed across the globe. Wasn't there a study that found patients healed faster if people prayed for them, even if they didn't know they were being prayed for? Something like that.

When she opens her eyes, Kim feels better. She's not sure how much time has passed, but from the sounds downstairs Steve's still messing about on his Xbox.

She climbs into the bath and sits shaking as she sluices herself down with the shower attachment, washing the filth off her nightie. The warmth and pressure of the water against her skin makes her feel a little more human.

The sudden sickness seems to have burnt itself out. She slowly climbs out the bath and grabs a towel that's seen better days.

And suddenly she's crying. Pressing her face into the roughened material, she can finally release some of the pent-up hurt that's lain hidden under her cold fury. Like lancing a boil.

When she comes downstairs Steve thinks she looks like a little girl.

Police Helpline

'I have information regarding the abduction of the child. I know where she is being held. The house has a blue door with the number seven, or seventeen, or twenty-seven on it. There's a woman looking after her. There is also a man in the house, but I do not see they intend to harm her. Please do not dismiss these messages. I have received many through the years, ever since I was a child myself, but this is one of the clearest I have ever—'

'I keep trying to call the local police but they never pick up. It's just a recorded message. I saw the lass with a man who used to go to the bookies at the end of our road. He disappeared for a long time, but I'd know him anywhere. He wears a grey hat—'

'That girlie is dead, mark my words—'

'Believe that the Lord has a plan and that His purpose, no matter how obscure it may appear to our limited human eyes, is for the best—'

'I want to report a burglary—'

*

'I saw that Tonya on my TV. She was at the back of the crowd in that film that was on Tuesday night about the cars with the bald man—'

'I feel so bad for the parents. It makes me so sad. I lost a child once. Leukaemia. It plays on my mind so much even now. Will you please pass on my sympathy. I sometimes feel like walking over to Archway Bridge. I stopped myself, but I can think of little else—'

'Fuck you cunts (unintelligible) you (laughter)—'

'I'm not sure, but I think I saw someone in a big black coat carrying a little blonde girl that afternoon. I really think it was the right day like they said on the news report, as I had to take my niece to the dentist the day after. She got on a bus – the woman, I mean, not my niece – but I didn't see the number, which is why I didn't call before. I feel terrible about that now, but I didn't know it would be so important at the time. She only caught my eye because the scarf wrapped around the little girl was such a pretty salmon-pink colour and I wondered where I might buy a similar one—'

'I'm sure you've thought of this but is there a way you can check computers to see if anyone has put the kid up for sale on the dark web—'

'I have her. I can do whatever I like to her, when I like. She's tied up in my attic, nice and tight, just like her tight little—'

'Tonya is alive. I don't know who has her, only that it will be because she knows too much because they run a child sex ring on that estate and politicians and celebrities all go up there for—'

Tonya

Where is it?

Where are you? Where are you, Mr Chocolate?

There's got to be chocolate somewheres. Mum hides chocolate in the high bit of the cupboard. And she hides the rainy-day money in the freezer in the frozen peas packet because I saw her but it's a secret and I can't tell Daddy because he's a knob head.

Where are you, Mr Chocolate?

It's not here. Pull the chair. Quiet. Quiet. Don't let The Woman hear. But she's asleep again.

She snores like a pig!

It's not up here. Just bottles.

Don't wobble!

Mummy

'DON'T TOUCH THAT!'

Her little face crumples, then a wail, followed by piteous crying.

'Oh! I'm sorry, Izzy darling, I didn't mean to shout. I'm so sorry. Don't. Hush now. It's okay, sweetheart.' I make my voice softer, higher, 'I didn't mean to. Give it to me. Please. You must never, never touch this. Do you understand? It's bad. It can hurt you.'

She continues to sob and shuffles away from me on her bottom to squash against the pantry door. Her thumb disappears into her mouth, which is a new habit I need to address. But at the moment, the priority is to calm her. I have found the best way to do this is to leave her by herself for a little while. If I try to embrace her, she stiffens and the cries can turn to screams.

She hates it when I shout. I frighten myself, to be honest. I hate the shadow that creeps into the words.

But the child's wilfulness gets her into all sorts of trouble. She bangs on her bedroom door when I lock her in; she tries to bang on the front door if I leave her unattended for a moment, no matter how many times I warn her that it is dangerous outside. This time I found her playing with a bottle of Michael's whiskey. I must have forgotten it.

I put it in the back of a kitchen cupboard for safekeeping.

Anything could have happened. She might have broken the bottle. The thought of glass slashing at her tender skin makes me queasy. What if she drank it, the alcohol poisoning her blood?

I shiver. How I hate that evil liquid. It turned my Michael from the sweet man I married into a beast. His soft-spoken, caressing words erupting into profanity. His warm hands suddenly brutish. A hug, in a flash, a rib-crushing threat. I would plead and beg and struggle against him.

And I gasp for air and claw at his fingers, but he is too strong, and my thoughts and shouts are the same desperate, 'STOP! STOP! STOP!'

I breathe.

That is in the past.

I will keep this child safe from harm. I stretch up and check the bottles on top of the fridge.

She watches me and I see her face harden from fear to defiance.

'Izzy, stop sucking your thumb right now, please. Only babies suck their thumbs.'

I swear she shoves it in deeper.

Kim

A couple of days after Christmas, Steve says, 'We need to clear up this crap.'

Kim snaps, 'Then fucking clear it up.'

The crap is mainly plastic – a chaos of colours and shapes designed to pierce the soles of your feet when you shuffle down to put on the kettle of a morning. Darryl and Tonya's toys. Now she's not here to keep her precious cache safely away from her brother, they're all mixed up.

Steve's crap is corralled in his van. Kim's in the bedroom. She has to lock away her make-up, or Tonya's in it the instant she turns her back. Used to be. The times she smeared Kim's lipsticks and eye-shadows all over her face. Once she drizzled nail polish on her bedroom carpet and got her arse tanned for it.

Kim walks up to Tonya's room, hardly bigger than a cupboard really, to gaze at the discoloured patch, like she's visiting an ancient ruin. She sits on Tonya's little bed. Strokes the fur on her Simba – her favourite toy before the *Frozen* mania kicked in – as gently as she might touch a relic. And she sends out a plea, 'Please, help us.' To what? The forces of good? Darryl's superheroes?

Ayesha says she's never questioned Allah.

'But you must have,' says Kim, stopping before she lands herself in it by saying the unsayable.

Her friend knows what she means.

'When Mo was born, you mean? Because he's how he is?' asks Ayesha.

That's exactly what she means. Whenever she looks at the twisted teenager strapped into his mobility-scooter-chair thing, she wonders what sort of god could let it happen – a mong, a spaz, an abortion of a kid.

But Ayesha manages a tired smile, 'Allah's will, innit.'

Kim silently calls to something out there, 'Please, let Tonya be safe. Please, bring her back to us. Just fucking please.'

She wonders if those attuned to such things may sense a slight lifting of pressure, a brightening of the light, as her heartfelt prayer is offered up.

Or not.

'You've got to get out, babe.' On a fucking loop for the last week.

'Give it a rest, Steve.'

'You need some fresh air.'

'Fuck off, will ya.'

Before she leaves the flat that morning, Kim has to find Steve's van keys for him – which he says have gone missing, but they're on the table right in front of him – and remind him to take the rubbish out because it's bin day. It took her years to drum it into him that the bin men came on Mondays. And don't start her on that 'bin person' bollocks, because when was the last time you saw a woman stupid enough to do it? Then, last month, the bastard council changed it to Wednesdays.

Her back's killing her and she can't even neck an Ibuprofen because of the bloody invader inside her, currently attempting to somersault in what tiny space is left in her insides, bouncing off her womb lining and sticking his limbs out at all angles, so her belly's like a scene from *Alien*.

There's not room for Steve with this one. Her body shut down on him even before Tonya went missing. They tried. She spread her legs, resting her forearms on the kitchen table as he shoved himself in behind her. But they had to give up. Battering her cervix wasn't exactly knock, knock, knocking on heaven's door as far as she was concerned. He was reduced to mercy hand jobs, or an occasional blowjob if he begged enough. Or a thank-you gobble if he actually remembered the bins.

All that seems from a different life now.

When Kim finally drags herself out, she clenches her teeth and juts out her chin a little, preparing to push through a mob. Not that there's any snappers or journos around now – they've moved on to someone else's trauma. But even when people aren't obviously staring at her, Kim catches snatched looks, and the flickers of blame shimmering in the cold air.

She's good at this bracing. She's had practice. She's been made to feel like scum before. Her mother often looked at her like she'd crawled home through shit.

When she tried to tell her—

Dave did this. Dave did the other. He's starting on Heather. Mum. Mum. Do something, Mum—

The look froze her. She turned to stone as her mother started screaming at her, 'Dirty fucking liar. You wicked little cow—'

And that stuck. Hooked deep inside her.

Her sister never backed her up. Heather said it never happened. Easier that way.

Kim didn't blame her. Pretend, wish, swear Dave never did it, perhaps he didn't. It hadn't happened. End of. In some fucking fairy-tale world, Dave's the sort of big brother who'd stop other lads hurting you.

She let Heather's lies slide away, but she swallowed her mother's words whole. That old poison runs in her veins now. She hears the imagined judgements in her mother's nasal voice.

And she swore, vowed, made sure she would never make Tonya feel like *nothing*. She was her princess. Tonya was tough and fearless and brave. Is. Is! She's a tomboy, a rogue. Tearing up and down the stairs, roaring around with the little lads on the estate.

Christ, it's quiet without her.

Tonya can be her own knight in shining armour, her own prince. Although she might need someone to rescue her now.

But the kid can be kind as well as fierce. She'd play with Mo for hours. He must be missing her, although Ayesha says it's hard to tell.

Is it that little kids don't notice mangled limbs and weird, twisted faces? Don't they judge like adults? Tonya revels in Mo's attention. She adores the kid. Although he can be rough.

He bit her quite badly the last time they played together. But to be fair, Tonya bit him first.

Kidz Klub
WhatsApp Group

Kidz Klub
We would like to assure parents that we will be open as normal on Monday after the holiday break. We have been working with local police to ensure the club is a safe environment. If anyone has concerns about their children or our safety measures, please contact Sylvia directly.

Cathy
I feel so bad for the mum
Shes not on here is she
Should we do a card for her

Mai
Are you kidding me? She's a total nightmare.

BB
You should be shamed Mai

Mai
Who's asking you? She's a nasty piece of work. And her kid bullies my Matthew.

Linda
It could happen to any of us. I feel awful about it.

Mai
It could happen to any of us if we'd been pissed and not looking out for our kids you mean.

Bruce
Sylvia, can you have a word?

Sylvia
We will not tolerate abusive or bullying comments on here. Parents will be removed if they continue to send messages like this.

Jenny
Is the February trip still going ahead?

Lluul
Can you remove me from this group please

Mummy

Deep in the night, my friend Nina comes to me.

I wake with familiar pangs of regret and mortification, rubbing my eyes like I used to as a child to stop my tears, remnants of the dream, which is more memory than fantasy, squeezing out like a blackhead.

One of Mammy's lessons – 'Thou shalt not covet.' Although I suspect she did. As comfortably off as we were compared with many others, the role of a farmer's wife could not match Aunty Kathleen's position and wealth. Kathleen married a banker. So did I, in effect. Someone in finance. But I yearned for things money can't buy.

I am back at my friend's chaotic flat, Nina's workmates and neighbours toasting her wonderful achievement with Buck's Fizz and Bloody Marys at this most civilised 'Baby Brunch' – another hateful American invention along with Halloween and ostentatious clapping. Nina parades around with her newborn daughter, holding out the infant for blessings and kisses.

Along with my glass of celebratory bubbles, I swallow down a wicked impulse from the bad fairy hidden behind my smiles, itching to wish illness and bad fortune on the gathering. Better still, for Nina to drop down dead of a massive haemorrhage, suddenly, without pain (for she is my friend), right here in her messy designer kitchen, as I step in to save the little one from dashing its brains against the slightly soiled granite floor. My mammy would be appalled by the state of it.

Instead, she turns to me with that simpering look of pity she has worn for months, ever since I confessed my yearning for a child of my own, and hands me the wriggling bundle, all freshly baked and delicious.

Everything else fades.

I am amazed by the child's Disney rosebud mouth. It is so ridiculously perfect. My own slackens in wonder. I hear others cooing and asking questions in the background.

Someone strokes the baby's face and I brace against the intrusion. It's one of Nina's friends from college, a girl I met once at a New Year's shindig, along with so many other shiny new work colleagues, because Nina has always been so social and well-liked and I am just the lonely charity case she keeps on to prove what a good, kind person she is. She probably warned them before I arrived – 'My anorexic friend will be here. Please don't say anything and try not to stare.'

But I trump their newly minted friendships. Our connection goes right back to our school days, where we practised our writing, the Catechism and kiss chase together. Oh, the illicit thrill of that game! We lost touch for quite a few years in between, but then we bumped into each other in Selfridges' bistro. After her initial shock – for I had lost so much weight even then, crawling from my hideous chrysalis, totally transforming from my plump, imperfect school days, lasers treating the acne scars and the dark hairs on my chin and upper lip – we discovered we had both fled the restrictions of small-town Irish life and settled in north London. And we started up where we had left off.

I realise I have turned away from the woman trying to peek closer at the baby's face. Rude, I know, but I don't care. My need, so raw, turns me into a vampire, a dark star consuming all light.

Nina laughs nervously as she reaches for her daughter, but I hold on to the small body, squishing it close to mine, hugging her tight against my new dusky pink Reiss dress – for I had so wanted to make a good impression – long after the polite amount of time has expired.

Nina's husband, John, puts his hand on my shoulder and as I shrug it off, I hear myself say, 'No!' It comes out low and menacing.

My legs start quivering. I refuse to look up at the adult faces congregating nearer, sensing the disturbance, a hint of potential danger, and I stare down, resolutely, intensely, at the child in my arms.

How long this stand-off continues, with John flustered, embarrassed, panicked now, prising my fingers away from the baby, whispering, 'Come on. Come on now, love. Give her here. Come on—' I cannot remember. But I am unable to rid myself of the contraction in my belly, the wash of mortification that accompanies the scene.

I am not sure what happened next.

I was never invited back.

I get up slowly, my head throbbing. I didn't wipe off my eyeliner properly last night and the smudges make me look sordid. But I can smile at my ugly face in the mirror nonetheless.

Because now – finally! – I am a mummy.

How shall we celebrate this holy festival? The Epiphany.

Tonya

She lets me put on the princess dress and the crown and she brushes my hair. A lot. And I do a dance and a sing for her but she don't know the song which makes me laugh cos *everyone* knows the song.

And I try to teach her the words, like I do Mo, coz she really don't know it – 'If you like it then you should-a put a wing on it. Oh-oh-oh-oh-oh-oh-oh-oh-oh-oh-oh-oh-oh-oh-OH!' And I teach her the hands and she does it with me. But she does it funny.

And she tells me about a bloke called Michael and keeps saying cheers and she cries.

And then she goes and has another lie-down.

I wish she'd do more dancing with me.

Mummy

I once believed I could not want for anything if I had my own child. But there is still a hollowness. My heart yearns for my Michael. How I wish he could share this with me.

Who else could hold me and soothe me and kiss away my fears?

I did not realise it would be so hard as a single parent.

I'm afraid the old habits come out to play. Come out, come out, wherever you are!

I see plumes of dark smoke trailing from her eyes, her ears, her mouth. She stands in a toxic cloud.

When I wake, mid-morning, mid-afternoon, I can't tell, I see clearly what I must do.

She must be exorcised.

No time like the present.

Now I seem to have filled the bath too full, although I have made it nice and warm for her. I didn't consider that my arms and chest would need to be in the water with her to keep her down and I'm sweating.

She kicks and splashes but I manage to contain her churning.

'It will be all right, darling,' I tell her. But her eyes are wide as she struggles against me. She looks so little, but it takes all my strength to hold her under.

I slip as the water washes and sloshes across the bathroom floor.

'This is for your own good, sweetheart. Hush.'

She stills for a second. There are bubbles from her nose.

Her innocent spirit has been clogged and defiled with so much filth. Now she will be purified.

I explain, 'I will wash away your sins.' I doubt she hears. Bubbles from her mouth.

As her arms go limp, I see tiny, tiny bubbles in her eyelashes.

I tell her, 'You will be cleansed of all those bad influences.'

This is my duty as a parent.

As the water quietens, she splays motionless – an angel preserved in a Glacier Mint. Like this, she is beautiful.

Silent.

But she thrashes and bursts upwards, taking a giant gulp of air, catching my chin with the force of her skull.

The shock dazes me. I feel a wave of nausea and the bite of anger, as if I might hurt her, although of course I never would. My arms fall to my sides, shaking after the effort.

I can do no more.

She has been immersed.

He sees my intention.

An exorcism. A baptism. It will have to do.

Perhaps she is too young. I may be expecting too much. But I can educate her and show her the righteous path. In time, she will welcome the Holy Spirit.

Against the taps, hugging her knees up to her ribs, she looks at me like a half-drowned cat.

When I come round, I'm not sure if I've dreamt it all. It's only when I manage to get up and see the pile of wet towels on the bathroom floor that I see it really happened.

I lug the heavy load down to the washing machine. I place the empty bottles in a recycling bag and haul it outside. Then I take the organic meat out of the fridge, chop the vegetables and add the stock. Something nutritious. Something healing.

I carry the chicken soup into her room on a tray.
    She scowls, and shouts, 'Go away, YOU!'
    But when I go back after my cup of tea, she's finished the bowl.

Kim

There's a numbness in Kim she recognises from the bad times, back for an encore. For days – weeks, is it? – she's shut off her feelings so she can put food into her stupid mouth to keep going. For Darryl's sake, for the baby's sake. She's kept herself more or less together. Refused to go under. And she bites back the fury she feels whenever Liaison Woman shows up, telling them absolutely fuck all.

Now, all of a sudden, not so much a thaw as a river smashing through ice. The bit inside her that she thinks of as the old Kim resurfaces.

In Holloway Road, a whey-faced fat lass needles her by staring. Kim refuses to look away first. As the girl eyes her up, passing judgement, she mutters, 'Bog off back to Greggs, you fat, frigging munter,' then realises she's said it louder than she intended.

In his pushchair, Darryl gets wind of the sea change and cranes his head round to gaze up at her.

'Maccy D's, buggerlugs?' she suggests.

He grins.

She's shoving chicken nuggets into Darryl's greasy face when she hears them, because they mean her to.

A loud teenage skank and a couple of mates, raking over her life. Because she's a local celebrity now. National, even. She watches in case they start taking selfies with her in the background.

They clock her watching and giggle, exchange sly looks.

Kim takes a big breath and marches over to their table.

'Got a problem?'

Two of them, just kids really, look down, fiddling with the remains of their fries.

Not the one cocky little mare who locks eyeballs and nods at Darryl, 'Kept hold of that one, yeah?'

One friend laughs, hard and false.

Kim hears herself shout, 'Fuck you!' as she shoves the floppy nugget box in the girl's face. She grabs the one who laughed by the hair extensions, yanks back her head and spits right into her face, 'And you can go fuck yourself as well!'

She stomps out, wondering if they'll have the balls to follow. They don't.

Propelled by a righteous anger she starts off for Ayesha's. Waiting at the traffic lights on Seven Sisters she touches her belly. When the new baby comes she'll do anything it takes to make sure he's safe and the nasty little slags and the newspapers and the social workers and the frigging police and Liaison Woman can all fuck right off.

She's got enough on her plate. The due date's next week. How the fuck is it the middle of January already?

What Kim didn't notice in McDonald's was the quiet mother and daughter at the table by the bin. The girl filmed the charming little scene starring Kim and the three bitches. She's already posted it.

It goes viral.

Kim hears what the trolls are saying about her 'latest shocking outburst'. She can't not hear, because people break their bloody necks to tell her any time she ventures out of the flat. Ignoring the bit when she went for the first girl, some try and make out it's a hate crime, because the one she grabbed by the hair was black. As if that had anything to do with it.

Whatever.

But when she sees the post, she has to agree with Steve – she looks proper mental.

Mummy

I finish the sentence and close the book. She turns over to face me and says in a sleepy voice, 'It's nice.'

'The story?'

'The way you say it. It's nice.'

I hug the compliment and read another chapter.

Kim

Sandra's the sort of 'friend' who can suck all the air out of a room. In that, as in so many ways, she's the opposite of Ayesha. If you ever make the mistake of asking how Sandra's doing, she has a comprehensive list of physical, financial, mental and emotional complaints. Kim's always felt drained by her. It's just unfortunate that Sandra's lad goes to Darryl's free playgroup thing and she lives nearby, otherwise Kim could give her a wide berth.

Until now, when circumstances absolutely demand it, Sandra has never once asked how Kim's doing, wanting an actual answer, rather than waiting for a breath so she can start on with her own grumbles.

And this is the woman standing in front of her now, the signature over-teased, dyed-black hairdo and severe black eyebrows blocking her way into the Nag's Head market. Sandra's asking questions with her 'concerned' face on. It's a look you might confuse with 'constipated', particularly as the eyebrows make her look like an Angry Bird.

Kim doesn't have the will to escape, because Sandra channels the skill of all vampires, mesmerising the victim, sucking the spirit out of her, feeding on what's left of her energy.

She struggles to stand upright, balancing the pregnancy on shaky legs, rocking slightly. Sandra's power increases as Kim's wanes and the questions come at her like a swarm of wasps. She fails to answer even the basics.

How can she say how she feels? How is she bearing up? Is she actually bearing up? Then there's the loaded question, 'Is there any news?'

Kim shakes her head.

'Oh, I'm so sorry, Kim. It must be awful for you. How long is it now?' The tone drips with saccharin, a nasty frisson crackling beneath the surface. 'Five weeks is it?' A shadow of something plays on Sandra's shiny, lip-glossed mouth. The market atmosphere seems to dull as Kim realises that, at some level, Sandra's enjoying this. And all of a sudden, she bolts, pushing her way past, rudely, roughly, mumbling excuses, making yet another enemy.

She's not sure how she gets home.

But she can't rest there either. As soon as she opens the door, Steve grabs her elbows, steers her backwards and sits her down in the shabby armchair. She can see by his face that it's not good.

'Listen. Just fucking listen.'

And he kneels in front of her and reads out message after toxic message – another wave of it – a spew of hatred and bile. Some of it doesn't even make sense, but the intent to hurt, to pour salt into their wounds, shines through clear and dandy.

Kim can imagine these tossers enjoy indulging their worst selves, their cruellest, least generous impulses, splurging it all out in an orgy of spite. It's like her Uncle Mick used to say, 'God's a skinhead – he puts the fucking boot in when you're down.'

Trolls, spewing out things you could never breathe to another, for they'd recoil in disgust. Words you daren't say, because they'd reveal pus in your soul. And these are the actual words in post after post, tweet after tweet. All directed at Kim.

She suspects the sad fucks get off on it.

Why has Steve decided to make her listen? Can't he bear it by himself any more?

He's shaking now as he forces out the words, going white around the lips, muscles strained around his neck, his body tensing. And in a powerful half sprint, he's up off the floor and thundering towards the stairs, galloping upwards to the bog, where she hears him dry retch.

She continues to sit, feeling little. The terrible thing has already happened. These fucking amateurs can't make her feel worse than she already does. When it comes to beating herself up, she's the pro.

Tonya

The Woman has a garden. There's trees and everything.

She won't let me go in it. She says the germs will get me if I do.

She tells me if I'm good we can go out when it's warmer, when the germs are gone. Don't care.

I make my face sad so she'll give me the chocolate drink. But she won't. She don't laugh and say, 'Give that girl an Oscar,' like my mum neither. And she says she ain't got no chocolate but she has coz I've seen it up in the cupboard.

Mummy

Mammy is off with Aunty Kathleen somewhere shopping. Daddy is in the kitchen with Margaret. You are supposed to be upstairs 'recovering' from the measles. But 'recovering' is boring – just a lot of lying around with the curtains closed.

You hear your daddy singing. You love his sweet voice. So you climb downstairs and creep nearer to listen, not wanting to disturb him. Margaret is on his knee, her legs swinging in time to the song, and he is singing to her and stroking and stroking her hair. And it hurts so much to hear and to see.

You hate your sister. She bosses you around. When you play together in the Wendy house she's always the mummy. 'Because I'm the eldest,' she tuts, when you say that's not fair.

The kitchen smells of Dettol. Tea towels folded neatly, drying by the Aga. It's warm. Upstairs is cold.

Daddy strokes Margaret's arm. You have never seen those rough hands tender. You only see them heave and haul and punch and pummel and launch your mammy through to the middle of next week and wrench a calf out of a cow. You have felt them hard against your ears and the back of your knees often enough. Vicious hands. Hands that slaughter.

The song ends on a sad note which fades until there is a space where it was, and he tilts her face up to his gently and kisses her so sweetly and he notices you watching and jumps up and Margaret spills from his lap and shouts, 'Ow!' Then suddenly you're being dragged back to bed and he's hurting your arm and you try to tell him, to explain it was the song, but he snarls, 'Don't you dare say one word, you ugly little bitch. Get back to bed this instant, you spying little whore.'

And you can't move your arm the next day and you wear a sling for a week or so.

I feel myself shuffle across my lovely deep carpet, my limbs heavy and sluggish. It's hard to keep my head upright. My eyes itch with dryness, my throat itches with tears, which seem perilously close to the surface.

It's as if I am without a layer of skin.

Too much drink is never enough.

I find myself staring into a distant memory or a far-flung future, displaced from the moment. Sometimes I sway with fatigue. My muscles shake as I reach up my arms for the teabags. When I stoop for the dustpan, I fear my thighs will not be able to bring me upright again. I ache in all my joints.

My head wincing.

Her chirruping and tuneless singing grate – snatches of pop songs no doubt, although I can't recognise any of them. The way she clatters through my rooms!

I would shout, 'Be careful!' if it were not too much effort.

I find it difficult to engage the child in any worthy pursuit. She seems bored by the educational games suggested by the child development websites. I do my best, but without a hint of encouragement from her.

I must home school her. I hardly know where to start.

I give her the earphones and set her down in front of the TV. I so wanted to be a good mummy, yet I am forced to resort to this crass form of babysitting because I find I'm so tired. I would love to go up to my bed, but I don't trust what she might do in my absence and she wails if I lock her in her room. Instead, I lie on the sofa and put on the eye mask.

I must doze for a couple of minutes.

When I try to sit up, I feel unwell and flop down once more.

Poisoned with drink.

Dear God, please help me. I am failing You. I am failing her.

Kim

Teatimes are hard. Darryl seems not to notice his sister isn't around any more, but it's when Kim misses her the most. The absence sits heavy alongside her.

She used to look forward to settling the kids at the kitchen table after Tonya got back from school. Sometimes Steve would come home early from a job and join them, his long legs getting in the way as he perched his muscular bulk on a chair that looked too flimsy to hold him.

The kids were always excited when their dad was around at mealtimes, mainly because he was daft as a brush with them. Food in, fun out – that was Steve. He'd make Tonya laugh so hard, she'd snort orange squash out her nostrils.

And Tonya would do what they called her gobble and gabble routine – telling them all about her day and her friends and the teachers and yapping on about what she'd played and what she'd read, because she loved her books – she got that from Kim. And she'd manage to eat everything on her plate at the same time as chatting – Steve said she must be able to breathe though her ears – and it was always boisterous and noisy, like a proper family, although there were far too many swear words for them to be like the families you see on the telly. They don't even swear on *EastEnders*.

Now teatimes are so fucking quiet.

Steve avoids coming back early these days. Darryl still squeaks and points and chatters on, poor little sod. But Kim's lost the heart to play along, although she does her best to fake a smile now and then.

Ayesha comes round to paint some henna patterns on her hands. Kim couldn't be less arsed, but it helps her friend feel like she's doing *something*. She brings Mo. He's strapped to his mobility chair, head lolled to one side, watching a *Peppa Pig* DVD alongside Darryl. With no Tonya, without her making him play her games, he's retreated into a cartoon world.

'You sure he knows she's gone?'

'Yeah, I think so.'

'How can you tell?' She wonders if that's too cruel a question.

Ayesha considers. 'Little things. He's quieter. Khalid reckons Mo don't look at him properly now. I told him, "Who'd want to look at your ugly mug?!"'

Kim looks at her cigarette lighter, fighting the urge for a fag. She chews her nails on the hand Ayesha's not working on instead.

'Steve won't look at me.'

'He'll come round.' Ayesha stops making her intricate lines and pats her shoulder.

'Will he though?' says Kim.

'You still shagging?'

Kim rolls her eyes.

'Nor us. Be thankful to Allah for small mercies.' She winks, which Kim always thinks looks a bit odd with the robes and all.

When she finishes Kim's hand, Ayesha gets Mo's plastic beaker and gives him a sip of juice. His head thrashes as he latches on to the spout. She braces against him as he tugs at it like Skid's mental Jack Russell-cross mongrel.

What would Kim do if one of her kids was as fucked up as Mo? Could she cope as well as Ayesha seems to? Come to think of it, Tonya might be well fucked up by now. But she'd take that. Better than never knowing. Better than never seeing her girl again.

The pains start soon after Ayesha leaves, and Kim almost welcomes them.

Tonya

Yum, yum, yum. Bunny likes chocolate. Bunnies like carrots. In the wild. Wild bunnies. Grrr!

But there is no carrots in the little room.

There's no chocolate neither.

This sweet stuff tastes like – dunno.

It smells weird in here.

Mmmmm. Sip, sip. One sip for me. One sip for Bunny. Some of it gets on his long furry ear. Silly Bunny.

I tell Bunny, 'You need discipline, you little heathen.' Then I bash Bunny. Smack, smack, smack!

'Go to bed with no tea, young lady.'

But Bunny ain't a girl. He's a he. But he goes to bed with no tea neither. And then we laugh.

Mummy

I suppose I should find it amusing to see whiskers of sherry around her lips, but when she blatantly lies and tells me she hasn't touched the bottle, which she's obviously taken from the pantry, it riles me.

'There is no hiding the truth, Izzy. Lies are always found out in the end.'

She refuses to look at me and strokes her toy rabbit in a manner I find somewhat enraging.

'Izzy! Are you listening to me? Our Lord always knows if you have been a good girl, or a bad one.'

She pipes up, 'Like Santa?' and I'm unsure whether this is bare-faced cheek or a genuine question.

'I will ask you one more time – did you drink the sherry, after I told you never to touch those bottles?'

She tilts her face down and shakes her head.

'Do not lie to me, young lady.'

She looks up and I see her chin jut out in that unattractive, combative manner.

'You expect me to believe you, when you're covered in it?'

She shrugs, which enrages me even more.

'You wilful little liar!'

'You're the liar!' she shouts, scooting away from my raised hand, as if I would ever hurt her. 'Liar, liar, pants on fire. You said there was a puppy!'

I am surprised she remembers the original story I made up to persuade her away from the shop, away from that awful woman, to come along with me. But her cleverness does not impress me. As my mammy would say, 'So sharp she might cut herself.'

I send her to bed without serving the mackerel salad. Good for both my skin and a child's brain development. I refuse to reward such bad behaviour.

She has dirtied her bunny, so I put it in the wash, and when she cries for it in the night, I calmly explain how she has brought this upon herself and suggest I may have to throw it away unless she treats it, and me, with a little more respect.

Tonya

I am hungry.

Darryl likes chicken nuggees. Yum yum.

I like ice cream.

Not that green stuff *she* puts on pasta.

I hate The Woman. She says my mum won't come for me coz I'm bad and she don't want me no more.

I am so hungry.

Kim

When Steve comes in they watch *The One Show*, her pacing and bracing against the back of the sofa when the need takes her, then some crap Steve's following about knob-heads who get crap tattoos and go on the show to cover them up with even worse ones. She has no sympathy for the daft twats. Every one of hers means something. Tattoos aren't fucking doodles.

Then there's some other stuff she doesn't really clock.

Then it's time.

Steve takes Darryl round to Ayesha and Khalid's, carrying him wrapped in his mini duvet rather than wrestling him into the pushchair. When he gets back he says, 'He didn't even wake up. You got everything, babe?'

'Yeah.'

Apart from Tonya.

His hands look unsure as he grabs the van keys. He drives like he's taking a test. She keels forward up Hornsey Road and pants, resting her head on the dashboard.

'You okay, babe?'

She wishes he wasn't so polite. 'Okey fucking dokey.'

He holds her up halfway across the rip-off hospital car park and she squeezes his arm so hard he'll have bruises there for a week.

'Do you want me to stay?'

'For fuck's sake, Steve!' She doesn't know who he thinks she is any more. 'Course I want you to stay. You got me into this sodding mess.'

He attempts a grim smile. And the unsaid hangs there – she got them into the bigger mess.

It kicks off faster than the other two labours. Suddenly a torrent of pain. Steve looks like a kid caught in a thunderstorm.

The harder the contractions clench her, the more she roars. Her throat's not wide enough for the rush of hurt. The nurses, who have seen pretty much everything, ask her to keep it down a bit, watch her language, which is disturbing the rest of the ward. She screams at them to go fuck themselves. Then language disappears altogether and it's all guttural bellows.

She read in one of those misery porn magazines (*Other Poor Sods Have It Harder Than You*) how people (generally women, girls, female children) hover above the bad thing happening to their bodies, dissociating from the hurt and the abuse. They observe the pain from the top corner of a room.

If fucking only.

Kim's relationship with physical pain is the opposite of her reaction to emotional stuff, which she generally tries to ignore. If anything, she embraces it – welcoming the tattooist's needle, any needle. And it's the same giving birth. She doesn't float above the tearing below, she dives right in, deep inside the gaping, blood-soaked, messy darkness of it. Welded to it, until the agony blots out all else. Until she's nothing but fucking pain.

She hears herself howling, but couldn't tell you what words make a pathetic attempt to contain and shape that noise because she's right inside the animal part of herself.

Her sense of time fractures. Parts of her body rip. The only thing she's sure of now is the pain, so she clings to it to stop herself shattering, dispersing.

And this is the only time she doesn't think of Tonya.

Afterwards, the quiet is too much.

Flayed, naked, skinless, boneless, she lies empty. A jellyfish. Less than animal – a thing. Wobbly as the newborn she's delivered. No longer sure of her purpose. It's some time before the fragments congeal into some sort of mosaic – something resembling a version of Kim.

Then she remembers.

And a new pain seeps through – different, more acute.

Loss.

Such a tiny word.

Giving birth to one child. Losing another.

Instantly, she wants her daughter more than anything.

She can't allow other feelings – feelings for the baby – to distract her from Tonya. Somehow, she has to find her girl, and for that she needs to ride this fresh pain in every breath. This. This. This. Like her own heartbeat.

She shuts her eyes for a second. Then she's out.

Her ten minute nap while they clean up the baby is as deep and untroubled as it's ever been. But then Steve gently shakes her arm and hands her a bundle. Their son. Nathaniel, they'd agreed on, from a telly show she'd liked *Six Feet Under* – all about death.

She settles him on her deflated belly, looks into the baby's squalling face. And feels nothing.

Mummy

The next morning, I oversleep a little. I must have somehow forgotten to lock her door again and discover she's not in her bed when I go to check. Thank the Lord the front and back doors are always locked.

I try to hurry downstairs, but find I have to walk slowly and steadily.

She is sitting on the kitchen floor, surrounded by debris. A confetti of crumbs and paper. She has pulled apart almost an entire loaf of organic spelt bread. The Manuka honey jar (24 Plus, not exactly inexpensive) is practically empty. I see a corner of crumpled foil from my Duchy unsalted butter sticking out from under the fridge.

Without meaning to, I start shouting. She seems oblivious, sitting totally still.

I inhale fully, gather myself and ask, sternly, 'What has happened here, Izzy?'

When I poke her shoulder she mumbles, 'Made a san-wich.'

I am at a loss what to do. Yet something must be done to curb this stealing and lying.

My dilemma is rudely interrupted when she suddenly heaves with disgusting gagging noises, as if to expel a hairball, and brings up a glob of bread and honey, spewing it down her nightdress and onto the heated granite floor.

I will not be able to get the bile stains out of the broderie anglaise.

After I've cleaned up her mess, I lock her in her room, put on yet another wash and spray my Red Roses to mask the smells in the kitchen. I have to shut the door because the sickly odour lingers beneath the scent, reminding me of worse smells, worse memories.

But I can't think of that.

We'll see if going without food today will make her think about what she has done. She will have to behave if she is to be rewarded with her breakfast tomorrow.

Kim

Steve's back at work when she comes out of hospital. Had to go in. He's had too much time off already.

Before she can face hauling herself and the baby to the bus stop, she sits outside the Whittington entrance, rummaging in the overnight bag for the packet of fags she hid right at the bottom.

She's promised herself just the one.

She joins the other dedicated smokers: an old boy and a bloke who could be his son, or younger brother, puffing in unison; a leathery old girl in her hospital shift, dressing gown around her shoulders to hide her bare arse, stoically pulling her drip on the trolley thing, ciggie clamped between thin lips; a young girl clinging to her fag as she coughs and splutters into her other hand. Almost heroic.

The navy-blue T-shirt from New Look hangs droopy and creased over Kim's deflated belly. She props the baby in the crook of her elbow and fires up her own fag, careful to blow the smoke away from his face.

She smiles to herself, remembering Tonya's exaggerated eye roll and tut when she saw her smoke – something she'd picked up from Ayesha. Five going on fifty-five, that little madam. Almost six, now.

Kim's got her a birthday card. She's hidden it in a shoebox at the bottom of the wardrobe.

She's giving up for good this time. After this one.

She'll get up in a minute.

*

She gets through the next few hours like a sleepwalker. She's not even aware of how tight she's been holding her body until Steve gets in for his tea, then she goes straight up to bed, leaving him to settle the kids – those she has left.

Mummy

It has been a hard week. Every single thing I have asked her to do has been met with a wall of sullen defiance.

Now she sits in the bath. Most nights I tend to leave her alone for a little while. Sometimes I hear her humming softly to herself, but as soon as she hears me approach or sees the bathroom door open the sounds abruptly stop.

She can't bring herself to reward me with a smile.

Bathing her has never been easy. She startles when I reach out to her. So I sit on the toilet seat and watch. She shifts around in the bath and turns her back to me.

No matter, madam. I will sit here until the water goes cold if needs be. And I will wash her hair, no matter what battle that entails.

She must be clean.

I count her vertebrae which poke through the hair sleeked across her tiny shoulders. She is all angles, all hollows, all bones. Beautiful. Like I imagine Kate Moss looked as a child. The same feral cheekbones and defiant pout. I could send her down the catwalk.

That is something I always yearned for.

If only my daddy had not insisted we ate every single mouthful of the starch-on-a-plate that appeared each dinnertime, I too might have had this wonderful start in life. My sister, being his favourite, was allowed to leave the table before finishing, but not me, *the porker*. Oh, to be slim! I might have avoided the shaming plumpness that made the other children laugh and taunt me as 'the Michelin Man'; blimp-like, ungraceful, my shocking contours corralled into my scratchy school uniform like an over-stuffed sausage.

It was torture. Yet now, obese schoolchildren are the norm and their terrible, lumpen parents seemingly without embarrassment. I agree with Jamie Oliver on this, although he is not exactly Mr Svelte himself. And his diction is appalling.

My voice coach corrected a multitude of sins, although Michael then accused me of 'talking like you're in a BBC costume drama'. He understood why I wanted to better myself, but he didn't like me losing my Irish accent.

Would I be able to send Izzy to elocution lessons? Apart from her bad language, the London twang isn't nice. For her to get on in life she has to be able to talk properly, old-fashioned though that notion might seem.

I always wanted more for myself. As a child, I had such a clear vision of who I might become – a model! I had the height. But puppy fat, swiftly followed by a cruel puberty and vicious acne, put paid to that dream.

'Spotty Muldoon!' laughed my daddy. 'She's an ugly little bitch, isn't she, Margaret?' And my betraying sister would arrange her lovely face into a smile to humour him, although there was no amusement in her eyes.

I would lie in my narrow bed, confined to my mean, humdrum life, stroking the marvellous contours of my sister's Barbie doll, imagining a different world – one where I would become a glamorous, more magical person.

I had only once felt chiffon, when Aunty Kathleen visited Mammy in that beautiful cerise blouse. I rarely had the chance to see anything so lovely. I remember fingering silk scarves in the only department store for miles. But a single touch was enough. I knew instantly that these were the materials for me. I desired a world wrapped in shimmer and gossamer.

Yet I was condemned to live in cottons and wools. Boring functional garments. No colour. No style. Doomed by an accident of birth.

My mother was not the least interested in fashion. My sister and I were parched for it. When Mammy went for one of her rare 'spruce-ups', I would sit and pore over the glorious, glossy magazines in the hairdressers. Months old and dog-eared, they were almost holy to me, for which I felt suitably guilty.

I miss Aunty Kathleen. So stylish. But I am grateful for the money she left my sister and I when she died. Breast cancer.

Even now, to my eye I don't look quite right in some of the lovely clothes Michael bought for me. I fear I never will. Designer dresses only look perfect on those honed to the bone.

I bear the acne scars today, harsh reminders of the taunts of 'Freddy' (I assume meaning Freddy Kreuger; so original) and 'the Bearded Lady' that blighted my teenage years – years marred by grotesque periods and facial hair and all the attendant horrors that my warped ovaries decided to bestow upon me.

A twisted, tortured reproductive system betraying me.

This child is blessed, although she doesn't know it and she does not care. There is no gratitude in her small, stony heart.

'Izzy.'

Her head turns and her huge Twiggy eyes look up at me.

'Time to wash your hair.' I make my voice trill.

She ignores me.

In a pleasing sing-song manner I ask, 'Shall we make it all nice and shiny?'

She turns away.

I would have adored lovely long hair like Izzy's, but Mammy forced me to have mine shorn. She cut off Margaret's hair and then mine. Always one for practicalities, as farmers' wives tend to be, although we didn't understand why she sobbed so as she yanked and hacked at us with the kitchen scissors.

Daddy was furious when he saw and gave her a pasting. He adored Margaret's hair. He was always stroking her long, dark locks, singing 'Scarlet Ribbons'. Singing and stroking. Stroking and singing.

Mammy wore sunglasses for a week.

I take the showerhead and run the water so it's not too hot, not too cold.

Then I struggle to make my hands kind, because I am so irritated by her, I might comb out the knots a little roughly.

Lucy West, Staff Features Writer, *Women's World*

If you ask me, she probably knows more than she's letting on. It wouldn't surprise me if some 'friend of a friend' had something to do with the 'abduction'. My editor agrees. There's something shifty about Kim. The bloke's okay though: sexy muscles and soft eyes, a winning combo for the photos.

Still, some of the comments we get when we publish an update are a bit much – our readers sure love to hate Kim. They blame her, quite rightly in my opinion, for failing to keep a close enough eye on her daughter. Although how many of us have done the same? I once lost Lola for a few seconds in a Harris + Hoole after I was distracted by someone from my spin class.

But I never smoked while I was pregnant. Yes, I did have the odd glass of Malbec, since you mention it, but the smoking is simply unforgiveable.

We do have a laugh at some of the comments, but others are just awful. I would never write that Kim deserves to die. Or gloat at her misfortune.

My deputy editor, Maurice, mocked me for being 'soft' when I said I felt sorry for Kim at the start. And he laughed harder when I said I could understand why she might not want to do an interview. I won't make that mistake in the morning meeting again. Especially not after Maurice said the only reason Kim was keeping schtum now was because he'd heard she'd done a deal with Cynthia Lea, 'agent to the stars' (or at least the numpties on *Love Island* and *Geordie Shore*), to 'write' a book.

Perhaps it's because she looks so unsympathetic. There's not one picture out there of her crying, which rings alarm bells, doesn't it. We choose the most unflattering angles, naturally – so many of the shots we use show her snarling at the lens; the constant V sign that we have to blur. It's a narrative we currently pursue, in the same way as reality TV shows help craft the storylines – but we do have plenty of choice. Putting it kindly, she's not photogenic. Unlike dishy Steve. Kim's punching way above her weight with that man, Editorial and Marketing can agree on that at least. Readers are jealous of that sort of thing.

Naturally, we've tried for an exclusive on several occasions – given her a chance to redress the balance, to put her side across, to garner some sympathy. She's turned us down along with *Loose Women*, *This Morning*, even *Lorraine*.

Every story we've ever run has been met with a backlash of 'serves her right'. Kim, our readers deem, is too downright unlikeable to deserve a happy resolution. Although, to be honest, the child is no oil painting either. There's something rodent-like about her mouth.

If she'd just issue a photo of the new baby, that might turn things around for her.

Mummy

She lets me paint her nails.

Oh, the first time Margaret painted mine! The best fun! We both laughed so hard as we raced to scrub it all off before Mammy came home.

My heart glows when Izzy informs me, 'You do it nice. My mum don't make it neat.'

I had enough practice doing Margaret's for her.

We read for a little while. Then, when I ask her what she'd like to do next she squeals, 'Let's do dancing!' so we jig about together and it's fun, it really is. And think of the calories we'll burn.

I tire long before she does.

When she's finally out of breath, I collect the shopping from outside, where I instruct them to leave it, slice a small banana for her and settle her with earphones in front of the TV while I lie down awhile.

Later, despite my nap, I feel hardly refreshed. And we have words after I explain, for the hundredth time, that it is too dangerous for her to go outside.

'Leave me alone, you!'

'Come here, this instant! Give me the bottle. That is not something for you.'

'Fuck OFF!'

'I am warning you, Izzy.'

'I ain't IZZY!'

'Where did you find that? Give it to me now, please.'

'Gerroff me! NO!'

I understand from all I have read about child psychology that there may be some 'acting out'. And, given her appalling upbringing, I am willing to overlook some of the terrible language, for now. But I simply can't condone the smirking and the disrespect.

I make her put her hands together, to pray – to ask for forgiveness. I start the Hail Mary, closing my eyes and kneeling on the carpet next to her, to show her how it's done, as my own mother had shown me. But, when I peek, after the third round, I see she's lost interest and is gazing out of the bedroom window, blowing a spit bubble.

She could not have hurt me more if she had slapped me.

She must work towards her confirmation, although I am not sure how that might happen, in the circumstances. And the little heathen seems to delight in ignoring the lessons from scripture. She can read, of that I'm sure, as I see her eyes follow the words when I give in and read them out loud to her. But she refuses point blank to do so herself, even when I grab her finger and run it along the pages of my old *Stories About Children of the Bible*. How I adored that book. All those lovely Ladybird books.

So, I am trying a new technique. I refuse to give her lunch or dinner until we finish a chapter. Some evenings she goes to bed without eating. I lock her in her room at night to stop her rifling through my kitchen cupboards, which I've caught her doing on several occasions.

It isn't cruel – it's a necessity. If I'm ever to allow her out of the house I must be sure she'll obey my instructions. I have to trust her not to run off or betray me.

'Train her now and this is how she will go – even when she is old she will not depart from her lessons.' I looked that up on a Christian education website.

She must respect me as her mother and her teacher. She must be educated.

This is what elevates us from the beasts in the field.

Kim

'Heads, shoulders, knees and toes, knees and toes.'

At first it is so far off, it's a memory, a fading dream. Then Kim hears Tonya's Siren call magnify, although it's not exactly hearing, rather feeling the words vibrate through her body, like those flash twat 'bone conduction' earphones.

That song has driven her to the point of screaming. Tonya was obsessed, chanting it over and over. Singing it to Mo and trying to make him do the hand movements, with him flailing about like he was having a fit. Tonya was so patient with the lad, Kim often thought she'd make a good teacher.

The refrain echoes, atoms of air vibrating in that precise, well-worn pattern. Drawing her.

And Kim wakes fully, knowing she has to follow it.

No matter that it's the middle of the night. No matter Steve's not there. She has no choice.

She half falls out of bed, drags on leggings, boots, rushes down for her jacket, locks the flat behind her and walks away in swift, jerky movements, leaving a panicky message for Ayesha, saying to come round quick, even though she knows she'll probably be asleep. Ayesha has a spare key for emergencies, just as Kim has one for Ayesha's flat. And she might be up with Mo, please God, or Allah, or whoever.

She doesn't say she's left the kids home alone.

If only Steve didn't have to go back to finish that rush job in Kennington, pulling an all-nighter for double wages. South of the fucking river.

She walks so fast, she's almost running. As her heels bash the concrete she feels the impact of the pavement up in her knees and what's left of her insides. Drizzle seeps through her hair. Blood seeps into the pad wedged between her legs.

She's no idea where she's heading.

She starts sweating under her fleece, feels it trickling down her back. Her milk's soaking through her bra and T-shirt. Breasts weeping for her baby boy. Heart aching for her girl.

She finds herself up near Crouch End, trailing round smart, tree-lined roads – usually only a twenty-minute run or so, but a world away from the estate. She pauses on Mount View, gripping the railings against the view spread before her, sending her cry over London, twinkling and unconcerned below.

'Tonya!'

She trudges on, intermittently shouting. An arthritic woman with an equally stiff-legged Labrador calls across the road, 'Have you lost your dog, lovey?'

She comes over to Kim, who's hooked between flight and freezing. The elderly dog ambles up and pushes her hand with his grizzled nose and out of habit she strokes it.

'I know what it's like. This one went missing last month. Found him in someone's garden all the way over on the Tottenham Lane side, didn't we, Jasper? Thanks to his collar. Is yours micro-chipped? I swear by— Oh!'

The shock of recognition silences the old bird's unintentional barbs. She sees it's that poor mother who lost her little girl. The one the awful tabloids have vilified. Jasper and his owner stare at the woman with the pale face and wild eyes as she makes her escape.

She gets colder as she circuits, making a loop around certain streets, drawn by an undercurrent of longing, or some strange, psychic magnetism. Because Kim feels she's close to Tonya. And she can't leave now, but she knows she needs to go home.

She's pulled in both directions – like two vultures are fighting over a length of her small intestines, dragging out the sinews and smooth muscle and mucus and gunk until it's as taut as a tightrope and she might snap.

They'll take away the kids she's left abandoned alone in their beds and Steve will hunt her down and squeeze the fading life out of her scrawny throat. And for that she might be grateful.

What if Nathaniel suffocates himself? What if Darryl wakes up, as he's given to doing in the middle of the night recently, disturbed by his brother's fretting, and finds her lighter and sets fire to the flat and roasts himself and the baby alive?

'Ladybird, ladybird, fly away home, your house in on fire and your children are gone', another of Tonya's favourites; so many of the old nursery rhymes full-on horror shows.

At her nearest, Kim is just two roads away from Tonya, who can feel the closeness of her mother in her dream.

One hundred yards as the crow flies.

Mummy

'No!'

'GO AWAY!'

'Won't.'

'Shut up!'

'Fuck off!'

'Bugger off, you!'

'Leave me alone!'

'Why don't my mum come and get me?'

'Why can't I go out?'

'Why, why, WHY?'

'You're NOT my mum.'

'Gerroff! Gerroff! Gerroff!' Repeated *ad nauseum*.

'I hate you!' Which comes out as, 'I ate you!'

Her favourite words and phrases. Not a very nice list, is it.

Plus, the infernal, 'Let it gooOOOO—' This screeched – until I put a stop to it – as if she's in pain.

I do not think I have had an uninterrupted night in all the time she's been here. Seven weeks is it? And I am fully aware, as I would tell Michael when he nagged and nagged at me, that 'self-medication' is not ideal. But needs must.

Tonya

It's quiet here.

Why don't Daddy come to get me? Why don't my mum come?

The Woman says they don't want me because I'm too naughty.

I wish I could go out to play but *she* says it's DAN-GER-OUS! And she says the school is still closed.

I wish I could play with Mo. I don't want him to get another girlfriend.

Mummy

Every cell hurts. If I lie completely still I can almost bear it. What I cannot bear are the scratches at the bedroom door. Are they real?

How long have I been ill?

Hours? A day?

I remember being so thirsty. I gulped water from the tap. That's how bad things were.

I should not have opened another bottle.

One glorious thought keeps me going – at least I will lose weight! I feel my stomach, satisfyingly concave, dipping from my hips as I lie on my back.

I fall into another dark sleep.

As I come to, I hear her knocking, whispering, 'Please—'

Later, wails, 'I'm hungry. I'm HUN-GRY!'

I push my throbbing forehead into the pillow. The silk reeks.

The next time I wake, I think I hear her say, 'Please, Mummy.' But it's too late now, after so many fights, where she refused, point-blank, to call me that.

I should have locked her in her room.

I reach across to my bedside cabinet for my glass.

*

When, at last, I manage to put my weak legs on the floor, straighten my twisted nightdress and totter to my bedroom door, using it to steady myself as I turn the key and open it slowly, I see she has curled against it like some dog. The ridges of her backbone confront me like an accusation.

Downstairs, she's made a total mess of my cupboards.

God forgive me for my failings.

Kim

The early commuters are already clogging the road and the murky charcoal sky is promising to lighten as Kim slots the key in the lock – to find it already open. Fuck. Now it'll all kick off with Steve. This will finish them, she knows it will. He might be an easy-going bloke, but after everything, he won't be able to forgive her this.

She pushes open the kitchen door in slow motion, a tightness high in her throat, and sees Ayesha sitting at the table, rocking the baby on her chest.

Thank fuck she got the message.

She won't look up. Kim takes a breath, then reaches for him, but Ayesha holds on.

'I'm sorry.' She trips forward with fatigue.

Ayesha doesn't move, doesn't smile.

'Ayesha, I had to.'

Ayesha hugs the baby tighter and shakes her head. She shoves the spare key across the table like she doesn't want it any more.

Kim's shoulders slump. And in answer to the unasked questions and accusations and silent anger, she says quietly, 'I heard Tonya.'

Steve never finds out.

Mummy

I am looking forward to making a mint tea to warm myself after the trudge from the car. I have been forced to park streets away, in this relentless drizzle too. But as I take one step inside the front door, I hear a male voice in the living room! I drop the Waitrose bags and bang my elbow against the doorframe as I stumble. Heart hammering, I squash against the wall.

My panic only lasts a split second, then I exhale, realising it's only the television.

She must have somehow escaped from her room again. Did I not lock it? Fatigue is making me slack. She has managed to switch on the TV all by herself. Such a clever girl to be able to work out the controller. It took Michael so long to show me how to use it, but then, I was never very good with technology. He mocked me – his 'dizzy blonde'. Hardly politically correct.

I peek into the lounge. She seems very quiet, for once.

No harm done.

I have prepared for these eventualities – her occasional, unsupervised forays downstairs – attaching a locking mailbox to stop her naughty little fingers prying open the flap; unplugging the phone if I'm not here, although she never seemed to realise what an old-fashioned telephone was for. Plus, the French shutters hide my front windows and our front hedge is high.

No one would notice she exists behind these walls. Even someone on the doorstep might not hear her through the triple-glazing, and she doesn't cry out as a rule. My warnings of what will happen to her if I find her screaming have sunk in, or perhaps she finally realises she is better off here with me than with that terrible woman.

She has somehow found the BBC news channel, which I was watching last night. Like any good mother, I would never usually let her see news coverage. I shield her from all the horror and violence in the world, restricting her viewing to age-appropriate programmes. Ideally, I wouldn't even allow her those, only she is not often amused by my lessons, or drawing, or card games. She has a stubborn gene.

The usual reports of death and destruction, man's cruelty to man, blare out, but I leave her to this for a moment – it might make her realise how lucky she is here, safe in the beautiful sanctuary of my home. I feel a pain in my side as I stoop to lift the shopping and struggle to carry the bags to the kitchen.

I haul my collection of organic vegetables onto the work surface and reach over to switch on the kettle. Too late I hear the terrible words, '— missing child Tonya Searle. The girl, abducted from a north London branch of Peacocks before Christmas—'

I lunge for the living room.

'—her parents, Kim and Stephen—'

She has scooted closer to the TV, with one hand, probably sticky, pressed against the screen.

Oh, sweet Jesus, no! I freeze.

'Police have no new leads in the investigation of the abduction—'

Thank God! That is something—

She looks round when she hears me, then swiftly turns her head back to watch. I trip forwards into the room, spluttering, 'Turn that off immediately!'

A photo of her own face appears on the screen. I can't see the controller. Her mouth drops open.

'Kim Searle has been subjected to a barrage of abuse on—'

Where is the damn remote!?

'Oh! Oh!'

There is a close-up of that nasty woman's face, and as I finally spot the controller in her other hand and grab for it, snatching it away, she suddenly screams, 'Mum! Mum!'

And that desperate tone is the final insult.

I don't remember exactly how it happened, truly I don't, but I must have accidentally caught her face as I wrenched the remote away from her grip to switch off the report. And there's now blood on her lip.

I rush away, like a coward. I can't bear to look at her crumpled face.

It takes me several minutes before I gather myself, breathing deeply in the pantry, sipping a little brandy for the shock, then I get the TCP from the cupboard along with a pad of cotton wool and go back in to tend to the cut.

She is sitting where she was before, still looking at the black screen.

Kim

She rides waves of exhaustion. Fatigue brings back some of the numbness, which is almost a relief. And the amazing thing is, Steve takes over. He steps up. He changes more nappies in two weeks with this one than he's done in five sodding years and more with Tonya and Darryl combined. He takes the baby from her leaden arms and walks up and down the three paces of the flat, back and forth, back and forth, gently bouncing him up and down against his chest to get him back to sleep. Hushing and soothing him.

Curled on the sofa, Kim watches. But she can't reach for the child. The only thing she feels for the baby is guilt.

Steve does things without her asking, or telling him, or shouting at him. The midwife's impressed.

And when her milk isn't enough, because this little devil's ravenous and demanding pretty much all the bloody time and it's too painful for her to let him gnaw away at her, Steve makes up the formula and shoves the bottle in the kid's mouth and turns to her and says, 'Try and get some kip, hey, babe?'

So she falls back on the pillow she's brought down to the sofa, closes her eyes and disappears for a few moments.

She comes round to find Steve on the floor, playing with Darryl, the baby in a tiny, fresh Arsenal Babygro – emblazoned with the slogan, I'M NOT OUT OF NAPPIES YET AND I ALREADY HATE SPURS – conked out in his carrycot.

Taking on the baby isn't the only thing he manages. He talks to the police and answers the phone and bats away relatives, mates and neighbours, saying they're not up for visitors right now, leave it a bit, yeah, and he posts regular Facebook updates, not that there's anything new coming in, but Liaison Woman tells him it's good to keep at it. Police are still sifting through hour after hour of CCTV footage, according to her. They're still trawling through calls and tip-offs. They're still bullshitting, as far as Kim can make out, when he relays these updates.

She can't stomach it, but he takes the baby outside and lets the photographers take pictures. Nathaniel's startled face, eyes and mouth perfect 'O' shapes in the flashes, will appear in newspapers alongside an old image of his sister, in another appeal for more information.

Steve has started talking to her in a quiet, polite voice that makes her feel like a visitor in her own home, some friend of a friend, perhaps, who's come to stay.

That night, as he lies on his side of the bed and she turns away, scootching over to her side, not that there's much space, she feels his foot reach across, his toes resting against her heel. And she can't help it, but she flinches, so he moves away and then there's nothing.

His breathing slows. Kim waits for unconsciousness, staring into thoughts that turn liquid and melt into each other.

Just a few miles away, Tonya twitches in her sleep like a kitten.

Kim's body jolts like she's been tasered and she's instantly wide awake.

She felt something touch her hand.

She shakes Steve, who groans and gets up and searches under the bed, like she's a big bloody baby herself.

For the rest of the night she keeps the light on.

Mummy

I fell in love with it the moment I spotted it on the Alex and Alexa website. Delicate blush lace. Frothy. As pretty as anything Audrey Hepburn might have worn as a child.

The sort of present I would have adored.

As I zip her into it, she reminds me of the expensive dolls I saw in the window of the department store when Mammy took us on the bus into town just before Christmas one year. But when I pestered for one, saying it wasn't fair because Daddy had bought Margaret a beautiful dolly, I got the pasting of my life.

This child wriggles so.

She could be dainty, should she choose, blessed with her looks if not her nature. As long as she keeps her mouth shut.

I turn her this way and that in front of the mirror. She doesn't seem interested in her lovely new dress. Or the sweet ribbon in her hair. Scarlet ribbons.

How many hours have I spent in front of mirrors? Michael would say too many. Monitoring my weight. Trying to fix my face, covering the ravages of the pustules that afflicted my adolescence. My reflection has always disappointed me.

In secret, I would gaze at myself when not much older than she is now. Like a budgerigar with a shiny surface, I couldn't tear my eyes away, seeing what my daddy saw. Grieving. To him I was always an 'ugly little whore', and later, when vile hairs sprouted on my body, thanks to my warped hormones, 'a hairy-arsed little whore'.

Mammy felt my obsession was sinful and dragged me from my examinations, calling me vain. In *The Nun's Story* they have no mirrors. Their hair is shorn. But when I said to Mammy that Sister Luke was not suited to the stark convent life and neither was I, she took the belt to the back of my knees, leaving angry red welts.

This child doesn't seem suited to this beautiful frock. At best, she tolerates it.

Within minutes, she has gone back to her solitary game, dancing her rabbit around the room. I scold her because she plays too roughly. Eventually, nagging becomes too wearing and I leave her to her own devices, escaping into *Sense and Sensibility*.

I'm annoyed to see her scratching her arm, as if the lace itches.

Margaret always looked so lovely in her dresses. Thanks to my vile 'puppy fat' I looked hideous in all my clothes. But my sister was a true princess. Lustrous dark hair and fine features. She walked like a queen, holding Daddy's hand as we went to church, Mammy dragging me along, nagging me to straighten my back and stop scowling.

I saw the way Daddy lit up when Margaret smiled at him. I was never so easy to love.

Ah, that school fancy dress competition. From a more innocent time, before ridiculous accusations of cultural appropriation. Margaret dressed as a geisha – a tiny doll-like figurine in sandals with cork stuck to the bottom. Her hair a magnificent contraption Mammy made into three huge buns like a giant cottage loaf. She had borrowed a dressing gown from Aunty Kathleen as a kimono and wrapped a scarf around her waist, tying it into a gorgeous big bow at the back. And the make-up! Again, borrowed – white face, blood-red lips, black elongated eyes.

I wished with all my might that I too could be transformed into such a beautiful vision. But no, one showy child was enough. Otherwise the church ladies might have thought our mammy vain.

I wore a dun-brown shift and was allowed a single white feather in my hair. A Red Indian. Boring. Galling.

Margaret won a prize. I started crying in a jealous rage.

'You can stop your grizzling right now, or I'll give you something to cry about,' warned Mammy.

I ask Izzy to take off the dress before dinner, as her table manners still leave much to be desired. For once she complies with little backchat.

She shoots me wary looks over her beaker. After several breakages, we've regressed to plastic instead of glass. When I reach across her to put down a napkin beside her plate, she ducks, making out I am some sort of monster. I ignore her nonsense, yet I suspect something has occurred.

Later that evening I discover the cause of her nervousness. As I fold her beautiful new dress, there! The result of her wildness – a tear in the delicate lace sleeve.

Kim

She takes to napping in the afternoons, which isn't a good thing because she's got to watch over Nate and Darryl. Even though she makes sure to lock the doors, she still worries that one of them might, somehow, be spirited away.

When Darryl's not at playgroup, she asks Ayesha to come round to keep an eye on him and the baby, like she's not got enough on. Then she crawls into bed and crashes out for ten minutes or so – before she catapults back to consciousness, shaking and sweating and sometimes shouting out, so that Ayesha runs upstairs, holding her long skirt high, to see what's the matter.

She's dead on her feet. So out of it it's like being stoned. She can't concentrate on anything. She'll start a cup of tea then forget where she is, what she's doing. She feels heavy and clumsy, like she's on a planet with different gravity.

Nate starts whining and she has to walk out of the room because she can't bear the baby's hungry cries screeching through her. She can't bear any of his cries.

So Steve has to take more time off work to help out, although that really means do everything. Kim would panic about the money if her attention wasn't so totally shredded.

She hopes that just one night's proper rest will put this weird brand of exhaustion behind her, help her get on with things again. But when she goes to bed she lies rigid, too tired for sleep.

Each time she sinks a little, her muscles spasm and she's startled awake with a lurch like she's falling.

Then she lies on her side and worries about Tonya.

And she tries not to panic about her emotions when she picks up Nate – as in, there are none.

Around four in the morning. The time people slip away in hospices. She's not asleep.

She hears the baby bleat and on automatic swings her legs from the bed and pads across the synthetic carpet that makes her hair static. She peers into the crib and watches the baby's mouth open and contort, seeking her out.

Her breasts brace for the onslaught. She's about to reach for him when her response simply withers. She stands, Medusa-cursed, looking at its mewling, gummy face. She feels a weight on the top of her head like a headache starting. There's a contraction in her chest around her heart.

The baby's noises change, building into the insistent hunger alert. And Kim stands and looks and does nothing. It almost doesn't register when the tone turns from squeak to squawk to desperate scream.

She holds on to the side of the cot to stop herself from sinking.

And that cry could break the hearts of a thousand women whose arms would reach past immobile Kim, to soothe, to succour.

But she can't. She just . . . can't.

The cry is impossible. Darryl joins in.

Then Steve's at her side, hungover with fatigue and resentment as he shoulders her aside and reaches to lift the furious shrieking bundle, and he says to her, 'What the fuck, Kim!?'

And she has no idea.

Mummy

The next day I hear her talking to herself in the kitchen – a chirrupy noise, unlike the others. Quietly, fearful of disturbing her, I peer around the door to watch.

She's crouching down, fascinated by something on the floor. She addresses it with baby-speak, trilling nonsense words. Her tone is kind.

She pauses and looks round, sensing I am in the room

'What have you got there, Izzy darling?'

'Nothin.'

'No-*thing*. And I doubt very much it is nothing.'

I notice how her body tenses as I step towards her. She tries to hide whatever it is she is playing with, spreading the skirt of the cute smocked dress I bought for her – Little Alice, another online spree – so I cannot see.

'Show me, please.' Not sharp, not loud, simply firm, as you must be when you train a child.

'S'mine.'

I pull her away to find a woodlouse on its back, legs scrabbling at the sky. I scoop up the vile insect in some kitchen towel, unlock the kitchen door and fling it out. She's too fast for me and scoots under my arm as I'm closing it. But, instead of running down the garden screaming for help, she drops to her knees and begins searching for the creature in the wet grass.

I watch for a few seconds before I grab her arm and bring her inside. She doesn't resist much.

*

That night she braces against my touch when I attempt to brush her hair and curls herself into a tight ball on the floor like a hedgehog.

I give up. I'm exhausted.

Sometimes I feel as lonely with her here as I did before I had her.

Then I have an idea. The more I consider it, the more I think it might help. I decide we might have a little celebration. There is no reason it cannot be her birthday some time soon. I can pick any date – it is only a white lie. And it is such a dark time, just after Candlemas.

In preparation, I ask her what she would like for her birthday and she immediately says, 'A llama! A real one.'

I give the matter some thought.

I could take a chance and order a rocking horse. The Christmas gifts weren't a hit for very long; she soon got bored with them. Such a short attention span.

I could lock her in her room when they make the delivery and turn my music up loud. They would only need to lift it into the hall. Perhaps we won't be able to put it in her room – I might not be able to drag it upstairs by myself. But I wouldn't want a rocking horse cluttering up the lounge—

Then, divine inspiration!

'Izzy?'

Nothing but a sullen silence aimed in my direction as she starts fiddling with her crayons, sprawling on the carpet and doodling rather than drawing on the paper.

'Izzy, sweetheart?'

As usual, she refuses to acknowledge her new name, but I can tell she is listening.

'Would you like it if we got a kitten?'

I'm tired of looking at her sulky mouth. She could transform her face with a sweet smile, as long as she keeps her lips together to hide that tooth.

Her silence grates. At moments, I want to slap her face.

Of course, I never would.

A kitten might change everything.

Kim

Kim can't move her arm. It's trapped and hot. She pulls against a heavy, clammy weight, realising Steve's turned in his sleep and managed to pin her underneath him. It takes all her strength to push him onto his side and snatch her hand away.

He barely stirs. He sleeps the sleep of the dead and Kim used to envy him that, although she tries not to wonder where his mind now travels. She catches him making odd noises in his sleep, but he claims he can never remember his dreams and she daren't push him because she can't bear to know the truth.

She rubs her bicep, and as the numbness starts to fade she feels pins and needles, then shooting pains careering up and down her arm. And she thinks, at some point in the future, when the numbness and exhaustion start to wear off, this kind of pain is the least of what her heart might feel.

She props herself up against the pillow and looks at him, slumped onto his back again.

His face is more familiar to her than her own. Ayesha says it's 'full of character', then she cackles, because they both know that Ayesha's Khalid is sexier, more conventionally handsome in his exotic, smouldering way. Although he's so useless with the kids, Kim could never be bothered fancying him.

Unlike Khalid, Steve's a godsend as a parent. Genuinely kind. Sure, he's a bit daft – hopeless with money, which causes most of their ructions. When they talk about providing for the kids' future he laughs, and says, 'Someone's got to die soon, babe. Or we could win the lottery.' Given that

Steve's lot are about as flush as her own, an inheritance is as unlikely as a win, seeing as he never buys a sodding ticket.

As well as fancying him, she used to love him. Proper, 'in love' loving. That diffused with the kids, which was fine. Now and again she worried about his drinking and they rowed about him smoking weed, but she always felt she could rely on him if it came to it.

Now it's really fucking come to it, yet she currently has no idea what she feels about him. Within the space of five minutes she wants to kill him, then aches for him to hold her tight and tell her everything will be okay. More often, she feels dead inside and wonders if she'll ever want to fuck him again. Then she feels sorry for him and for herself. Something else she's lost.

Occasionally a fury flares out of nowhere and she has an urge to do violence, like she could angry-fuck him, hurt him, punish him for not finding Tonya and bringing her back home, but that's got nothing to do with the actual fucking.

Blaming Steve makes no sense. And if she can wish him dead on a regular basis, when he's the one who's done nothing wrong, she can only imagine how hard he hates her.

Only Steve doesn't really do hate like that. He's more generous, though God knows how, given that, while not as fucked up as her family, it was hardly *The Waltons* with his mob either. And if Steve doesn't want to hurt her, that's just another thing to make her feel even more guilty. And Kim being Kim, that makes her hate him a little more.

Plus, how the fuck's he managed to put on weight at a time like this?

She's always liked his bulk, his washed-out blue eyes, his big nose.

She'd say, 'You know what they say about a bloke with a big conk?' And Steve would chip in, 'Big nose – Man-Sized Kleenex.' One of their corny double-act jokes when they've had a few. It tickles them and that's all that counts.

It hurts her to see the strain etched into the lines around his eyes, the dark skin underneath, like that time she punched him when he snuck up behind her and grabbed her arse and she lashed out – a knee-jerk reaction. He didn't even have a go at her for that and most men she's known would have KO'd her.

Kim jumps. Without her realising, Steve's eyes have opened and she quickly turns her head. Weird. When he looks at her these days, properly seeing her, like now, it makes her feel embarrassed.

Tonya

'Thankyou-thankyou-thankyou.'
    She's got big blue eyes and long gold hair and a real CROWN!
    She asks me what's her name, but I don't know yet.
    'Just Princess.'
    She tells me it's my birthday – The Woman, not my princess doll.
    Then she says, 'Cheers!'
    And I ask her when my mum's coming. But she don't know.
    And after a bit she starts crying.

Mummy

Before me stands an angel holding an immense fiery staff. Beautiful and terrifying in equal measures. I know I am found wanting before this mighty being, but it is not clear what I must do to prove my worthiness.

I am to follow.

Tripping and stumbling, I try to keep up with the light, but it trails ever further away from me, graceful, unforgiving, and I fall and the brightness wanes even though I crawl towards it as best I can.

The angel fades, and I am left alone in absolute darkness. I wake with tears in my eyes and a gnawing emptiness inside me, which is hard to bear.

And I know she is to blame. The girl is at the root of all my pain – this crushing disappointment. There is something bad within her that spoils everything.

Yet I do not know what I am to do with her.

And I reach for my glass, but it's on its side by my pillow and there's a nasty stain on my duvet cover.

Kim

It's a dull, shivery afternoon. As Steve escapes into a late stint at work, she goes round to the station alone. Ayesha minds the kids, which makes Kim feel guilty because she knows she's taking advantage of her friend, although she can't see an alternative.

There's something about police Kim can't stand. It gets right under her skin. It might be from the time of paranoia, when she and her mates hated anyone in a uniform, any figure of authority.

But it's more than that. The whiff of power and bullying, feeling out of control, at their mercy, reminds her of Dave. Watching her brother's eyes for that look. Holding her breath, waiting for him to strike.

She sits across from one of the uniforms now. There've been so many she can't keep track of names. Plod One. Plod Two. Fucking Liaison Woman.

And she's pretty sure this one's only going through the motions, meeting her to 'update her on the investigation', to tick some box.

He tells her what they're 'currently engaged in' – apart from 'thoroughly checking the established timeline' they're also 'approaching and enlisting members of the local community' aiming to 'seek further assistance'. Kim wonders if some of her knob-head neighbours constitute a local community. Or if the line of questioning – 'Have you seen her?' 'No' – assists anyone.

He says the DI has put out a press release saying, 'We continue to work with the family' and Kim realises this, right here, is what that means: sitting in a crappy room with an even crappier cup of coffee, lying to her face about 'possible developments'.

Every uniform glosses over what they continue failing to do – get fucking anywhere.

Tonya's still missing.

Kim bites her nails like she hates them, foot tapping against her chair leg.

He says they've warned the trolls to 'refrain from posting inaccurate theories and speculations, potentially harmful to the investigation' and to 'cease and desist writing threatening posts'. Naturally, this 'unhelpful' vileness is aimed mostly at her.

They would like her to make a statement to add to this, saying how distressing the family finds the comments, basically asking the trolls to lay off. She refrains, declines, and when pushed, tells him to fuck off.

If the scum think they're getting to her, she reckons they'll just carry on. It's best to ignore them, like she'd ignore school bullies. Only when physically provoked would she then punch them in the face.

On the way back, the bloke of indeterminate age who lives opposite is hanging out his window as usual, smoking a spliff the size of a Cornetto. Muttering. Most of it's unintelligible, but she catches the phrase 'my business slapping up against your business', and where she'd usually shout something like, 'Is your mother proud of teaching you that trash talk, you fucking wanker?' (and yes, she does realise the response would be more eloquent without the swearing) this time she hasn't got the energy to react.

Mummy

'Pwetty. Pwetty.'

She's cooing, pressed against the French windows. What has she seen?

Surprisingly, she doesn't brace as she hears me enter the room. She turns and points, inviting me to look. The sweetness is almost painful. How long has it been since she initiated any contact with me?

I daren't break the spell by talking, so I walk across and look to where she's pointing.

Snowdrops have emerged in the back garden. Late this year, thanks to the grinding cold.

Mammy loved the delicate beauty of the flowers; she said they reminded her of nuns at prayer, bowing their bashful heads. Not showy. She did not approve of 'blowsy' flowers, although garish daffodil yellows and iris purples bloomed across her face often enough.

The snowdrops tremble in the breeze, their fragile stalks bending deeper.

'Would you like to go and see?'

She looks at me as if it's a trick question.

'If we go outside, Izzy, you must promise not to make a noise.'

She looks straight into my eyes.

'No talking. No shouting. Understand?'

She nods.

'Promise.'

'Cross my heart and hope you die.'

I let that slide. She may have simply confused the phrase.

I am trying to be less touchy. Michael often accused me of being a 'drama queen' if I 'overreacted' or was 'hypersensitive' in his less than humble opinion.

I unlock and unbolt the back door and take her hand. For once she doesn't resist and we walk down the three steps to the garden.

It is woodland damp, which makes the cold bite deeper. She goes straight to the snowdrops, crouches and starts patting them. I stop myself from saying, 'Don't touch them.'

She's smiling. Then she sees a spider and a small 'Oh!' escapes.

I tense, but she doesn't squeal like I might have at her age, my sister Margaret taunting me – 'Little Miss Muffet!' – as she thrust a spider in my face. For someone so beautiful, she had an ugly heart, my sister.

Still, I caution her, 'Hush, Izzy!'

In a loud stage whisper she says, 'Hello. Hello!'

It's a small noise for a big city, but I cannot take any chances. I grab her hand and when I start to hurry her back to the kitchen I feel her pull against me. I stoop and whisper, 'Let's leave the spider to make her web, shall we?'

She refuses to move, so I'm forced to pull a little harder.

'Remember, you promised you'd be a good girl. If you misbehave, the kitten won't come to see you.'

She tries to snatch her hand out of mine.

'Izzy! Come along. Now.'

And this time, I pull more sharply than I intend and the quiet is shattered by a loud, 'NO! Leave me alone!'

The next unfortunate sequence happens too quickly. She wrenches her hand away. I grab it back. She shouts, 'Bugger off, YOU!' I drag. She starts screaming, 'Gerroff! Gerroff!' I clamp my hand around her mouth. She tries to bite. I smack with my free hand. She wriggles and bucks against me. I almost lose my footing in the damp grass. She gets her mouth free and squeals. Dear God! I wrestle her up the steps. She flails, hands and feet against the doorframe. I fling her in and slam the door, sweating and shaky with the shock. And she launches herself at me from the floor, shrieking, 'I hate you! I hate you!' Kicking and punching.

So I have to make her quiet.

When she is back in her room, I spray the paraben-free glass cleaner on the French windows and wipe off the greasy hand and nose prints, the smear of blood.

I sit braced for the doorbell.

Half a bottle later, thank the Lord, it is still silent.

Kim

She's running along the pavement, her legs pistons, her heels striking the concrete. Something is chasing her, but she knows she mustn't look back. If she does, she'll lose everything.

She hurtles round a corner and sees she's suddenly in the Andover Estate. Home! Yet she can't slow down, because she has to slam her door on whatever it is behind her.

Some nights she makes it, only to find the thing she's running from is somehow inside the flat, threatening everything she has left.

She comes downstairs carrying Nate, Darryl trailing behind, and finds Steve's left her a card and a box of chocolates, probably from a Tesco Meal Deal.

She gets that sinking feeling. She knows what he'll want – he's old-fashioned like that on Valentine's Day.

She opens the envelope and is taken aback to see it's not one of his usual jokey ones. (Last year: 'There aren't many words to describe how I feel about you.' And inside, 'But twat comes close.') It's a 'To My Wife' card, crap poem and all. Something a granddad might buy.

She leaves it on the table, wondering what the fuck Steve was thinking.

She sticks on the kettle and puts the chocolates out of Darryl's reach. Does this odd offering mean he'll still be looking for a bit of duvet action when he gets in from work?

All morning, the card nags at her. It's like Steve has no idea who she is any more. He might as well have bought her a 'Get Well Soon' card.

But they don't make a 'Sorry For Your Loss' card – not for when your girl's missing, do they.

Mummy

It's so drab, so cold. A long, hard winter. How I'd love to travel to the Caribbean. To feel sunlight on my pale skin once more. Naturally I use Elizabeth Arden Factor 50 sun cream.

Michael whisked me away to Antigua one Valentine's Day. No one to send me so much as a card this year.

But how could I go away? I am tethered here by her needs and her surly, ungrateful face.

I need a break. I deserve a break. I have held myself on such a tight leash recently, as all single mothers must.

But the world does not revolve around her.

The room is spinning.

I am suffocating. I need air.

I run through the manor house, flinging open curtains, a fierce, beautiful Scarlett O'Hara. I would look so fine in an emerald dress.

'You live in a fantasy world. Life's not a bloody costume drama.'

Shut up, Michael. I don't give a damn!

Oh, but how my mammy pasted me when she found me wrapped in the net curtains she had washed and hung out to dry, parading up and down the hall. Displaying such vanity! That terrible vice. Another wickedness on the never-ending list of sins she compiled and tallied and held against me forever and forever more.

And then I was cast out from her Eden. Accused of being a wicked liar. Banished from her arms. The hard-hearted bitch!

God forgive me. I should honour her and Daddy, despite . . . everything.

Not one cousin, or aunty, or nephew called to check on me after I was exiled. Cut off and blamed by them all. I cannot forgive her for that. The venom she spread about me. She is dead to me now.

I was blamed for Daddy's death. I was banned from the funeral.

'You broke his heart with your wickedness,' she hissed, with worse accusations, until I shut down my heart against her, thinking, *Fuck you, Mammy!*

And I would sit and sob, curled in Michael's lap, until I could cry no more.

What I wouldn't have given to pay my respects. To hold his hand, cold though it would be, one last time. For I still loved him.

I was denied the chance to say goodbye to my own daddy.

What sort of God would do that to me?

I feel like screaming, but I can't because I will be discovered. The thief in the night. Although Our Lord pardoned the thief on the cross.

I cannot, will not, go to prison, although some will think I deserve it.

And Michael got his 'just deserves' as Mammy might put it.

You would not have approved of our relationship, Mammy. Sex before marriage! And yes we did, thank you very much, and how I sighed and enjoyed it, you old witch.

I cannot breathe, I need air, and I fling open the window and shout, 'Damn you, Mammy! Damn you, Michael! Damn you all!'

I come round with several nails broken and bleeding.

Reeling. Confused.

What have I done?

I am flushed, tangled in the sheets.

Then I see one side of the bedroom curtains hanging – as if I have swung from them in the night like some ape.

I feel a blast of damp, icy air the moment I unlock her door. It takes me a second to process what I see, but then I gasp and she turns, wobbling.

Her window is wide open. She's straddling the gap, her body half inside the room, one leg dangling over the lip of the frame.

How did she unfasten the window? I had assumed it had been painted shut long ago. Where did she find the strength?

But—

Oh.

Did I do it?

I can't remember.

I daren't move in case I startle her. She might fall and break her neck.

She glares my way, her fingers gripping the woodwork. She does not look well. I fear she'll be light-headed. I can't remember the last time I fed her.

'Izzy!' My voice rasps and she shuffles her bottom another inch away from me. She looks down, teetering on the edge, the leg still inside swaying precariously above the carpet. If she moves any more she'll surely tumble. I could never cover the distance from the door to the window to grab her in time.

Is she trying to escape? Or does she mean to fling herself away from me, no matter the danger?

I try to sound calm. 'Izzy, darling, please come here. Come to Mummy.'

She shakes her head, her bottom lip jutting out. She leans her messy hair against the frame.

I swallow hard. 'I'm sorry, sweetheart. Come away from the window.'

But I've no idea why I'm apologising to her. She should be the one saying sorry to me for her appalling words last night – toads spilling out of her ugly mouth.

I cannot think of that. I must think clearly despite the thud-thud-thudding in my head. What is it that hostage negotiators do?

Then it comes to me. 'Izzy, would you like some hot chocolate, sweetheart?'

Her expression changes. There is a questioning keenness along with the mistrust.

I can't leave the room. If only I could go to the kitchen and bring the drink to her, the smell would do the trick. All I can do is try to lasso her with my words.

'I'll warm some nice milk and put in some sugar, shall I?' Of course I have no sugar. 'One or two teaspoons?'

She stares belligerently.

'And we'll froth it up, shall we? Make it nice and creamy and yummy?'

I can tell she is thinking about it, suspended. At least next door's lime tree hides her from the prying eyes of neighbours.

But she might scream.

I find I'm leaning heavily against the door, as if I too might plunge.

'Shall we get the chocolate together? Will you help me make it?'

I wish I could promise her biscuits, but she knows too well that I have none.

Her body seems to slump and I take one cautious step forward and she whispers, 'Two.'

'What's that, darling?'

Her hollow eyes look up to me. I strain to hear her answer.

'Two sugars.' She sees my face and quickly adds, 'Please.'

Kim

Kim first met Ayesha when she was rooting through the sports kit in TK Maxx and the smiley woman started ferreting about on the rail next to her. Kim was a bit put out, to be honest, because of the black flapping robes. Ayesha looked like a giant bloody bat.

'They've got some new Nike leggings in over there,' the dark-skinned figure gestured with her head to the next rail. 'I won't get in them with my thighs, but they'd fit you.'

'Oh, er, thanks.'

'I never find bargains here,' said the woman, although, when Kim looked at her properly, she saw she was more of a girl, really. About the same age as her, perhaps. Her face round, with the smoothest skin Kim had ever seen.

'My mate Rania always comes back with some designer stuff that's perfect, innit. Just don't happen for me.'

Kim wondered what her hair might be like under the veil thing. She surprised herself to find she was smiling back and when after a bit more chit-chat the woman said, 'Fancy a coffee in Costa?' she said yes.

After ten minutes or so she was even more surprised at how normal the conversation was, with Ayesha showing her pictures of her bloke (proper smouldering, that one) and her kids, Faisal and Mo (one gorgeous, one – Jesus!), rattling on about people they both knew on the estate, because it turned out they lived round the corner from each other, that's how she'd recognised Kim.

Kim and Ayesha have been best mates ever since. Come to think of it, Ayesha's probably Kim's only real mate, as such. Steve's got all his old school friends nearby, but Kim's are back up north and apart from the odd Facebook ping, they don't keep in touch. She'd cross the road if she saw some of the old crew now – doesn't want to get dragged back into that.

Steve was shocked when Kim first told him about her new friend.

'What, one of those pillar-box women? You're joking me.'

'No. She's not like that.'

'You watch yourself.'

It's taken a few years, but he likes her now, Kim can tell. He makes Ayesha a cup of tea now and then, but he's still a bit shy when she's around. Doesn't swear as much.

Since Tonya, Ayesha's been at the flat nearly every day. Kim has no idea what she'd have done without her over the past weeks. She's put up posters of Tonya in the mosque, says the imam is praying up a storm for her.

'Do you think that'll help?'

'Yeah, I do. It's like *Ghostbusters*, innit.'

'What the fuck?!'

'You know, all the bad thoughts create the monster thingy.' Ayesha piles more sugar into her tea, although she's always saying how she needs to lose weight. 'All the good thoughts, all the prayers and hopes and wishes and stuff, that dissolves the monster.'

'That's not how they got rid of the Pillsbury Doughboy.'

'Yeah, it is.'

'No one prayed. Have you even watched *Ghostbusters*?'

'A bit of it. Anyway, the imam will get Tonya back – you'll see.'

Kim shakes her head. The imam's prayers never helped Mo.

Tonya

I'm tired. The Woman tells me to put my hand in front of my mouth when I yawn. She reads me the story about the princess in the tower. I tell her we live in a low-rise not a tower but she don't know about them. And she says I don't live there any more. But I do.

I like the story. And I like her voice all whispery and posh. She sounds like a real princess.

It's nice in the bed. It's all soft.

Mummy

It has been a peaceful day. I close the page and settle to sleep. How many times have I read this book? I find Jane Austen so soothing. Michael mocked me, but I do wish I lived in that world.

I first saw my Michael striding across the heath like a hero from another time. My dark, dangerous Mr Darcy. He had excellent technique – the Nordic walking instructor said so. I had joined for an introductory lesson, thinking it was a way to meet people and exercise. I wanted to tone up my upper arms, which had become a little floppy. Not flabby, but nonetheless they could do with a more defined shape, although obviously not muscle-bound.

I also yearned for some green. I missed the rolling fields of home. I didn't think I would – although the countryside gives an illusion of space, in reality I couldn't bear the constrictions of that life. I came to London to stay with friends of Margaret, the over-stuffed, crowded city providing so much more freedom than the miles of nature that pressed in on us. Suffocating.

My sister fled the coop several months before I escaped. She phoned often enough, offering an olive branch after our fractious years, asking how I was, telling me she was worried about me, urging me to join her. How she was enjoying her adventurous new life, sharing a house with four other girls from the same art college she attended. She knew a lot of people in Kilburn and that's where I ended up after Daddy died, her new, exciting friends all bohemian types in shades of jolly eccentric, or plain outrageous.

I was asked to model for one of those artists, but I declined. Modesty is a quality much underrated in such circles. And I could not bear the thought of appearing as a slashed, warped Picasso or gross Bacon abomination.

Margaret and I were living off the money Aunty Kathleen left us in her will. It wasn't a fortune, but it was our own, to do with as we wished. I was wondering if I might take up further education, just as Margaret had quit her job in the local chemist to study art. For me, literature perhaps, as I so loved to read. Spending so much time curled up in my room with a book was another reason I wanted to get outside in the fresh air; emerge from my fusty cocoon.

And that day was full of promise, with a low sun casting cartoon shadows, making Michael look like a daddy longlegs as he approached. And he was so helpful as he showed me how to hold the Nordic poles, his beautiful long fingers wrapping around mine, explaining how it would turn me into 'a four-wheel drive on the grass'. And he smiled when I was so hopeless at it and the tutor, I felt, was a little exasperated.

He invited me for a coffee in Hampstead after the session. I knew I looked my best, all rosy from the walk. It led to a drink. There was hardly a pause in the conversation as we discussed home – its warped politics, archaic morality and vicious judgements. I was tipsy on excitement, garrulous and brave.

He said I made him laugh. He said he'd never met anyone like me, 'so delicate' as he put it, and I loved him almost immediately for that alone.

We had a date a few days later and spent an entire night talking and talking and talking. He too had a vulnerable side. His parents were 'emotionally unavailable' and in their own way as crushing as mine. Rich. They'd moved to the British Virgin Islands, a fact which made us giggle together, for at that time, ludicrously in this day and age, I was still, technically, a virgin.

My Michael was not put off by my lack of experience. Nor when I laid my hopes and my dreams, my nightmares and terrors, at his feet. My only ambition after meeting him, to be his – to create a family together.

We took things slowly. He understood the demons of my past. He trod lightly. And I loved him for his sensitivity.

And he was such a fine-looking man! It was easy to love him for that too. There was not one ugly part of him. And the first time he held me in his arms it felt like home.

And he told me I was *beautiful*.

A miracle! Soiled and sullied and scarred as I am, to him, I believe I was.

Tonya

We do the song together, 'Rain, rain, go away, come again another day.'

She says she'll buy me wellies and when it's spring we can go in the garden. When it's dry. When it's warmer.

I tell her, 'I miss Mo!'

She asks me who Mo is. I tell her he's my boyfriend. She says I'm too young for a boyfriend. But I'm not.

'But I don't miss Darryl.'

She says, 'Who's Darryl?'

'My *brother*.'

I don't have to share my toys with him any more. Ha ha ha! That'll show him!

Kim

Since the baby came, Ayesha's seen a change in Kim. A change that frightens her.

'Give him a break.' That's all she says.

And Kim's out of the blocks like fucking Shergar. 'What do you mean, give him a break?'

'He's hurting too.'

'Yeah – poor, poor Steve.'

'Don't be like that.'

'Like what, Ayesha?'

'You know.'

'No, I don't know. He's being a total arsehole. He's doing my head in. He blames me for Tonya. You know it.'

Ayesha rolls her eyes. There's no point pushing anything with Kim like this.

'And I'm so fucking tired of it all and the fucking police aren't getting anywhere and I can't fucking stand it any more. I want to stab him in the fucking eye!'

'Don't say that.'

Kim glares at her. 'Why? Because you *fancy* him?'

'Just stop it, will you.' Ayesha's never seen Kim so agitated. She's blowing smoke right at her, ash flicking all over, dangerously close to Nate's face.

'You always have, haven't you. Always secretly fancied a slice of Steve pie. Always here when I'm not. Funny that.' She jabs the fag towards her.

Ayesha gets up to leave. Of course she's never been in the flat when

Steve's there and Kim's not about. But there's no point reminding her of that when she's in this mood. She'll get Khalid to call Steve later and tell him that she thinks Kim needs help.

'Truth hurt, does it? Running away now?'

The door slams.

When Ayesha's gone, Kim wonders if cutting herself wouldn't have been easier.

Mummy

My favourite part of the day is reading to her as she nestles against me, her head on my shoulder. This small oasis of peace. She likes tales of animals. I check in case there is a cow in the stories. I can't abide the creatures.

I leave her when her eyes grow heavy, to read my own books.

Austen understood so much more than romance, although the rom-com aspect of her work is why they put her work on the stamps and her face on the bank notes. No matter how much Michael teased me, I like to imagine I'm part of those well-to-do families, with suitors and sisters in abundance.

I always envied my sister Margaret more than I loved her. It didn't help that Mammy drummed it into us both how we should put each other first and look out for each other. Our loyalty must be to God and family above all others and all else.

My sister was to be admired, looked up to, obeyed, for she was the eldest. And how, despite those lectures, I did adore her. As she was adored by Daddy. And why wouldn't she be? Her fine features, her pretty face. Her shiny hair, so unlike my own unruly, mousey mop. She was a totally different creature to me: slim yet curvaceous, where I was simply disgustingly fat. A blob. Her face, her body, all graceful, feminine undulations. The way she walked entranced me. Jiggly. Almost sinful.

I saw the way boys looked at her. Hungry eyes. I yearned to be so wanted. I saw the way my daddy looked at her.

My jealousy burned brighter as the years progressed, yet despite some low-level bickering we would only really fall out if I touched her things or tried to borrow her clothes or make-up. Then she would scream, 'I'll tell Mammy!' and that threat was enough to keep me in line, frightening me into keeping my 'thieving hands' to myself.

An unusual family, just the two of us, but Mammy's 'women's problems' put paid to dozens more, for which, I suspect, she was secretly grateful.

Margaret is childless. Her sin put paid to that.

She lives with her husband, a run-of-the-mill sort, who looks even less appetising than his job description: Administrative Services Officer. They have a small bungalow in Southend. Not the nice part, if such exists. Nowhere near the sea.

I only know of her life, her circle of Zumba friends, her annual TUI trip to the more commercial areas of Italy or Spain, from her Facebook page.

She has run to fat. Serves her right.

I've never visited, I couldn't look her in the face.

I've prayed for her, naturally. Yet my heart made its own decision as it hardened and set against her.

'You're as bad as them,' she wailed, noisily crying into her disgusting, germ-ridden cotton handkerchief, meaning, of course, Mammy and her cronies; the small-town judgements.

They never knew. I kept that secret for her – even though she had kept too many secrets from me.

When she asked for my help, I was shocked. But I owed my sister loyalty. At one time she had saved me by offering me a safe harbour.

She had also betrayed me by saying nothing. But I forgave her for that, for her lies – lies of omission.

And I collaborated in her sin.

I failed to persuade her to change her mind. The silent, strangulated voice deep within me wanted to shout, 'Why can't you have it? Why can't you give it to me? Why can't I love it and bring it up as my own?'

It remained an 'it'. Boy? Girl? Unspoken of, unknown.

I took her to the clinic and returned to collect her, but I couldn't bring myself to go inside. I texted her that I'd arrived and sat in the little white Renault Michael bought me, watching her walk across the road in slow motion, her beautiful face made hard and ugly by what she had done.

I couldn't look at her then, nor find the words to speak to her. I could barely drive.

How could she flush away something so precious? A soul!

We sat outside her flat in Kilburn for a long time, both staring ahead. And she said, in between sobs, and this I can never forgive, 'It wouldn't be fair. You need to have a child for the right reasons. You can't bring a child into this world just to have someone to love you.'

I knew she wasn't talking about herself.

After that last, stilted farewell, mascara running down both our faces, she did her best to try and heal the rift. Dozens of letters and calls over the months, years, although I guessed it cost her to speak to Michael, begging him to bring me to the phone. Still prideful, another sin.

Then I changed our number and eventually she gave up.

Tonya

I know the names of the flowers. She points and I tell her. I know them all. Pansies. Roses. Bruce Forsythia.

She laughs and asks how I know so many.

'My granddad's got a lotment!'

I like it when she laughs. Then she gives me chocolate.

She brings us hyacinths for in the house. Three pink ones. I tell her, 'My mum don't like them. When's my mum coming to get me?'

She don't laugh again.

Kim

She must have dropped off for a few minutes. She feels pissed when she comes round, with the dream clinging to her like those fake cobwebs from the ghost train that time she went to Blackpool with Steve, before the kids, although she's never liked going back north. Too many reminders. She scrapes hair out of her face and drags it back into a tight ponytail to stop herself from grabbing the scissors and hacking it all off.

These feelings demand medication of some sort. She's not sure she can tolerate them for long without – something.

But that wouldn't bring Tonya back.

She goes to the bathroom to splash water on her face.

Steve blunders in behind her and pisses like a fucking donkey. His bladder should be in the Guinness Book of World Records.

Hearing activity, the baby stirs and starts its crying.

Steve signals her with his eyes. She stares him out.

'Well, I'm a bit busy at the moment, aren't I?' he growls.

She remains static, dripping water, denying the demand from the cot in the bedroom. This morning, there's no way she can even look at the baby, let alone touch it.

'For fuck's sake, Kim!'

She sees the hurt and confusion in his face and mumbles, 'I'm sorry,' which is rare, for her. But, despite the push from him and the pull from the baby, she braces her feet on the lino and glares back at him, defiant.

As he stomps past her to see to it, she stumbles back to the sink and looks in the mirror. She sees a long, drawn face. Like an old woman. Like a witch. She sees black thoughts etched in the lines, seeded by the dream.

This is madness.

It's a way out.

The new thought draws her with a dark, insistent logic.

A life for a life.

The baby for Tonya.

She needs to get a fucking grip.

Mummy

She seems happy enough watching her lurid programmes. Sometimes I hear her singing along to an irritating jingle, but she's silent the second I step into the room. Her shoulders rise towards her ears if she hears me enter. I wouldn't be surprised if she hissed at me.

Surely she can't miss her awful excuse for a mother. Some of the things that have come to light about her are beyond belief.

So why does she hate me?

I shouldn't be drinking, I know.

In the night, or perhaps it's the afternoon – it gets dark so quickly at this time of the year I find it hard to tell – my mammy comes to me.

Mother of all living. My dear mother. Smother. Moth. Her.

Too much whiskey. I don't even like the taste, but we've run out of brandy. Michael's getting slack. Ha!

My mammy would grasp me too tightly and crush me to her chest. She would hug me until it hurt and I would try and wriggle away, but I was too little.

It was my daddy's hugs I yearned for.

And I tried to tell her—

But my mammy turned against me. Told me that I was no child of hers. Accused me of being a wicked liar.

Margaret didn't back me up.

And my mammy attacked me and drove me from the house.

I cannot, shall not be like that with the girl. I am a better mother than that.

Then I wonder if this is why Izzy doesn't like me touching her. Her mother must have hurt her too. Of course! Why didn't I realise before?

I admit, there were a couple of times in the early days, when I was ill, and I misjudged an embrace. But she can hardly blame me for that.

Why can't she love me?

I take another bottle.

'Give and take.' In every golden wedding anniversary interview, in every evening newspaper, when such things existed. 'You have to compromise.'

Compromise is sacrifice by another name. A gentler name.

I sweep up the broken glass. Wrap it in kitchen towel and carrier bags. Carry a box of empties out to the bin.

I forgot to put on my make-up! My vile, naked face on show for anyone to see!

'Losing it', as you'd say, Michael, my love.

I pray for hours. Please, let the answer be different. Surely my Lord, who loves little children, cannot require this of me?

And this demand has nothing to do with the Lamb of God, the milk of all kindness, Christ – but everything to do with his Father, the original advocate of capital punishment.

And I know which one is telling me what to do now.

Each morning for the last week – the lost week – I wake with the awful, leaden certainty of what He requires of me. I always knew my Lord would demand a terrible price for the gift of a child.

My heart canters as I slowly push myself up to sitting. I wipe sweat from my forehead and lean back against the brass bars at the head of the bed, pressing hard, as if I might rid myself of the thoughts.

Mine is a God who gave His only son and watched him suffer, hour after hour, ignoring his anguished pleas. A Lord as bitter as vinegar.

Now I will be nailed to the cross.

For am I not Sarah? Izzy, my Isaac? And, in the absence of Michael, I must also be Abraham. It is left to me to make the ultimate sacrifice.

I must take the girl and cut her throat. Sacrifice her. Let her go. This is what my loving fucking God demands of me.

Tonya

'Doo-doo dee-doo, doo-doo-dee-doo, be a *good* girl, doo-dee-doo, dee-dee-dee, let it go-ooooOOO!?'

Kim

Steve takes Darryl out after breakfast, so Kim crawls back upstairs into bed. She won't sleep, but it saves the energy it takes trying to keep her head up.

She should be with him today. Try to help him through it. Share their . . . grief, is it? Fucking no! Get closer by talking about their feelings? Just . . . listen to him? But there's nothing left inside her that might do any of that.

Ayesha's got the baby. Again. She jokes that it's to put Khalid off trying for another.

'A couple of nights of this one squawking and he'll think twice about hitching up my nightie,' she grins. 'Give you a rest for once, hey?'

They both know that's not what it's about. But Kim finds she can't say thanks. The word, any meaningful words – sorry; I love you; please, God – like ashes in her mouth.

She allows herself not to feel guilty about Nate, for once. How can today be harder than all the others? They got through Christmas – managing to survive the silence where Tonya's excited yabbering should have been. Somehow they get through each excruciating twenty-four hours.

Horror turns to boredom soon enough.

Nothing's changed. But it is harder this morning.

Her sister rang earlier to say, 'It would have been her birthday, wouldn't it?' and Kim slammed down the phone on her.

Today is Tonya's birthday. Not 'would have been'. Fucking IS.

*

About half-past eleven, the door bangs open downstairs and she hears a baby's noise that doesn't sound anything like Nathaniel. Darryl's giggling and twittering and Steve's saying, 'Come on, buggerlugs. Let's get in and show your mum.' His soft voice sounds well chuffed. She imagines him smiling. She's not seen that in a long while.

Then there's a high-pitched yelp. What the fuck? She shoots up to sitting.

There's a kerfuffle on the stairs and then Steve's in the doorway, carrying Nate, Darryl getting under his feet as usual, and a small, mad ball of fluff starts scrabbling up the duvet towards her. Steve helps it, giving its little legs a hoist, and then there's a puppy on her head, its tongue in her ears, her eyebrows, and she scrunches up her face as its claws tickle and scratch at her neck.

'Steve! No! What? Fuck!'

She wrestles the thing onto her lap as she scootches up the bed to sit properly.

The puppy dances demented circles of joy, little legs going nineteen to the dozen, and Steve's looking at her with such . . . need.

'It's for Tonya. For her birthday. For when she comes home.'

She swallows. He waits. She feels like one of those Roman geezers – it's thumbs up or thumbs down time. But what she says just comes out without any planning.

'What we going to call it?'

He grins. His shoulders come down a bit. 'Elsa. Got to be, ain't it?'

Once upon a time one afternoon, when they went to Newquay for a long weekend – last July was it? It feels like decades past – and it belted down, raining horizontally, and once it hailed so hard, she feared it might put someone's eye out, Kim had told Tonya a story about 'Denzil Slobbalot, King of the Cornish Pasty Hounds'.

Squashed together on the bed in the self-catering chalet – with the bloody heater on, they were so damp and perished – Steve had listened as intently as the kids, although Darryl was just riding the up and down-ness of her voice.

'Where'd you hear that?' he'd asked as she finished.

'Just made it up,' she said, like it was nothing.

'You should write it down. Make a storybook. Get someone to draw pictures of that Denzil.'

But she knew that no one could ever draw the dog as clearly as she pictured him.

Kim doesn't know why she can't get Denzil out of her mind. She bungs soiled newspaper into a bin liner, then mashes rice in with the puppy's feed, like they told Steve at the animal hospital, because the poor little sod can't take anything too rich. She doesn't really know why she starts calling her Sausage, but 'Elsa' catches in her throat. Tonya's favourite name. At least two of her dolls and one of her toy lions are called that, along with the actual Elsa doll. Kim can't make herself say it.

Ayesha won't hold out her hand for the puppy to sniff. But it licks her when she's distracted and she squeals as if she's terrified, but she's really laughing, then she scrubs her hands as if they're radioactive, and the furball thinks it's the best game ever.

Darryl waddles towards the pup and Kim watches, on guard in case he grabs and hurts her, or she goes for him, but both small creatures seem quite gentle with each other. A rare gift.

She was a bit worried in case the health visitor disapproved, but it turns out she's got three dogs herself, so it was okay.

She reaches for the dog food and looks down at the puppy, instantly wiggling around her legs, pinging up to get her chow. She's a proper Heinz 57 – half poodle, a weird smattering of Staffie around her haunches, and perhaps a quarter feather duster. And a miracle crosses Kim's face – something like a smile.

But when Nate wakes up because of the noise, and shrieks at an atom-splitting frequency, the darkness crawls out of its hidey-hole and envelops her again.

Mummy

The ringing makes me jump. Chest thudding, I screen the call before rushing to pick up when I hear Doreen's voice leaving a message on the machine.

I check my face in the mirror next to the phone, look away quickly, replying, 'Thirteen weeks. That sounds perfect.'

They have a kitten available. I had totally forgotten. It has only been a week or so since I registered my interest, but then, they always have kittens available. Not a feral this time. I can't cope with anything else wild in the house. I already have a child I cannot tame.

'No!' panicked, 'No, I can come and collect her.' Heart thudding, 'This afternoon? That will give me a chance to get some cat litter and food ready.'

Doreen sounds weary and relieved, which is pretty much how she sounds every time I speak to her. Hers is the classic, worn ragged, charity-worker voice.

She never had children either. Doreen sublimates her maternal urges by spending night after night capturing feral felines in littered alleys behind the horde of north London kebab and chicken shops.

Donations pay for her petrol, cat food and vet bills. Thanks to Michael's many bonuses, I made substantial transfers into the charity's account. And I have already been vetted as a suitable foster mother. For cats.

'Shall we say around three?'

I am to meet her at the vet. We will get everything in order there. I rush to the lounge to tell Izzy the news.

'Izzy.'

She doesn't turn from the TV.

'Izzy, darling.'

I fear she's picking her nose.

'What would you like to call your kitten?'

She looks round, then, seeing no kitten, turns back to the screen.

'We'll have her by this afternoon. She's a little tabby. Thirteen weeks old.'

I can tell she is listening. I perch on the sofa and talk to the back of her head.

'She had a bad start in life too. Her mummy abandoned her, so we will have to look after her and show her that we love her.' I reach for her hair and divide the strands into three. 'And you must be very, very gentle with her when she arrives because she will be nervous.'

She doesn't tug against me as I start plaiting.

It's strange to see Doreen again after so much has changed for me. I'm almost afraid to look into her tired brown eyes in case she spots my secret – I am now a mother!

'She's in with the vet just now. How's your Michael?'

'Fine. Yes, fine.'

'And what did he have to say about you taking another one?'

'Oh, you know . . .'

'This one's a real sweetie.'

'Aren't they all?'

'And you're looking well yourself.'

'Am I?'

I should be. I spent enough time before this little outing putting on my face and arranging my hair to disguise the ravages of so many bad nights.

'You are indeed. Have you been on holiday?'

If only.

To my relief, the door to the consulting room opens before I have to make up more answers and the vet, Mrs Clarke, comes out with the carrier. She smiles at Doreen and hands her the container, without looking directly at me. I assume she has not forgiven me for returning the feral cat, but her 'bedside manner' has always left much to be desired.

'And she's all yours. Just bring her back for her booster jab.' This directed to Doreen.

I peer in through the front of the carrier, as the little one meows and paws through the gaps in her prison, bright as anything.

Mrs Clarke adds, 'And then we'll arrange the neutering.'

Over my dead body, we will.

I do not enjoy the drive home, with the kitten's insistent high-pitched demands. I turn on the car radio, which makes her squeak louder. Apparently she is not a fan of Classic FM.

As I shove the front door shut with my hip I call out, 'I have her!' and I'm so excited, I dash up to unlock Izzy's door before I take off my coat and she hurtles out past me, down the stairs, to throw herself on her knees in front of the cage.

'Shall we let her out?'

Izzy nods, her mouth hanging open.

'Let's get her into the kitchen. We must introduce her to one room at a time, so she doesn't feel overwhelmed.'

Only now I think I should have tried that technique with the girl.

Unleashed, the animal instantly takes to Izzy's petting. I let her spoon out the fishy kitten food as the small tabby thrusts her head against the girl's hands, purring insistently.

Izzy makes noises I have never heard before.

'She likes you.'

'Look. Look!'

She's thrilled to see the kitten wolfing down its food as if it has never been fed before.

'Can you hear her?' I take Izzy's hand. 'Here.'

I place her palm on the kitten's side so she can feel it purr. A perfect mother–daughter moment.

'Oh! Oh!'

'Gently. You mustn't frighten her.'

'She's all soft!'

'Have you thought of a name?'

'What?'

'Pardon! It's "I beg your pardon" not "What". Have you come up with a name for her?'

Izzy looks confused.

'What are you going to call her?'

She sits and thinks, patting the kitten.

'Be careful. She's not a dog.'

The animal gives herself a few cursory licks and trots over to the cat litter tray and immediately makes use of it.

'She's pooing! She's pooing!' squeals Izzy.

'Shush! Don't disturb her.'

'But she's pooing!' she exclaims in a dramatic stage whisper.

I have to get up as my knees are complaining. I remove my coat and start to make a cup of tea.

'Elsa!'

'Is that her name?'

Izzy nods and trills, 'Elsa. Come here, Elsa.' She looks up at me. 'But she's not coming!'

She's obviously never had a cat before. I say, 'Let her get used to us. She doesn't know her name yet.'

Izzy, who rarely responds to her new name either, looks up at me again and smiles.

And the ache in my heart eases.

I put on my rubber gloves and swiftly dispose of the animal's grotesque mess.

Tonya

My name is Izzy. I have a kitten. I love my kitten. Her name is Elsa. I love Elsa. I love my mummy.

Liar liar, pants on fire.

My name is Tonya. I am five and three quarters years old. I love my kitten. I love Mo. Me and Mo are getting married. I love him a millionty, billionty.

I don't love *her*. She ain't my mummy. I AIN'T IZZY! She makes me do writing.

Mummy

The first time I let the kitten into the living room, she sharpens her tiny claws on the edge of my sofa.

I shout, 'Stop that!' and both the kitten and Izzy startle.

I fill a plant spray bottle with water, shooting a jet at the kitten's face if it ventures near anything precious. She squeezes into a tiny gap behind the television speaker and refuses to come out, the cunning miss, as if she knows I can't spray near electrical equipment.

Izzy giggles. Her spirits have improved immensely since the arrival of Elsa.

She comes close when I am catering to the kitten's needs, preparing her food, or clearing the disgusting litter tray. She seems to have an unhealthy obsession with the animal's bowel movements.

And so I have a new tool to curb her more regrettable behaviour.

For every, 'Don't want to,' I counter with, 'Fine. But naughty girls are not allowed to feed kittens. Naughty girls must go to bed.' For every grumpy refusal to engage with me, or answer, or smile, I can lock her in the bedroom, away from her little friend, explaining, 'Naughty girls can't play with kittens.'

It is enough to stop most of the whingeing and complaining. For now.

Kim

Days pass. Some are harder than others, but all teeter between panic and desperation, exhaustion and mania.

When Kim drags herself downstairs, she sees Steve's left a card on the table alongside a pot of blue hyacinths. He must have kept them in the van overnight because the rip-off estate shop has never sold anything remotely living. Her name's on the card, but it's not her birthday.

She lets the puppy out of the big cage Steve borrowed from the animal charity, chucks a handful of crunchy bits in her bowl, and rips open the envelope. The generic flowery card reads, 'Hope these cheer you up. Love ya babe. Steve xxx'

She's confused. A bit gobsmacked, even. The gesture isn't like him. He's either pawned something or he's shagging someone.

She turns to make a brew when she's blindsided by the perfume. That time her cow-faced mother put a bowl of hyacinths on the window sill. From her gran, was it? Kim tries not to inhale, but the stench of the flowers is too strong. She's instantly back in her mother's grease-spattered kitchen and her innards churn and she has to flump down on a chair.

Back there is the last place she'd want to be. Apart from right here, without Tonya.

She puts the plant on the windowsill and props the window open, even though it's still brass monkeys outside. And it's nearly April.

She goes through the motions of getting breakfast for Darryl, then it hits her. The gift, the card – it's for Mother's Day.

She sinks back down on the chair and reaches for the fag packet, fiddles with it, then puts it back.

Upstairs, the baby cries. She shudders.

Mummy

I am trying to reread another of my Jane Austens when the little madam stretches her claws towards the throw on the side of my sofa, darting away before I can grab the water spray from the side table.

Izzy laughs, loud and wild. It's an odd sound that I have only heard since the kitten's arrival. She seems delighted by every exasperating thing it does. I find the animal's presence more stressful than I'd anticipated. She is always into things that don't concern her and her mischievousness makes Izzy manic.

The animal reappears and stalks my foot, which I find is jiggling.

'Elsa! No!'

She ignores me and shoves her bottom in the air, inching forward.

But that's enough distraction, enough reading. I must get on with my day. The kitchen is in desperate need of a deep clean and I am in desperate need of exfoliation – my elbows and heels are a sight!

'Izzy, darling, what would you like for lunch?'

The girl shrugs her shoulders in a gesture I find maddening.

'Would you like some spaghetti?' I can usually start a conversation regarding food.

She considers. 'Yeah. No green stuff.'

'Yes, what?'

She glances up. 'Yes, *please*.'

'With tomato sauce? No pesto?'

'Yes-please. Yes-please. Yes-please.'

I wonder if this is sass or enthusiasm.

'Ouch! You naughty animal!'

Elsa swerves, having pierced the skin on my ankle, and dives under the bookshelves. I grab for the spray, shooting it after her. The kitten hurtles out and dashes into the kitchen, the kink in her tail signalling more wickedness. I follow, squirting the water at her head. But I am brought to a sudden halt by Izzy's angry voice.

'Leave her alone, you!'

She thunders towards me like a baby rhinoceros, skidding to a halt right in front of me. She bounces on her tiptoes and reaches up. I'm surprised, half expecting a cuddle. Instead, she snatches towards my hand and wrestles me for the spray and there's a small scuffle and she falls and, just my luck, bumps her head on the door handle.

God forgive me, my mother's words pop into my head, but thankfully not my mouth. *Serves you right.*

It's another silent meal.

Tonya

Here is a rose. The rose is pink.
Here is a cat. Her name is Elsa.
My cat is brown. And orinje. And wite.
I love my cat.

She made me write that. And told me off for things I didn't spell right.
I hate The Woman.
My eye is blue and green and purple and it hurts.
Rotten bloody rotten stupid woman.

Kim

She always knew she'd be a crap mother. No talent. No role model. No 'aptitude'. That from her maths teacher, who'd hit her hands if he found her secretly counting on her fingers in class.

Crap at maths. Good at English, though she'd faked being crap, otherwise it'd provoke the chants – 'Clever cunt! Clever cunt!' – and another scrap on the school field.

As she unloads the washing machine and pushes Sausage away when she tries to catch the edge of the towels with her teeth, she thinks of other things people have said about her.

'Easily led' – her gran. The nice one.

'Arsey' – Steve.

'Fucking psycho bitch!' – Skid, after she punched him in the face for bringing blow to the flat.

The thing she says to Steve most often is, 'Fuck you, Steve,' or variations on the theme. But she'd say that in affection, joking, as much as she'd say it in exasperation. Now she can't even be bothered to dredge up a friendly 'fuck off!'

'Nasty little cow' – her mother.

'Honey' – her brother's favourite endearment. Said as a piss-take. Said as a command. It makes her shiver as she pours liquid into the washing machine.

And the words she should have said: 'No. Stop.' But they never escaped her filthy lips.

The tabloid headline: 'SCUMMY MUMMY'. That confirms some of

the worst things she thinks about herself, although it's less a thought, more a feeling that seeps into every nook and cranny.

She hangs the damp load of washing she's already done on the clothes-horse, paying more attention to memories than watching what her hands are doing. She's avoiding going into the living room for another useless session with Liaison Woman, who's on the sofa talking to Steve.

But mainly because the baby's in there.

She called Tonya 'Princess' – as in warrior princess, not some pink doll in a puffy ballgown. But then came the obsession with *Frozen* and she decided she wanted an actual princess dress after all.

What sort of aural crack is in that fucking song? Tonya sang it day and bloody night. Kim would find herself humming the sodding thing. It got so bad she made up her own words, 'Kill the bitch, freeze to death—' But she never sang that in front of Tonya.

She and Steve had a little song as well. He'd sing the opening notes from the *Top Gear* theme tune, 'Duum doodledoodledo doodle do duum—'

And she'd shout out, in time to the beat, her answer: 'Bollocks-bollocks-bollocks-bollocks bollocks-bollocks—'

Tonya would laugh, knowing that Kim tried not to swear so much in front of her. She did her best most of the time.

This routine from the magical time: before.

She switches on a second load, then trails through to the living room and her daydream's broken as Steve starts shouting, 'We know that. What else are you even doing?' Liaison Woman stays weirdly calm, balancing her mug of weak tea on her knees, and explains how police are 'pursuing multiple leads'. She assures them that hundreds, perhaps thousands of 'leads' have flooded in since the appeal aired on Tonya's birthday. Steve quietens, like a starving dog who's been tossed a small bone, but Kim knows, she just knows, it's all bollocks-bollocks-bollocks-bollocks.

She avoids Steve's eye as he tries to hand her the baby.

Who are these people who swear they saw a man drag some little girl along an alley, into a car? Why didn't they come forward immediately? Why didn't the bastards throw themselves under the wheels to stop him, which any right-minded person would do?

Who are the self-proclaimed psychics who see Tonya's body in some skip in Acton? On a Greek island? Spirited away by gypsies in some warped fucking fairy tale?

Who are the repeat callers who waste hours of police time?

Kim reckons most of these leads spawn from the shoal-like movements of human plankton, stupid shits full of spite and self-delusion, fuelled by the desperate need for recognition and attention.

Her leg jiggles and she itches to reach for her lighter.

Steve dumps Nate on the sofa and stomps into the kitchen, rifling through the fridge as soon as the policewoman leaves. He can't stop eating these days. His six-pack is starting to drown in fat. He doesn't seem to notice, shoving another slice of pizza in his mouth, possibly to push down the accusations he could throw Kim's way.

He asks her what the health visitor said when she came and she mumbles something about it all being good.

She feels queasy as she fiddles with her fags and tries not to look at the sofa where the baby lies.

If she catches sight of him, the hairs stand up on her arms.

Mummy

The echo of Michael is upon me. The book abandoned in my lap, words blurred.

For months I would wake each morning and lie there, for perhaps half a second, confused, wondering what was wrong. Something bad. Something missing. Then the shard of fear – Michael!

Pain followed, something clawing inside the hollow cage of my chest, scrabbling at my heart.

Grief holds its own brand of yearning. His absence, a cruel pain; an acidic burn high in my chest, cutting off air, like the time I broke my rib after another argument accelerated into another fight with him – about the usual.

Drink. Drink. Drink.

My afternoon nap has caused more harm than good. Shame clings to me.

'I am telling you, I am NOT having an affair!'

Michael – burning with indignation. Beyond angry with me.

He surprised me scrolling through his text messages, his emails. He snatched the phone away from me, quite roughly, shouting, 'Stop this! Are you bloody insane?'

And I screamed back. Nuclear rage. Certain of his guilt. Certain he was mocking me.

I recall it was some anniversary. Always tricky.

Now, I can't remember exactly – was that the anniversary of Daddy's death? The banishment? Or was it a year after we gave up the violating medical interventions? My mind doesn't keep track of the actual date these things happened, but my heart always knows.

I gave up my dream of becoming a mother for this man and he repaid me by committing adultery. A mortal sin!

Only, the morning after the row, I wasn't so sure that he was cheating after all. Things get muddied in the night.

Even now those memories, the words, slap me. 'Whore! Bitch!'

Dear Lord forgive me, they weren't his accusations.

Mine.

'Who is the whore? Who is the bitch?'

He denied it, of course.

I turn to hug my pillow, mortified.

When I come downstairs, I see a purple-red stain spreading across the cream rug. Like a bruise. Like blood. How many times have I warned her?

'Izzy, darling, don't be so giddy.'

Although giddy hardly covers it – she's almost savage, tearing around after Elsa, chasing, sliding on her socks. The way her crooked tooth is revealed with her mouth so wide as she shouts and laughs makes me recoil. Would we ever be able to get it fixed? What would I tell a dentist, for she'd have no records.

'Izzy, just calm down now. You'll frighten her.'

She is like the animal. A short attention span. No sense of consequences.

Truth be told, the kitten seems just as possessed. Ears flattened, eyes demonic. Sticking her bottom in the air, she scoots away from the child, careers around the sofa.

Tomboys.

I was never so loud. So . . . uncontained. I liked sitting quietly, reading, or listening to the radio with Mammy. Waiting for Daddy to come in from the cows. Waiting for Daddy to notice me.

'Izzy, stop that right now! Look at this mess!'

She pays no heed.

'I will not tell you again.'

She mocks me.

Now this! The stain from the cherry juice will never come out of the carpet.

Kim

After a lot of nagging and cajoling on his part, they go out – to the big Wetherspoons that used to be a cinema. The one where Kim had the Christmas drink or two that came back to bite her on the arse. Ayesha looks after Nate and Darryl, swearing she doesn't mind, which makes Kim feel worse, because when she's not around the baby she feels a weight lift. And that's another notch on the long, damning list of wrong things about her.

Susan next door takes the dog, who swoons with joy when she sees Susan's 'little man', Bobby; a soft as shit Bill Sikes dog. Sausage is growing fast, shaping up to be a miniature sideboard – square, with a leg on each corner. She already bosses Bobby around. She saw off a husky four times her size on her first walk round the estate, yapping at the stunted blossoms that fell from the trees like dandruff.

Kim stands in front of the bathroom mirror and thinks about putting on some mascara. She's forgotten what she looks like. The shock is that so much of her face – the nose, lips, cheekbones – conjures up her daughter. She's not managed to do anything except zone out when Steve calls to see what's keeping her.

He's on edge when they walk into the pub in case anyone says something, but Kim doesn't register much. She sits slumped and sips a ginger beer, like she's a kid again. She daren't start drinking.

Kim's slippery slope – from cheap cider, via cheap vodka and speed, to heroin – took a couple of years. You don't just wake up one day a sad-arsed addict. It takes many tiny bad decisions to get there, to sink to their level, because, for a short time, you think you're better than them.

The first time you piss yourself on the way home. Perhaps have a nightcap to take away that sting of shame. The next time, make a joke of it. Another time you might yank down your drawers by the side of the road. Then you don't much care one way or another.

The first time you give Dealer Mick a blow job for a wrap—

The time you shack up with Mick's mate Daz, partly because he's got an inside on the supply line, but you also sort of like him—

Then you don't care that you never really liked Daz's mate, whatever the fuck his name was, hated him really, but needs must—

Then the other faces. And the bruises—

Kim knew what this sad trajectory was called: 'normalising the abnormal', AKA being a weak-willed, dirty slag fuck-up.

Here, have another wrap to forget.

When Steve goes back to the bar to get another pint, a woman Kim's never seen before comes up to the table, and looks at her so oddly, like she's possessed or something, that Kim stares back, flummoxed.

'You're her, aintcha?!'

Kim says nothing, waits, doesn't move and doesn't even brace.

The woman staggers a little to her right, then suddenly hisses, 'Cow!' draws back her hand and slaps Kim full in the face.

As her head cracks against the back of the booth, part of Kim's brain agrees. Yes.

Steve shouts a lot and the woman is bustled out by an apologetic barman, while Kim continues to sit very, very still.

No, she doesn't want to press charges.

As soon as they get home, Steve's straight on the Xbox. He mutters a goodbye when Ayesha leaves, but doesn't look away from the screen.

Kim trudges upstairs to check on the kids.

Darryl's making whistley-snorey noises like Sausage when she sleeps.

She has to force herself to look at Nate.

'Fuck!' She pulls back her hand like she's been burned.

A trick of the light. Shadows on his head.

Shadows that look like horns.

Andover Estate Closed Facebook Group

Winnie Harris
5 hrs 🌐

That Kim was in the pub last night. Out drinking when that little girl could be anywhere!

Marcia French Don't surprise me

Olive B Nasty woman

Sunny Gayford She qwas always off her head when she pick up that kid fom school

Reg Offreiter Get all dealers off this estate. Not good for our young people.

Dan E Boi That terrorist bitch is always round there flat. Shell be beheaded innit. LOL.

Khal Mohammad Not all Muslims are terrorists

Frank Brown Not all vegans are twats.

Miss Thing OMFG! Get a life peeps!

MotherofDragons365 Scummy Mummy is about right for that slag

Remi Okafor If anyone has any information about that little girl they should contact the police.

Shakin' Bacon If anyone ahs information about Muslim terrorists donlt bother – they bend over backwoods for that lot

👍 2   2 Shares

👍 Like   💬 Comment   ➔ Share

Mummy

She has defied me once more, in the most shocking, hurtful way. Screeching profanities. Kicking my shins. Flailing about so aggressively, like some *beast*, she knocked my statue of the Virgin Mary off the shelf.

Wicked.

She must learn.

I vowed I wouldn't be like my mammy, but sometimes, I now see, a tight leash is essential. Discipline is what the child obviously lacked in her previous life, that's why she is so wilfully opposed to me. 'Folly is bound up in the heart of a child, but the rod of discipline will drive it away.' Mammy's regular lecture.

But now I see she had a point. Spare the rod, spoil the child.

So much nonsense is spouted these days about corporal punishment: teachers cannot administer the cane; a parent can't stop a child from dashing into traffic with a swift slap on the bottom; a lie can't be corrected with a ruler across the palm. And so we reap the nastiness and selfishness of so many unchecked brats.

No one likes to hit a loved one. It is called tough love for a reason.

I couldn't help but raise my voice as I instructed her, yet again, 'Thou shalt honour thy mother!' But, as I shut her in her room to cool her temper, I heard her sneer back at me, 'You ain't my mum!'

We'll see if she's so cruel and vile after another night without her little furry friend, or her supper.

I haven't got around to replacing the bulb in her room yet.

I used to be afraid of the dark, but Mammy said that was sinful because God's light is everywhere.

I try to ignore the kitten's plaintive mews but then she claws at my leg. Why is everything so demanding?

Tonya

I'm hungry. I'm cold. I hate The Woman. It's dark in here, like that time the leccy was shutted off because of Daddy, and Mum said Daddy was a silly twat.

I am bloody, bloody hungry.

I broke her stupid doll. I'm glad. Serves her right.

Are you hungry, Dunny? I am so hungry.

Mummy

'Don't touch that!'

Little heathen.

We are told we must 'bear with each other and forgive one another', but often this is very trying.

She fingers the statue of the Virgin Mary as if it's worthless. I have only just repaired Our Lady with superglue. She has no respect for the symbol, for me, for anything. She treats the icon like some toy.

Despite the high hopes I fostered, bringing the kitten into my home – with the resulting disruption, mess and stench – it has not healed our fractious relationship.

She can be a nasty child.

The solution comes that night. I have tried so hard to ignore it, but as I feared, there is no easy way out.

The voice of God is not a sound. There is no Brian Blessed booming down from on high. No walls shaking. Nevertheless I quake as His words pass silently through me.

The Holy voice has an intimate resonance: words your bones immediately recognise; a truth as deep as your heartbeat.

But these words are no blessing.

The demand, again, more insistent this time: 'Make the sacrifice.'

I do not want to hear this. It is too cruel.

My eyes might weep, my hands might clasp, but I know with an awful certainty that my appeals and prayers will be disregarded.

I don't want to do this. But I must. I have to sacrifice the gift my God has given me. I must sacrifice my Izzy.

Perhaps she was never truly mine.

We are doomed to this endless series of fights and disappointments, for she is full of sin.

I must give her up to save myself.

There's a tiny pulse just under her left eye. She has the same dark circles there as me, as if we really are mother and daughter. I bend forward to ease the pressure on my knees. I've been praying so long by her bedside they ache. I lay my head on the pillow next to hers.

She smells yeasty. How long is it since I last bathed her?

My breath, ragged with the pain in my heart, lifts wisps of hair from her forehead.

Apart from the soft rise and fall of her chest, she reminds me of one of those pale, waxy-faced Victorian children, dressed in their Sunday best, posed rigidly alongside their families in portraits. Dead, of course.

And it would be so easy to do it now. No eyes to accuse me, for they would be covered with the soft duck feather pillow as I push down, my body crushing the air out of her, perhaps a rib cracking.

Or would it be so easy? Might she buck and claw? My muscles have softened as I've lost weight. Stress is so slimming! Would it be enough if she fought for her life? Of course, she too is weaker now than she was when she first arrived.

But suffocation is not what our Lord demands.

I stand too quickly and sway, light-headed.

She makes a murmur in her sleep and turns towards me.

In her face I see the struggle – a battle between my pure, simple angel child and the base, corrupt little animal. When she's awake, that feral nastiness is uppermost. In sleep her features are sweeter.

A small, wicked part of me thinks it is so unkind to offer me my heart's desire then snatch it away in this inhuman manner. Although, if I have faith, she might be saved yet.

She *will* be saved. Surely?

But the images of what I must do, how she might look, are too horrible to contemplate. They flash into my imagination – a conflagration! I try to stand, to get away, but my knees buckle. I slump onto the mattress and disturb her, so her eyes flicker open, but they close immediately. I don't think she saw my face, which is just as well.

I can't tell how long we might have left together.

I must bathe her tomorrow.

Kim

In her dream, she's fucking Steve. When she wakes, she can't imagine that ever happening again. She can't even remember when they last did it.

The sun's out. It's one of those bright, chilled days that promise proper spring, at long bloody last. She feels a lifting of her spirits and immediately feels ashamed for it. The dog's having a mad half hour, and she can't help but smile at it. Then her stomach flips with disgust when she forgets for half a second and is about to call Tonya to come down for her breakfast.

The instant she tastes the hot chocolate she's made for Darryl, checking it's not too hot, she wants to heave. Will her girl ever eat chocolate again?

She sets off to Morrisons, leaving Nate nestled against Steve's barrel chest as she stomps the pavement like an invading Roman centurion, avoiding hostile eyes. And it happens again. Like it does a couple of times a month. In the busy supermarket, rammed with kids, half a hope flares.

She catches herself staring at a girl messing about in the stationery section. One of those shiny jackets Tonya wanted from H&M. Kim's gaze is so hard, the kid turns around. She looks nothing like Tonya really. She doesn't even see Kim, but she feels the laser beam of attention. Then she turns back to her friend, or sister, and they chatter on, as the mother leans on her trolley, talking to someone on her phone. And Kim wants to shout, 'Don't you know you can't turn your head for a second?! You can't fucking blink!'

She forces herself to walk away to the tills.

Traipsing the shopping home, her hands start to go numb because she's forgotten her gloves and she thinks, *Tonya hated the cold.* And that thought hits her deep in her belly, still wobbly and tender after the birth. She has to lean her arm against a garden wall, her feet suddenly unsteady.

Tonya hated the cold. Past tense.

She can't allow that thought to cling, so she says it out loud, like some proper nutter bastard, 'Tonya hates the cold. Hates it!' And despite everything, for a second, it seems true.

But she can't hold on to that belief. A sheen of sweat coats her upper lip as she strides on. She starts panting as she rushes back to the flat, turns into the estate, fumbles for her keys and staggers back inside, slamming the door on air that now seems poisonous. She leans her forehead against the kitchen cupboard.

She'd know if Tonya had really gone, wouldn't she?

Sausage dashes to her feet and woofles around her. The dog's hoping that Kim's back to feed her, or get her lead and take her for a walk.

Steve shouts, 'You okay, babe?'

She forces out, 'Yeah. Fine.'

She unpacks the shopping, her movements jerky, shaky. And she remembers fragments of the early morning nightmare that woke her – an old fairy tale, Hansel and Gretel. Although it didn't feel like a dream.

She feels proper weird.

Upstairs, she pops her head into Darryl and Nate's room. Steve said they should either have the baby in with them or put him in Tonya's room, and that set off a nasty screaming match, for which Kim's not at all sorry.

Darryl's crashed out for a nap. The little sod was up at five this morning, woken by the bloody baby, and they never got him back to sleep again. She strokes his hair, which is starting to curl, it's so long. She likes it. Even Steve's coming round to it, although he's warned her that if it ever gets close to a Hoxton bun, he'll take an axe to it and chop it off himself.

She turns to the crib to check on Nathaniel and swings back round quickly. Can't breathe.

What she saw, she can't have seen. It's impossible.

She turns back, slowly, dreading what she'll find.

The baby's on his back, long lashes, a fuzz of peachy down. A smooth, round skull.

Whatever was there on his head has gone.

It must be an acid flashback or something.

She has to get a grip.

She tries to shake it off. Decides to go for a run, even though her sports bra is far too tight with the milk glands still heavy in her breasts. Thudding out the estate, she heads up along the glorious beauty of the scenic Hornsey Road.

She won't acknowledge the cold, doesn't want to be reminded of her daughter's dislike of it. Like a little cat, Tonya would often sit squashed against one of the radiators. She loved her electric blanket 'a millionty, billionty much!' and had it on most nights to warm her bed before she got in.

Kim shouldn't be running so soon. Her knackered womb could drop out. She could rupture something.

Her lungs hurt as she breathes hard. Smoking karma. It's the only thing she enjoys, though. The only thing just for her.

But she'd give up more than the smoking, swearing, all her bad habits, if only the bastard who has Tonya would give her back. If only fucking God would listen, she'd go to church.

If only.

What wouldn't she give to get Tonya back?

Kim's mind is suddenly full of a terrible idea.

She ups her pace. Not a great decision. Her pelvic floor is fucked. But she has to get away from her thoughts.

Up past the mini Tescos, the Factory gym, Elthorne Park, with the pissheads huddled round one bench. Then the cut through Ashley Road, the crap end of Mount View, then, within seconds, the magical posh end, with the manicured front gardens.

But she can't outrun the insane thought.

And her mind's so full of Tonya, she can't, won't think of Nate. She has to do this thing for her girl, who might be cold somewhere.

In the old days, running would soothe her mind. The natural endorphins used to calm her unstable emotions and stop the drug itch. No such luck now.

*

When she comes in, sweating heavily, Steve pauses from his game with Darryl, looks up and sees her eyes are strange.

Her face shuts him down before he even asks her if she's all right.

After her shower, she gees herself up and peeks in on the baby. It's a half-second glance. And it's okay.

She breathes out, relieved.

What the fuck was she thinking!

But, as she closes the door and turns away, she catches it again in her peripheral vision.

Sees the thing she can't be seeing.

On the baby's head. In daylight.

Horns.

Tonya

This house smells weird. The Woman smells weird.
I don't like the smelly candles.

Mummy

Violence in the air, like the stink of sweat and lightning. A metal tang of blood. A young dog fox panting on the side of the road. Ribs shattered. A gaping wound. It snarls as the creature hops closer, snapping as the thing nears.

One parry. Two. Three. As the beak impales its cruel hook deep into the gash, the fox lays down its head and exhales one last time.

This is one of the worst dreams. Oh, there are many to choose from, but this is eviscerating in its clarity.

The confusing, fuzzy dreams of violence are bad enough. But the night of the fox—

He ran it down. Murderer!

Me, hysterical.

Back in our kitchen, Michael's raised arm. My tears and desperate cries. The pummelling.

I stagger to the bathroom and find I am scouring my teeth with far too much pressure. The dream leaves me shaken each time it resurfaces.

Michael knocked down the fox in his company Audi. He was never the best driver – overconfident, as so many men tend to be. Yet he left it to me to put the creature out of its misery.

And I did.

I am nervous of what is to come.

I light the Jo Malone candle – Pomegranate Noir. Too much for daytime, I know, but I have run out of the Frosted Cherry Limited Edition. They serve an important ritual, I feel, along with their practical application to disguise putrid odours – like keeping the votive candles alight for you, Michael, and my father, God rest their troubled souls.

My daddy was the best daddy in the world. A huge bear of a man. And what a voice! He could lure the angels out of the trees with his rich tones. How he'd sing and put Margaret's diddy, dainty feet on top of his almighty galumphers and dance her around the room as Mammy bleated, 'Watch out! Be careful! You'll have the ornaments off the dresser!'

She often spoke in exclamations, did Mammy, hand fluttering to her wizened heart to keep it inside her.

But he'd laugh at her and keep waltzing Margaret round and round, threatening the good bone china.

And how he would hug my sister tight as he put her to bed and tell her she was the most beautiful child in the whole wide world. And in the next bed, my dark feelings would simmer.

But Mammy might have had a drink and then she would scream at him that it was wrong and bad and evil for a father to show his own child such affection.

Certain songs remind me of him. He could make you weep with his version of the popular tunes, his notes carrying all the pain and yearning of his harsh younger life. One of fifteen children!

I remember Daddy stroking Margaret's hair, stroking it so much it would fly up to meet his hand, like my heart rose to greet him whenever he came in, frozen from his work in the fields. He did not see me. His eyes would always search her out.

But this memory's all mixed up now.

I told Michael how I ached to be more like Margaret, so my daddy would smile at me that way. To be slim. To be loved. Then Michael would hold and console me. But it might turn into something else. He might hold me too tight, crushing me.

And with his hot breath on the back of my neck he would tell me how he loved me, while committing the sin before we married.

I was his Eve, leading him into temptation.

And even after we were joined in God's eyes, sometimes I fought for my life against my own husband, lashing out, without meaning to, but his bulk would suddenly morph into a dangerous thing and I could no longer bear him touching me.

And, afterwards, Michael would whisper to me and try to soothe my sobs and say, 'I think you should see someone,' by which he meant, of course, that I was broken and fouled beyond his repair and I needed some head doctor, some trick cyclist, to poke around the buried memories.

But there's a reason why they're buried in the first place.

Only Michael isn't buried, is he.

The darkest scene in my dream. For I see his arm up – but it's not to strike me.

Forgive me Father, for I have sinned. It has been months since my last confession.

Michael's arm is up to ward off a blow. The bottle's in my hand and I'm jabbing it towards him. Always trying to stop me drinking. On and on. I bare my teeth and lunge and hit him hard over the head. The glass doesn't break as it does in the movies. Instead it makes a sickening clunking sound. He goes down, blood in his hairline. And, as he tries to stagger to his feet, I kick and kick.

Those awful words, 'Cunt! Cunt! Cunt!' They come out of my mouth.

The smell isn't so bad now it's cold. A stillborn spring. Sometimes it seems as vague as a dream.

They say you stop smelling things after a few hours. I think I saw a Febreze advert about it. So I'm not sure if it has faded, or if my senses have simply slid away from the odour.

But the truth is, Michael still reeks.

Kim

Horns!

She grabs Darryl and carries him downstairs. Away from – *that*.

The decision is instant. Final. She has to get the baby out of their home. To save Darryl. To save Tonya.

Two birds. One stone.

Some part of her thinking process realises this is wrong, totally mad. But—

She puts Darryl next to the sofa. He's sleepy and doesn't protest.

'I just need to do something. I'll take Nathaniel with me. Go for a walk. Watch Darryl, yeah?'

Steve's shock that she might want to take the baby anywhere confuses the part of his brain that might identify this as bad news.

The flashes and bangs on the TV screen mask the craziness in her voice.

There are flashes and bangs inside her head.

She straps the baby to her like some ancient washerwoman. The puppy dances around her, sensing an outing. She tries hard to ignore the desperate yaps, but if the noise carries on, she's afraid Steve might look away from his game. He might notice something's up. He could ask to come with her.

As the strange woman, who smells like Kim, but doesn't move anything like Kim, picks up her little harness and lead, the dog goes doolally with glee.

Kim needn't have worried. Steve glances up for a nanosecond, then turns back to his Xbox, slumping down so the new roll of fat squidges over the waistband of his jogging bottoms.

He doesn't ask how long she'll be.

She doesn't say goodbye.

She heads past the Old Laundry, the Old Dairy, everything old and used up round here, trudging on and up to the Parkland Walk. Kids say it's haunted there. It's as good a place as any. But she'll need to pick her spot. She hopes it's not busy.

She doesn't question why she's drawn up that way again. She doesn't know Tonya's sitting humming to herself, locked in a room less than half a mile away. Not with her mind, anyway. Perhaps it's sixth sense; a mother's sense.

She cuts down to the disused railway line along the path from Crouch Hill and is swallowed up in a tunnel of green. A low sun flashes sharp and silvery through the lacy froth of tight new leaves. She breathes in proper air, smells natural scents. The sweat chills on her back.

It feels right to be here. Almost calming. But what she might be about to do is so bad, she can't let the thought all the way in. Won't admit it to herself. Pretends this is just a walk, not a nightmare.

She slows her pace, places a hand on the bark of a tree, watches a little lad bomb by on his bike, followed by his mum on hers.

She fingers the plastic covering of the razor blade in her pocket. Walks on.

Nathaniel's a dead weight, the straps of the carrier tugging at her shoulders. She doesn't have to look to know how his head will be hanging, how his lips will look all pouty as he drools down her front. It reminds her of Steve when he used to crash out on the sofa after playing *Call of Duty* for six hours straight. Before the kids.

She tries not to think of the baby's face. Or what she's seen on his head. And she can't think about what Steve will do, what will happen if she does it . . . after she does it.

Nathaniel means 'God has given'. She looked it up. But God also takes away.

She's coming up to the bridge with the graffiti – artistic stuff, not like the crap scribble round the estate. The skateboard ramp's gone. Darryl loves anything like that. The noise, the movements, the big lads doing their tricks; it's cheaper than taking him to the pictures. Last year she sat him in front of the ramp in his pushchair and shoved a lolly in his chops and he was as happy as he's ever been.

He could show his little brother how to skateboard.

She has to stop thinking like that. This thing isn't his brother. It's not human.

What will happen to Darryl if she goes through with it?

The baby for Tonya.

She can't be serious. She's fucking doolally.

There's an underwater feel with the pale sun diffusing through the trees. It makes Kim think of fairy tales, although this wood doesn't feel ancient. Parkland Walk is like the bloody M1 on a Sunday with hordes of yummy mummies jogging, while Alices and Rories whizz up and down on their sleek new pushbikes. Per square metre it also holds the biggest concentration of French bulldogs outside of Crufts.

Sausage is tearing round like a blue-arsed fly, stretching the lead, whiffing *bats! foxes! other dogs!* A riot of smells. Passers-by smile at the animal's antics.

It could be a normal afternoon's outing: a woman, a baby, a dog. Although there's something off in the woman's gait.

As she crosses the railway bridge into Finsbury Park there's a darkening. The expanse of green softens with the failing light. Kim feels heavier.

She finds an out-of-the-way tree and stops to squat, leaning a shoulder against rough bark, unstrapping the baby carrier. The dog flumps down beside her, panting. Her thoughts seep into the growing gloom and she starts shivering.

She takes three deep breaths, like the meditation bloke showed her, then forces herself to check.

The horns are still there.

Mummy

I allow her to drink chocolate milk as a treat. A condemned child's last meal. She slurps. I wince a little. As usual she spills some on the table and gets a brown moustache. I try to wipe it off with kitchen towel and she pulls her sour face away from me and bats at my hands.

I'm glad that this will soon be done.

God will bless us with a fresh start.

Or it will simply be over.

I undo the back door and breathe in the dampness. Dusk. A time of moth wings and noises without origins. Leaves flitter across the lawn – the flowerbeds a ruin. I had to cancel the gardeners after her arrival.

I'll soon be able to make it lovely again. If it ever comes, spring will hail the greening.

She's by my side quick enough at the scent of the outside.

I have the gaffa tape ready.

She stands next to me looking into the fresh air, no doubt calculating if she can dodge past me to run out, but I slam the door and grab her shoulders and wrestle her between my legs, clamping her arms to her side, pushing her down with my knee on her back as I fumble for the black tape. I've already cut a section to go over her mouth – the first thing to cover with such a noisy creature. Some of her hair gets caught. But I can't worry about that now.

I stick a long section across her back and turn her onto her side – ignoring the sharp kicks, which catch my arm, my elbow – and tug it across her chest and then over again. I'm sweating by the time her arms are secured by her side. And still she squirms.

It's a little easier to half kneel on her chest and pull her legs and ankles together, looping them with the tape as fast as I can.

She thrashes like an eel, all will and muscle. Such fury in such a small package. Pure rage in her eyes. I leave her on the kitchen floor, grab a scarf and wrap that around her head so I don't have to see the hatred.

I catch my breath, then lug her out, down the steps onto the grass, smearing dank mud and mossy slime across her pink leggings.

She seems to go limp for a few seconds, before the bucking starts up again and the muffled grunts get louder.

The fresh logs I bought last week are already stacked under the tarpaulin cover, along with the barbecue fuel and the gas lighter from the kitchen drawer.

I half lower, half drop her onto the lawn, suddenly realising I should have lit the fire first. Now I'll have to wait until it catches, grows fierce enough to do its job.

Kim

She's not sure how long she stares into the twilight, but she's shaking uncontrollably now, desperately clawing at thoughts splintering in all directions. She hears Nate's breathing. Imagines he looks peaceful. The puppy's crashed out by her feet. She puts a hand on the dog's side and feels her warmth and resolves to get up and go back home. Just stop this madness. She reaches to pick up the baby carrier.

But—

She glimpses the small obscene protrusions on its head. Turns away sharply.

She will not let herself be taken in by this creature. It is not a child. It's a curse.

A small part of Kim's brain understands this is not true, can't be true, but she determinedly ignores that knowledge.

There's a smell of decay. Leaves and litter are rotting into the mud. Kim shudders. Tales from the crypt. Those zombie comics she read as a kid. Snaky visions of putrefaction deep beneath the hard ground. Bone-cold thoughts seep and chill her heart.

It's all muddled up.

She was carrying this thing inside her when her girl was taken. If she offers this one up, Tonya will come back to her. An eye for an eye.

She can't go on without her daughter.

The last time she was here in this park with her girl the kid was rolling round on the grass, patting it. She showed her how to make a whistle with a thick stem and Tonya blew and blew, trumpeting and marching all the way home.

Kim's resolve is that of the Ice Queen. She has no choice. Something's been determined beyond her. She sits with her back against a living tree, but she might as well be buried, crushed under unforgiving earth.

She can't bear to see the baby's face again. But despite willing herself not to think of him, she remembers his mouth blowing a tiny bubble. She closes her eyes because she doesn't have the strength to look away for much longer.

She can't not hear his small sigh.

She has to steel herself for what comes next.

The baby for Tonya. A sacrifice to the old gods.

She reaches for the razorblade. She's still not sure if she means to cut herself.

Mummy

'Your trouble is, you only half think things through.' One of Michael's favourite criticisms. Sometimes he softened it with a kiss, teasing me: 'Silly girl. What are we going to do with you?' His judgements stung.

'If you want half a job doing—' That, one of my mammy's.

I pace. I wish I could pray. Perhaps if I say the words out loud it will help focus my mind.

I light the screwed-up paper, which will catch the kindling, which will catch the logs, which will catch her hair and skin and—

Oh, God—

The smell of the smoke makes me think of Bonfire Night – not at home, never at home. It would frighten the herd. But the time I went to my friend Patty's house and her daddy lit the fire and her mummy had made dark toffee and the few squibs and rockets they had were amazing.

And her mummy told us about Catherine wheels and I wondered how it would feel to be tortured as she was, like so many of the saints – disembowelled and torn apart and set alight – and at the time I thought that my own mammy and Aunty Kathleen must be saints because of what they had to put up with, but then I thought, they can't be, because of the drinking, even though Communion wine and tonics like Sanatogen are allowed. So said Father Bell, who knew these things and always smelt of whiskey.

I stand over the girl and hear her whining in the back of her throat.

And I cannot do this.

But I must.

I look around, but there is no sheep, no ram.

An angel spoke to Abraham and told him he did not have to sacrifice his only son, Isaac, after all. God sent an alternative offering—

It was a test.

If I show my trust in Him, He will surely make things right.

But my heavy heart knows nothing will save the girl, because sacrificial lambs and goats do not miraculously appear in London gardens, do they? And I wonder if the whole story of Isaac was some warped metaphor about doing what your father says, even when he demands the impossible.

He found it impossible to love me.

My daddy wanted Margaret, not me.

I squirt more lighter fluid onto the flames to make them leap and I stare into the dancing heat.

You burn in hell.

Yet fire is cleansing.

But—

You cannot be cremated as a Catholic, so how could I burn her? Perhaps I've got it wrong.

Her body will be reborn. It must remain intact.

As the stone rolled away, resurrected from the tomb, as he was in life, so our Lord reappeared.

Surprise!

That is sacrilegious.

I pray but there is no reply.

I take another sip. She's shivering beside me.

I must slit her throat, then burn her. My God deems it must be so. And what else would I do with the body?

I stumble back to the kitchen to get the largest of my knives, to make sure I don't do this wrong as well as everything else.

And I freeze by the door. Because I can't. I know I will stand, turned to stone, then crumble to salt if I see blood trickle out of her, sinful though she is.

I take a little more brandy to steady my hands and leave her in the garden and I wait in the kitchen and after a long time just standing, watching my own startled, ugly face appear in the reflection of the door as it darkens to black treacle outside, my mind whirring, too confused to pray, I go back to the fire pit and grab her, ignore her muffled, terrified protestations and drag her back in.

She seems heavier.

I slam the door and roar with frustration.

Kim

She's shaking hard, like she's being electrocuted. She can hardly stand. Her muscles betray her and she has to lean against the tree.

A new idea comes to her.

She can leave the thing here, hidden in the undergrowth. In the chill, he won't last long. Not he. It.

And she'll walk away – disappear, without looking back. She won't have to cut its throat after all.

The relief is like a gift.

But she should have put it in the blackberry brambles along the disused railway line – so many places to hide on the steep embankments of the Parkland Walk. She knows she's not thinking clearly.

Looking around, furtive as a hunted animal, she sees a few drunks, the last of the dedicated joggers. She does not look down at the baby. No – the thing.

She turns to walk back the way she came, then stalls, muddled. Distractions flood her mind. She's not sure where she'll go after this. She just wants to leave, bury it, along with the thoughts tormenting her. What will happen when they find the body? Will Tonya really come home? But then she won't be at home to greet her, will she? She'll be in a prison, or some nuthouse. Will they let her girl visit? Won't she be abandoning Darryl? Steve?

But she can't think of another way to get Tonya home safe. Her thoughts keep circling back to the single mantra.

The baby for Tonya.

There's some power in the simplicity, no matter it makes no fucking sense.

And she turns back and squats. Quickly, roughly, she shoves Nate and the baby carrier inside a clump of holly and dead grass, scratching her hands as she pulls them out, as if the evil thing has scalded her.

And she grabs the dog's lead and hurries away, thoughts looping round and cannibalising themselves, but she only manages a few paces before the puppy strains at the lead.

She tugs. The animal plants her sturdy little legs and resists. Kim pulls again, more sharply this time, and the dog starts an insistent 'Yap! Yap! Yap!'

'Come on!' she hisses as she jerks the lead.

And, panic rising, she walks fast, half dragging the puppy along with her, furious at the noise and with herself, and even though no one would give a toss about a dog barking, she knows what she'd do if she saw someone dragging an animal along the grass like she's doing now, frantic to get away before the baby wakes and adds its wails to the dusk.

And she thinks to herself, *No! No! No!*

And the dog yaps and yaps and yaps.

Mummy

She lies trembling on the kitchen floor. I'm covered in a sickly sweat.

When the hormones made me flash and burn, Michael would sigh and say it was 'a tad unattractive', then when I cried, claim he was 'only teasing'.

And I would scream at him to shut his mouth.

As Mammy screamed at me – 'Shut your lying, dirty mouth, you wicked little whore!'

God made me this way. Lacking. If He had only given me my own child, my heart's desire, none of this would have been necessary.

If only I had been able to give my God what he demanded.

If only—

And then I think of Elsa! Divine inspiration.

A kitten, a lamb, a ram, a goat – no difference. An alternative sacrifice.

I rush up to Izzy's bedroom, which always seemed to smell of small animals even before the kitten arrived, and I see where the little cat lies curled round herself on the duvet, like a furry shell. I scoop her up. She stretches and yawns, displaying tiny needle-like milk teeth, then senses something is very wrong and I have to grab her tighter by the scruff of her neck as I dash down and start to run and stumble out the door and back across the lawn to the fire pit as she scratches and writhes ever more wildly and with a cry I fling her towards the flames.

And I see her arch and screech and twist just like they do in cartoons, as if she's running on thin air, and then she lands, just to the side of the fire, scrabbles horizontally, rights herself and hurtles into the bushes in a flash.

So even that is a failure.

I walk back in slow motion and sink onto a kitchen chair. When I get too cold I kick the door shut and start peeling gaffa tape off Izzy's leggings and then from her arms. She remains as still as a statue.

But I keep the scarf around her head until last, because I still cannot bear to look at her.

Late in the night, after the sniffling has finally subsided, she sleeps deeply, exhausted. I envy her. I am too wrung out to sleep.

I watch her ribcage rise and fall and wish I had been able to finish this.

Her hair is a little short along one side, where the tape pulled it out.

Kim

When she gets back to the flat, having failed, although she's no longer sure at what, Steve's still hunched over his Xbox controller. He looks up, slightly glazed, and she hands the baby to him as if it's a heavy burden and he shushes Nate's grizzles. She stands in the kitchen a moment not knowing anything, then, on automatic, opens the cupboard, takes out the bag of dog biscuits and chucks a handful into Sausage's bowl.

Then she goes back to the living room, slumps near Steve on the sofa and just sits.

For long periods Kim just sits. She tunes out, sometimes for a few seconds, and if she's lucky, a few minutes. Until she's skewered by memories. And the pain then is more a dismembering – losing a part of herself more essential than any limb.

She can't watch TV. The news is too horrific.

Comedies make her feel queasy. If there's anything that remotely tickles her, anything Tonya might find funny, she feels it's a betrayal.

So she sits.

Often she'll plonk Darryl down in front of his bright, bouncy shows and she can't even follow the plot of those. She forgets who the characters are, what the point is.

She's resentful when Steve seems to lose himself in his games, but she can't talk to him about it in case it's not true. Perhaps he's just sitting too, staring at the images. She daren't risk talking to him in case it develops into a conversation that neither of them are capable of.

Nate settles, propped on Steve's lap. His knees jiggle the baby as his hands dispatch aliens with laser beams. From her corner of the sofa, where she's curled around herself, holding her knees high and tight to keep herself together, she looks across to his rapt face, a bit fuller with the junk food binges but still her Steve. He seems to shoot and stab and explode away his anger in his virtual worlds.

He should stab and shoot her.

When Nate starts squalling Steve gives up his game.

And she hears, 'Where'd he get this scratch from?'

'What?'

'Here. On his forehead.'

She turns her head away, but Steve shoves the thing in her face and forces her to look. And she sees a raised red line on the skin of a perfectly normal baby.

She thinks fast. 'His nails must need trimming.'

Later, when he comes into the bathroom while she's in there cleaning her teeth, he demands to know why she pulls down the sleeves on her T-shirt so quickly, grabs her arms to check if she's been using again. And that would usually provoke an epic battle. But this time, when he sees the crazy map of scratches up her forearms – evidence of her attempt to abandon his son, to sacrifice his son – when he says, 'What the fuck?' she has nothing left to fight with.

In the middle of the night she lies rigid, reliving the feeling of horror, seeing what was on the baby's head. Horns. But in the morning, when her thoughts calm, when the baby's head is soft and smooth, she asks herself the same question.

What the fuck?

What the actual fuck?

Tonya

Darryl don't like the dark.
I—
I tell Bunny, 'We ain't afraid of no ghosts.'
Bunny's hurted.
'Kiss it better.'
I wish—
I wish my mum—

Mummy

Michael and I went on holiday to 'put things behind us' after a difficult period of rows and recriminations. St Lucia. I looked forward to the restorative yoga and rebalancing Pilates sessions. But after a gruelling flight that left me exhausted, I struggled to find the experience anything better than a let-down.

The view from our room was lovely enough, although the beach was much smaller than it appeared in the promotional photos – a victim of a recent hurricane I discovered, when I queried the discrepancy at reception, Michael tutting as I did so. But this was no bargain Sandals break. I was quite within my rights to hold the place to its claims of superior quality.

However, by then I had a much larger issue to contend with. Mosquitoes. No matter how much insect repellent I slathered on my skin, they would eat away at me, leaving me scratching, tossing and turning throughout the night. The irritation needled me throughout the day.

Michael sighed heavily each time I counted the red weals across the delicate skin of my ankles as we lay in front of the endless turquoise blue. He snapped at me when I accused him of ogling the girls in their bikinis – something I would never be able to wear. He even threatened to dine alone when I refused to join him at the beachside eatery, fearing more agony al fresco. In the end we ate, or rather he ate and I picked and pushed food around my plate, enclosed within the relative safety of the air-conditioned restaurant.

Then came the inevitable. After a little too much to drink that evening, he sighed as if exasperated, saying, 'You – you're the mosquito in paradise.'

Perhaps I should have stopped at three glasses.

I could not sacrifice my Izzy. It wasn't meant to be.

Now my only choice is to start afresh. I must build a new relationship with her, focusing on all the good. All her potential.

I will ignore the irritations that nag at me like those mosquitoes in paradise.

I begin by washing the kitchen floor, then ironing and folding her skirts.

Kim

For the next week or so, Kim forces herself to change and feed the baby, as quickly and efficiently as she can, careful not to look too closely as she does so. She assures the health visitor they're all doing well and gets rid of her as fast as she can. She finds she can stroke his face if she really tries. But she's still jumpy, more jangly than usual.

One teatime she comes back from the rip-off corner shop with the milk she forgot to buy earlier and jumps as she opens the door, hearing Steve scream, 'Sniper on the roof! Sniper on the roof! Down! Get *down*!'

Heart battering her ribs, she bursts in to find him shouting into the headset as he plays, thumbs bashing the controller nineteen to the dozen, probably instructing some dumb American teenager – who doesn't see too much daylight and has never had a living, breathing girlfriend – on team fucking tactics.

She punches him on his back and shouts, 'For fuck's sake, knob-head!' Steve looks hurt.

Later, in a fevered dream, she sees Tonya's body being riddled with bullets. It's a fractured night.

In the morning, she opens the door in her rank dressing gown, hair any old how. The postwoman hands her the packet and letters, clocking how rough she looks.

'Need an autograph?' croaks Kim.

She slams the door, glad to be out of the damp draft, and clutches the fleecy fabric of the ancient M&S dressing gown up around her neck.

She puts on the kettle and opens the letters first: a bank statement and a note from the headmistress at Tonya's school saying they're all still thinking of her. Both make her heart sink.

She slumps over her tea, warming her hands on the *Game of Thrones* mug she bought for Steve's birthday last year ('I drink and I know things'), and cuts the tape from the squishy parcel, trying to remember if he's ordered anything on eBay lately, even though the label's addressed to her. Come to think of it, Steve seems to have abandoned his hoody and trainer habit.

Since.

She feels the fear creep over her as she sees something that looks like white hair inside bubble wrap. Instantly, she thinks of Tonya. Not that she's not thinking of her all the time, only now, it's such a constant she doesn't exactly notice – like when they had building work on the estate for months on end and she only became consciously aware of it when the lads clocked off and the incessant noise of drilling and hammering stopped.

She snips at the Sellotape and realises it's just a toy. But as she reaches inside, somehow the softness freaks her out and she notices a tremor in her hands. There's something wrong about this.

The dislocation starts quietly.

Kim feels very slightly outside the confines of her skull, as if she's both inside and also just beside herself. Like it used to happen, as a premonition of some of the bad times. When she was little. Before it really cracked off.

In slow motion, Kim pulls the thing out of the wrapping. She turns it over. Slapped by disgust, she hurls it away as hard as she can.

It's a white unicorn with a white horn and a white mane and a long rainbow tail. And down one side of its plush, velvety fur is a streak of dried blood.

That's when the scream starts, wailing out of her like a car alarm, leaving Kim powerless, squashed on the floor against the cooker, Nate's cries echoing upstairs.

A neighbour calls Steve.

Mummy

The doorbell pierces my haze. The clock seems to say 10.37 but I'm sure that's not right. It can't be so late. No sounds from Izzy's room this morning.

I stumble into my dressing gown, fumble with the radio, turning it on loudly, so the classical music might drown out any noise, although she knows the consequences well enough by now.

She has been a slow learner.

I check her door is still locked, then descend the stairs, grasping the handrail, bracing myself.

It has been a long time since anyone called on me, although when Michael first went missing, I had to parry the concern: so many messages and calls and doorbells jangling my nerves.

The voice sounded worried on the phone. 'We've not seen him for three weeks now. We just wondered—'

'I don't know where he is.' I made my voice ground glass.

'No one here has had any message from him—'

'The last I heard, he was stumbling out of some club in Soho with a lap dancer young enough to be his daughter.'

'Oh, God. I'm so sorry.'

Michael's secretary, also young enough to be his daughter, apologised again for troubling me. I felt she put the phone down quietly at her end.

I forgave myself the lie. It was necessary.

There was nothing for another fortnight, then his boss turned up on the doorstep late one evening, awkward and apologetic – uninvited, obviously – almost giving me a heart attack.

Thankfully, I was presentable and hadn't yet removed my make-up, so I asked him in, hurried him through to the lounge and started weeping immediately, which took no effort.

It turned out I didn't need to invent an excuse for Michael's 'out-of-character behaviour', or offer theories as to where he might have gone. There was some paperwork I had to sign and apologies rained down upon me.

He said they would treat his disappearance as some sort of mental break-down, call it a sabbatical, keep the position open, theoretically. Unpaid leave, of course.

'Of course,' I echoed.

Thanks to Aunty Kathleen's money and Daddy's legacy, I do not really need Michael's wages. We invested wisely when that was a thing to do. I can now get by on dividends and the money from our London rental flat, which the managing agency sends through every month, with minimum administration on my part. If I avoid Kuoni holidays (hardly likely now, thanks to the child) and the outrageously priced cuts and colours at the boutique salon in Knightsbridge (which has the cheek to charge an extra four pounds fifty for a dishwater-weak cappuccino), I can continue living as before, albeit a tad more frugally. Now my hair is a horror, a multitude of sins covered with the Charles Worthington Root Concealer.

We saved so much money when I decided not to go ahead with more IVF.

'Have you involved the police?' said Michael's boss, perspiring over his drink – organic Earl Grey rather than a large glass of Merlot, for this wasn't a social call and so I wasn't required to provide lemon sole and tinkling repartee, as one of the corporate wives who entertained clients for Michael's investment bank would be expected to do in other circumstances.

'No, I haven't,' I snapped.

'Will you?'

'No, I don't think so. Should I?' I looked up at him, my watery eyes disguising the challenge.

His darted away in what I took to be panic. 'That has to be your call.'

As I suspected, the area of 'corporate finance' and offshore accounts Michael specialised in might not warrant too close an inspection. I never completely understood what he did at work. To be honest, it never really interested me that much.

I realised his boss hadn't come to accuse me of anything.

As I accompanied him to the front door, as he breathed fresh air, free from any demands I might have laid at his feet, he muttered, 'I'm sorry,' the relief in his face the only true thing I saw that evening.

'So am I,' I sighed. And that was the only honest thing I said.

That seems so long ago. Scenes from a different life. A different lie. Now I dread any approach to my door; even Ocado deliveries are stressful, although I wait to see the van driver pull up and scoot to the end of the path to collect the bags.

The doorbell insists. I hesitate.

I am not clear what I fear the most.

Police on the doorstep, naturally. I also have waking nightmares about that awful woman, as if she might materialise by some form of black magic, screaming and demanding I return her daughter.

My daughter.

Every time there's a short update on the news, my gut clenches in terror. Thankfully, nothing new has emerged since the very first reports. Just the tabloids spreading more dirt every so often, throwing a little more shade on the so-called mother, and muddying the waters.

But there's something else along with the terror of discovery that causes me to panic. My life and my looks pecked over in downmarket newspapers. Photos of my bare, startled face, shadowed and haggard, my hair a mess, no doubt, being wrangled into court. Stodgy prison food.

It makes me shiver. It makes me sweat.

And, again, like an electric shock, the doorbell.

Heart hammering, I manage to blunder down the last three stairs and swing open the door – to find an unshaven, foreign-looking man. Only when I remind myself to breathe do I see he's holding out a parcel.

'You sign? Next door, please? Take, please?'

When I do not reply, for these people with poor English infuriate me, he repeats this request, pushing the package further towards me.

I'm afraid I swore as I slammed the door in his ignorant face.

Kim

Liaison Woman comes round again. Steve tells Darryl, 'Look, it's Aunty Jean,' and Kim snaps, 'She ain't his fucking aunty,' and they tear a few chunks out of each other with their words because they're dreading what she has to tell them.

But it's not as bad as they both feared. The police could find no matches for the blood. It wasn't Tonya's, that's for sure. Using some new scientific technique investigators determined it was probably menstrual blood.

What kind of sick fuck would pull a stunt like that?

When Steve pushes for 'developments' she also tells them that officers are currently wading through new calls to the appeals number. 'Potential leads are still coming in.'

She does not tell them what most of those calls say, or what's being flung about on social media – she wants a bath after going through that shit.

Facebook and Twitter

Erica Wilde
@Wildstorm55

If my kid was as fugly as Tonya, I'd pay someone to kidnap them. LOL! #KimSearle #ScummyMummy

💬 1   ↑↓ 5   ♡ 33   ⬆

Caroline James
1 hr ☁

There's some sort of collection for that Tonya girl. Is it for the mum and dad? If so, they should get off their scrounging arses.

Kitty Jones Absolutely. It's disgraceful.
Matt Olsen I wouldn't give them a penny.
Aziz Hassan Isn't it for the investigation? Or a reward?
Edwin Stanley The police should be doing their jobs. We pay
   our taxes—

👍 2

👍 Like   💬 Comment   ➤ Share

Taal35
@Salat5

@Ayeshabeats What sort of sister are you, befriending that shameless kafir. You will not be pardoned, mushrikun—

💬 2   ↻ 0   ♡ 0   ⬆

Montys Python
@Lumberjackpanties331

@kimsearle1985 You look like the kind of dirty bitch who'd enjoy a good seeing to on your knees sucking my—

💬 9   ↻ 0   ♡ 0   ⬆

Em Fields
@emfieldsreal

@SteveOgamer420 I see your Missus round by the Holloway Argos doing H only last week—

💬 3   ↻ 0   ♡ 0   ⬆

Hazydayz
@hd7065442

@kimsearle1985 @SteveOgamer420 I have youre girl. Leave 1000 in used notes in a Tesco bag by the clothes recycling bin—

💬 1   ↻ 0   ♡ 0   ⬆

Shaylana Brady
2 hrs 🌐

Ditch the bitch, Steve-O. Pick me! ;)

Tracy C OMG! Steve's pretty hot!

👍 7   4 Shares

👍 Like   💬 Comment   ➤ Share

Flick Chappell
@fchappiesings

Did anyone else see the footage of her going apeshit in McDonald's? That slag should have her own reality show!!! #KimSearle

♡ 11   ⇅ 9   ♡ 23   ⬆

Simone Ward
@simwardofficial

WTF are the police even doing? There's a kid out there missing and they sit on their fat arses bleating about health and safety and human rights— #FindTonya

♡ 2   ⇅ 1   ♡ 4   ⬆

Sol Hernandez
@Solhernandez00

Who else thinks that Kim looks like Rodney Marsh? #KimSearle

♡ 1   ⇅ 44   ♡ 143   ⬆

John White votes Labour
@JohnWhite456110

Now we hear some essential CCTV cameras were down? Another Tory cut. The lack of infrastructure claims another innocent victim. #KimSearle #FindTonya

♡ 5   ⇅ 0   ♡ 2   ⬆

Mummy

Children are a heritage from the Lord. Offspring are a reward from Him.

But is this feral creature really my reward?

She has not forgotten the kitten, even though it hasn't returned since the bonfire incident. She draws pictures of Elsa. She never gets the nose right.

It doesn't surprise me. She always appears entranced by any animal in the stories I read to her. Which is probably why she becomes so silly when the butterfly flutters into the kitchen. And the window had only been opened a tiny crack, as it's getting so stuffy in here. April blooms with global warming.

'Ooh! Look! Look!'

'Yes, it's a butterfly, darling.'

'I know that!' she snaps.

I sigh and turn back to my chores. Even when there's the potential for a mother–daughter bonding moment, she ruins it.

She dashes around, almost knocking me over, trying to catch it, leaping upwards.

'Izzy, sweetheart, please calm down.'

I make my voice soft in case it will quieten her, but she continues with her frenzied movements, jostling my leg.

'Be careful, please.'

Mine is a good-sized kitchen with a central island, yet she makes it feel small as she careers round and round after the insect.

'Look, he's playing with me! Oh! Oh!'

I rarely see her so animated.

She jumps again and again, finally managing to clutch at the butterfly, but accidentally squashing it in the process.

And it is as if a battery has fallen out of her. Her face crumples.

The thing lies there, dusty and dead in her open palm. She looks up at me, shocked by the creature's sudden demise.

'I told you to be careful, Izzy. Now look what you've done.'

'Is he poorly?' She reaches her hands out to me so I can take a look. She rarely reaches out to me. Or consults me about anything, come to think of it.

I push one wing with the finger of my rubber glove. The butterfly does not move.

'I think you've killed it.'

'No. NO!' she shouts.

I cannot resist saying, 'I did warn you.'

'He can't be dead. It's not fair!'

'Throw that in the bin, please.'

She pretends not to hear and sits with the broken insect lying on her palm, staring at it for some minutes, pouting in that unattractive manner of hers. I turn back to scour the worktops.

She is very quiet which is a rare blessing. I begin to find my own soothing rhythm in the cleaning, glad that I'm burning off calories as I do so. Then I hear a sudden, 'Look! Look!'

And she's back on her feet, bouncing up and down. The butterfly is stirring in her hand. I peer down to look, delighted that she wants to share a moment with me.

The creature wobbles on its hair-like legs, then takes off on its jerky flight path.

'It's alive! It's back alive!' she shouts, clapping her hands. 'It's butterfly Jesus!'

I am not sure if she is being sincere, or if I should be offended.

Jean Hall,
Family Liaison Officer

Some people don't make things any easier for themselves and Kim Searle is definitely one of those people. She does herself and her cause no favours.

Steve, on the other hand, is a doll. Jean thinks Kim's lucky to have him. She doesn't harbour doubts about him. He has a cast-iron alibi, with the whole pub as witnesses at the time Tonya was taken. His work, his friends and his family all check out. He isn't harbouring his daughter anywhere, as far as they can tell. But nothing surprises her in this line of work. And it wouldn't be the first time a child was discovered drugged and hidden – to get a ransom, not that anyone's asked for one so far, or to milk money off well-wishers, not that Kim has many of those.

Steve makes her job easier. He's open with his answers. He wears his emotions on his sleeve. Polite, receptive to suggestions and grateful for any information, plus, he really listens to briefings.

Kim does not. She comes across as crude and aggressive. A total liability with the media. Plus, they're having enough problems getting the press and public on side as it is. The general consensus is that people are baying for Kim's blood rather than focusing on the abductor.

Jean sighs to herself as she heads out to the flat for another gruelling meeting. The team's desperate for a new photo of Tonya. Kim's been tasked with asking around mums from the school, or neighbours on the estate, to see if anyone has caught a recent image of Tonya playing with their own children.

One good image can spearhead an investigation, catch the public's imagination.

It might have been easier if Tonya had been a pretty blonde, but the girl has her mother's hard-set face. A determined look, if you want to put it nicely. The current photo they're choosing to circulate is one where she's laughing – but she looks wild. Pointy tooth crying out for a brace. So many of the rejected photos feature her scowling.

Jean finds all interactions with Kim wearing. She opens the car door and steels herself. The woman resists advice, and does not warm to any offer of sympathy. If Jean's lucky, Kim will be sullen and appear a little absent. If not, there's often a simmering threat of violence.

Addressing Steve is far easier, but her training requires her to look both parents in the eye.

The flat's a mess as usual, but she's seen far worse. Darryl's inherited Kim's scrawniness, like his sister, but he appears to be thriving, hitting all his developmental milestones, according to the social worker's report. He presents as a happy kid. No signs of neglect or abuse.

Although Jean wasn't surprised when the drug allegations involving Kim came out.

As she drives back to her office, Jean organises her thoughts. Kim's friend, Ayesha, was round at the flat again. They've checked her, along with her husband, Khalid, an IT student. Both seem blameless. And they have their own cross to bear with that disabled lad.

Cross to bear – Jean catches herself and wonders if that's racist. She's glad she hasn't said the phrase out loud in a team meeting.

She notes to herself how she'd never seen Kim hold the baby until today.

Mummy

She is no fun.

I try to encourage her but she sits deflated, seeming not to see the puzzle pieces.

The next morning it lies there like an accusation, gaping holes taunting my mothering skills. I touch the stiff, shiny cardboard, turn over a piece featuring a fluffy duckling or chick.

Oh, how I loved this one – with the lambs and daffodils and the brightly coloured eggs. She seems bored by most of the stories I read to her about the cave and the miracle, central though it is to our faith. Although there was the promising interaction with the butterfly and yesterday she pointed as if she recognised a picture of the Easter Bunny.

So now I use the felt-tipped pens I bought for her, not that there's been a lot of drawing recently. She will do some colouring in if cajoled, although it's rare for her to stay within the outlines.

I rally myself with a black coffee.

I draw a doll's face on one of the eggshells to make her laugh – bright red cheeks and big blue eyes with spider's leg eyelashes and yellow hair parted down the middle on each side. I make frills and squiggles in pinks and yellows and blues. So pretty! I draw two tiny pink ears peeking through the yellow and hold up the fragile shell to admire my handiwork.

When I go to waken her in the grey mid-morning I say, 'I have a surprise for you, Izzy.'

She writhes in her bed as if she is cramping.

'Izzy!'

I do not mean to snap, but still—

She turns over to me, staring vacantly, lolling on her pillow, showing no interest. She is such a limp lump these days.

I ignore the rebuff. 'Would you like to know what the surprise is?'

She looks at me but doesn't move.

'Oh well, perhaps I shan't give it to you after all if that's how you feel.'

'What?'

'I beg your pardon?' I correct.

'What is it? The surprise,' she whispers.

'Come downstairs and see!'

The progress down is slow going. She seems so listless. She has hardly ever been a bundle of laughs, but these days her whole body seems grumpy, although now she's even slimmer than when she arrived she looks so much better in her pretty dresses.

I sit her on a chair at the table and ask her what day it is.

She shrugs her shoulders in that most irritating way of hers, then doubles over, as if her tummy hurts.

'Sit up straight, please. It's a very important day today, Izzy. It's Easter Sunday!'

She looks blank.

'Easter Sunday,' I say again.

Nothing. Not a flicker of recognition despite all the schooling I've given her on the subject.

'Easter eggs,' I offer.

She looks up at me.

I take the little wicker basket I've prepared and present the eggshells to her with a flourish. She holds one as if she has never seen a decorated egg before.

'This is the day Our Lord rose from his grave.'

She rolls the egg in her hand and says quietly, 'Like the White Walkers?'

I'm not sure what she means or how to answer her, so continue, 'These Easter eggs symbolise the new life, the everlasting life of Christ! Our redemption!'

She turns over the one with the face and picks it up.

'Easter eggs?' Suddenly alert. Hungry, animal eyes.

'Yes, darling.'

'But they ain't chocolate.'

Later, I sweep up the eggshells and wipe clean the table. I turn up the radio so I don't have to listen to her protestations.

She spoils everything. So different from the time I was a child, when I so looked forward to my decorated egg after church.

All this hope for a fresh start, crushed.

Tonya

My belly aches. My head hurts.
   I want a drink. I shout, 'Mummy.' But she ain't my mum.
   The Woman doesn't come.

Kim

She got away with leaving the kids home alone. She got away with dumping Nate in the park – or trying to. She's also somehow managed to keep both boys alive, despite those days when she was so out of it, off her fucking head – as much as she ever was on the scag – anything could have happened.

So Kim resolves to 'make amends', as they say in those sad, grey NA and Al-Anon groups she attended for a while. Step Eight, or Nine? Too many fucking steps for Kim to manage.

So she puts Steve and Darryl's tea on their plates, sees to the baby's never-ending needs – in one end, out the other – shops, cleans and even tidies up a bit, as degrees of guilt settle on her, weighing her down. Her latest mad round of thoughts dumps all the blame (for Tonya, for fucking everything) at her feet again – telling her, convincing her that if she wasn't so wrong at the very core of her, bad things wouldn't keep happening to those she loves.

Yet the thing that sends Steve over the edge and breaks some part of him isn't that she ignored him and the baby for so long, or that they never shag now, or even that she was the one who lost Tonya. It isn't the accumulation of all the truly rotten things she's done, all the bad things she's responsible for. It's something tiny – a final grain of sand on the hefty pile of shit he could and should blame her for.

It's the day she forgets the shopping.

And he's dying for a brew before he sets off to work, as it pisses down like it's the end of the world, Noah-stylee. And when he opens the fridge and finds there's nothing in it – it hurts him.

The argument starts out small.

'Did you get some milk?'

Kim sneers, 'Can you see any in there?' She's trying to make amends; she's not suddenly, miraculously a brand-new person.

'If I could, I wouldn't be asking, would I?'

The nastiness in both their voices ratchets up.

'So why ask if you know the answer?'

'Because I was hoping, just for once, that you might have thought about something other than yourself.'

'Cry me a fucking river!' She clatters her plate into the sink. 'I just forgot, that's all.'

'Perhaps you lost it on the way home.'

'Fuck off, Steve.' The nasty dig sounds nothing like Steve. 'That's not fair.'

He shouts, 'Not a lot about this is fucking fair, *babe*!'

'So fucking sue me.'

He goes quiet, and she thinks it's fizzled out for a second, but then he turns from the fridge and comes right up in her face and says, quietly, so she knows it's serious, 'I've had enough.'

She's so surprised, she can't even reply.

He walks past her and up the stairs.

She slumps on the sofa and waits for the next bad thing to happen, as she knows it will.

He comes down with his sports bag. Call her psychic, but she guesses he's not off to play football.

'I'll stay with one of the lads for a bit.'

'What?'

'I'll pop back, get some more of my stuff tomorrow.'

'But—'

'I can't do this any more.'

They eyeball each other for several long seconds. Kim has to look away first.

She hates the whine in her voice as she says, 'But what if Tonya comes home and you're not here?'

Again, he looks right at her, which disturbs her as much as the bag in his hand. And he says so faintly she hardly makes it out, 'But she's not coming home, is she.'

It's not a question.

About half an hour after he's closed the door behind him, Kim starts shaking.

Mummy

I hear her shout, but I don't go up to her. She must learn that she is not the centre of the universe.

Later, I hear her call more quietly, politely, but I have just painted my nails and I don't want to smear them.

When I finally go in to see her, it's apparent that she's ill.

This must be my fault. I must have brought some bug into the house – where else could she have picked it up?

But what if the poison and pollution is within her? Or this might be a punishment for a sacrifice I could not see through.

She disturbs my sleep in the night as she coughs in great hacking barks. Then I hear her moaning. I go to her room and feel her forehead, which is burning up, her pillow damp and sweaty. She's wheezing.

I'm worried. What if it gets worse?

Then it hits me – how can I take her to a doctor?

In the morning I apply my make-up in a rather slipshod manner and as soon as the shops are open, I leave the house on shaky legs and buy a batch of children's medicine from a chemist I never usually frequent. Although I don't ask for advice, for I simply want to pay and hurry home, the pharmacist says, 'Is it this flu that's going around? If it is, you probably need to take your kiddie to the GP.'

'A virus,' I proclaim, although I've no idea if it is.

'There's a lot of it about,' she replies, and advises rest and warm drinks and says to go to hospital if her temperature doesn't drop within a day, or the breathing becomes laboured. 'Youngsters and the elderly are more vulnerable,' she cautions, and she lectures me against relying too much on Calpol, as if I would.

When I get back, Izzy does seem worse. I forgot to leave her a glass of water.

Could I take her to hospital? Make up some name or pretend I am a visitor to this country? According to the Mail Online, 'health tourists' get faster, better treatment than those of us who live here and pay our way.

What if she starts talking? Would they think her strange tale is a fever dream, or would the police arrive as I waited to see a doctor?

I stand next to her bed watching her struggle for breath. There's a raspy, gurgling noise. Her skin seems scalding.

Is it because it is unseasonably warm for May? Or is God burning her because I could not?

I try and force water into her mouth to quell the fever and I pull up a chair for the vigil.

Some time later during my fitful sleep, I realise that I too am succumbing and I have to take to my bed. I didn't think to stock up on Night Nurse or anything else small hands might find, and so my muscles cramp and complain as I sweat into my own sheets.

I feel myself dehydrate. I'm desperate for a drink – yet I find I can't even force myself to the bathroom taps.

When I stagger to the sink some time later, I am shocked by the sight in the mirror.

I'm unable to think.

I try to pull myself along to the other room, her room, then wonder why I need to go there. I feel as if I might have dreamt the girl, and finally there's a time when I forget there is a child at all.

*

I can't stop shaking. My teeth clatter together and my bones complain. I hug the duvet around me and bring my knees up to my chest.

Michael, please get me some water.

I vaguely wonder if Tonya – no, *Izzy* – has the same virus. But it's beyond my ability to get up and make it across the landing. Those few steps could be miles. It's impossible either way. I am caught like a fly in amber, pinned to my pillow by this punishing contagion. The sheets are wet. I daren't think how they've become so. I need to roll away from the clammy vileness, but I can hardly turn myself over in the bed.

Where is my Michael? I need you, darling.

Is this flu or worse? The only other time I have felt so bad was when I had measles as a child. But that was a burning. This infection chills my blood.

Some time later I am trembling all over, as if possessed.

It feels like retribution. My penance.

Tonya

I am so thirsty.
I am so—
I am—
I—

Kim

She doesn't see him for two days, which drag even more than all the other days. Then he blusters in, fusses the boys, pats the dog, grabs a few things then fucks off again. It's a kick in the gut.

She assumes one of them will contact the other – if there's any news, or when he wants to spend time with Darryl or Nate.

Liaison Woman pops round – Jean, her name's Jean, she keeps saying it and Kim keeps forgetting it – and she finds herself telling her that Steve's not staying at the flat right now, although she wonders if the police might try and make something of it.

But when she sees Jean's face go all soft and concerned, Kim's furious with herself for confiding in the bitch.

She and Ayesha spend hours picking over Steve's walkabout, analysing how he's seemed the past few weeks, coming up with theories about where he's gone, stalking him on Facebook to see if he posts anything.

'Has anything happened?' asks Ayesha.

'Like what?'

'You know, something bad to make him go?'

'What? Worse than the usual?' says Kim, plonking Sausage down off her lap. 'I'm just surprised he didn't go before.'

Mummy

It is so quiet.

When I finally stumble out of bed, some hours – days? – later, I slowly make my way to her room. Thoughts of her have disturbed my rest, insistent and nagging. My legs shake as I stagger across the landing and my hands fumble with the key.

She is lying on her back, duvet on the floor, arms at an unnatural angle on the tangle of the bottom sheet, looking like a tiny, wizened old lady. Her skin has taken on an ungodly hue, the texture of cheap leather, which puts me in mind of those ancient corpses discovered in our peat bogs.

I lower myself to sit on the side of the bed and the movement jolts her position. I still myself, watching for her breath.

'Izzy?' My voice a scratchy whisper.

She looks so peaceful.

I start to rise, to get a drink. It takes a great effort.

I leave her in God's hands.

In slow motion she opens her eyes.

I spill as much water on the sheets as I manage to get to her lips.

I have to go down the stairs one at a time. Walking on boneless legs, I make it over to the table as if I am on a tightrope. I collect two spotty bananas from the Alessi fruit bowl.

It takes a long time to make the steep climb back. When I open her door, she's not there.

My legs have had enough and I slide down the side of the wall, unpeeling one of the bananas.

I hear the tap run in the bathroom.

She eventually reappears, her nightdress wet down one side, her sodden hair dripping on the carpet. I am so tired I cannot summon the energy to tell her to fetch a towel and turn off the tap.

She wobbles over and reaches out her hand to mine. For a second I think she will stroke me, as a kindness, but she takes the second banana and hunkers down next to me to gobble it, leaving the skin discarded in her lap. When she moves, it falls on the carpet.

After a few minutes I feel the sugar enter my system and rally myself to say, 'Pick that up, please.'

She reaches for it with fingers like chicken bones.

We are cautious around each other for a few days. I provide small, nutritious meals and we both spend hours resting. It is marvellously noiseless.

I brace myself for an onslaught of guilt, expecting it to arrive at any moment. I am surprised when it does not.

She watches me warily.

But she is at her sweetest and most malleable when she's so weak, waiting patiently, yet eagerly, for me to give her food. Rewarding me with a smile.

This is how you train an animal after all.

Halfway up the stairs one night, she plops down on her bottom, breathing heavily. I stoop to lift her the rest of the way. Her arms wrap around my neck. Bless her! It feels wonderful.

I have waited a long time for a spontaneous show of affection.

To keep her so tender, I must keep her hungry.

Tonya

I hate The Woman. She makes me kneel and put my hands together.
I pray hard that she'll drop down dead.

Kim

'He'll be back – like Arnie, innit,' says Ayesha. 'He just needs some space.'

Kim fears she doesn't have the energy to fix things. Steve will be yet another thing she fucking loses.

But he does come back – two and a half weeks later. No big decision has been made. He's not even had a change of heart. It's just that Skid's missus told him it was time to fuck off because she was sick of seeing him moping around on her sofa when he got in from work.

And then they settle into something that passes for a life.

Ayesha's round a couple of days later. As soon as she opens the door Kim smells it – rich and spicy and comforting – and that's before Ayesha's taken the top off the big casserole dish.

Steve's in the kitchen like a whippet after a rabbit.

'Curry, is it, Ayesha?'

'Yeah, made it for you, Steve. A welcome home. Save you wasting away, innit.' She grins and whips off the pan lid like a magician. 'Ta-da!'

'What's this?' He prods towards it. 'Chicken, is it?'

'Goat.' She smacks his finger away from the pot.

'Goat?' He doesn't sound sure.

Kim takes the pan, wondering how the bloody hell her friend has time to make food like this and do everything else. With sleepless nights giving her a headache, if she even manages to pick up a ready meal Kim feels she's overachieved.

The next morning she hears two Muslim women talking outside the playgroup building. The really fat white lass, whose billowing robes make her look like she's in full sail, is yabbering on about 'dividing the feast' – for her family and the 'poor, needy people', and she looks over at her as she says this, so Kim sees fucking red and marches straight round to Ayesha's, dragging Darryl along, so he has to trot to keep up. And as soon as her friend opens the door, before she's even had chance to open her mouth to say hello, Kim shouts, 'So I'm a fucking charity case now?' and stomps away, doing the 'talk to hand' gesture when Ayesha calls after her.

It's only when she sees a report about Eid al-Adha on the telly that night, explaining how the tradition is to divide the feast food into three – for family, friends, and the poor; to honour how Ibrahim was willing to sacrifice his son, Isaac – that she realises Ayesha wasn't bullshitting when she shouted to her retreating back, 'No, it's because you're my mate, you daft cow.'

And Kim realises she's heard the story of Allah and Ibrahim and Isaac before, with different names. And it makes her feel queasy and ashamed. Would she really have sacrificed her boy? Is she totally fucking insane?

Later, she walks Sausage round to the park via Ayesha's – to take back the dish and to say a sorry she actually means.

It's the last proper meal she and Steve have for a long time.

Nothing else happens during the hours, days, weeks that follow. Time, somehow, passes. May, June; words to mark the passing.

Except a grinding despair drags at their spirits, like scummy water sucking filth down the plughole.

Mummy

Summer blooms in the garden. Anger blooms in my heart.

I ask her a question and she will not answer me. It is enraging.

I kneel to pray, to ask for forgiveness, because I was not paying attention to what I was doing and accidentally caught her face again.

And I am near tears so often these days. Stung by her insolence. She – whose own slatternly excuse for a mother injured, neglected and ignored her. Let her go. Let her be taken.

Oh, I would never allow anyone to take her from me. I would hold her tight. I would fight for her. I would give my life to defend her. She is my most precious possession. God has blessed me. He heard my prayers.

I always knew there would be a miracle.

A toast to the miracle!

Michael told me I was foolish, deluded, to get my hopes up. He thought my dreams were hopeless because he didn't have my faith.

She is all I have ever wanted. Yet she torments me.

Her rejections. Her slights. Her sneers. Can she not see how much I treasure her? I love her so much, it hurts to breathe.

Why can't she love me?

I can hardly bear the way her eyes impale me as she stares at me across the kitchen table.

Who does she think she is?

She has come from *scum*!

Here, she has everything she could ever want. She has a fresh new start. Opportunities. All that was denied to me. She is finally safe, away from those terrible influences.

I cannot bear it! This spiteful face judging me as I sip my wine, my small aid to help me through this bitter life.

Wine for those who are in anguish!

How she seems to resent me.

But Michael warned me. Always looking for the reason why we shouldn't do something, weren't you, dear Michael. Telling me why I shouldn't pursue my dreams—

'It would be like babysitting someone else's child – but for years,' he said of adoption. 'You just don't know what sort of terrible start in life they've had.'

'But surely that's the point, Michael. We have so much space here and the means to give an orphan a wonderful fresh start. Allow them into a different world . . .'

'They're not orphans. And we don't live in a country house,' he interrupted. 'This isn't some bloody costume drama.' So snappish. 'They might be brain damaged or psychotic. You aren't given the full information.'

'Are you suggesting a child might murder us in our beds? For giving them a good home?' I made my voice light, but I harboured dark thoughts.

Looking at this one's nasty little face, now I am not so sure.

'You know you would not be able to give a child back,' he said of fostering.

'I gave back the foster cats,' I say out loud. And, yes, I know he cannot hear me any more.

Perhaps his doubts showed that he never truly loved me, let alone Our Lord.

They had not loved me either. The cats.

Or perhaps he knew me too well. After all, I was indeed secretly contemplating how I might leave the country with a fostered child – leaving him, our home, leaving all my lovely things behind – if it came to that.

My marriage became bitter and black as stewed tea.

And then, no more Michael.

And then – this gift of a child.

But—

'You hurt me, madam!' is what I mean to say. 'Please, please love me.' The words sound fat and sluggish in my mouth.

I pour myself another drink.

Tonya

Bored, bored, bored, bored. Bored, bored, bored.

Kim

Kim's laid low, surprised she can feel worse than before.

This is a new circle of bastard hell.

She lies wrung out, her lungs on fire, propped up in bed, hacking and spitting into bog roll, because they've run out of tissues, and Steve goes to see to the baby for his early morning feed.

When he comes back in, Nate's slumped over his shoulder and Steve's face tells her something's wrong.

He grabs his phone, awkwardly balancing Nate as he jabs in numbers. And the adrenaline kicks Kim out of bed. An instant mess of clothes and fumbling. Steve's shouting. She's coughing. Darryl's crying.

But not a peep out of Nate. The baby is eerily silent.

It's the first time Kim's been in an ambulance, which strikes her as odd given her fabulous fucking life. Steve's following with Darryl in his van and Ayesha's going to meet them at the hospital, because, amazingly, the ambulance came within ten minutes and she hadn't managed to get over to their flat by then.

In A&E, Kim struggles with the slew of questions and Steve has to deal with it. Sleepy Darryl pipes up, 'Anty A-sha!' when Ayesha appears to collect him. She says to Kim, 'I'd give you a hug, but I don't want none of your germs,' and Kim rasps her thanks as her friend takes her eldest son.

And she wonders if God's going to take the other.

Punishment. Karma. It's what she deserves.

She fears she might pass out, but there's no such relief, and they sit and wait by Nate's bed, or rather, Steve paces and she rocks herself in a plastic chair, bashing her head against the wall whenever another coughing fit shakes her bones.

Then he sits down next to her and grasps her hand and she feels, for the first time in bloody ages, that they're back in this together.

But they're left alone with the fear. The doctors whose job is to manage that fear are too busy dealing with other patients and desperate parents. Too many. The NHS is so fucked, the fear rampages round the wards unchecked.

Steve keeps going out to pester the receptionist, this nurse, then that one, anyone he can grab. Until, after hours and hours of nothing, and so much bustle and noise, with sleep grating at her eyes and the cough ripping out her lungs, someone in a white coat appears and announces that Nate's breathing is better.

And the relief is so deep, it shocks her.

She's amazed at how bright the June sunshine is when she leaves the hospital to pick up Darryl in the morning. A real lick of warmth in it, even though it's so early. Steve's had to go to work. She hopes he doesn't fall off a ladder and kill himself after that awful, sleepless night. And when Ayesha opens the door, she's worried by her friend's face.

Something else is wrong. Is she fucking cursed?

'Sorry,' says Ayesha.

Her muscles tense.

'I didn't see him do it.'

And she rolls up the sleeve on Darryl's *Transformers* hoody and Kim sees where Mo has bitten him.

Her voice cracks as she says, 'He'll live.'

Then she bursts into hot, splashy tears, which surprise her as much as Ayesha.

Mummy

I am drifting off again as the words flood my mind.

'You've got to lay off the booze, love.' Michael's words. Said kindly, which made it worse.

I tried to justify. 'I need it to get to sleep. It's my medicine, Michael.' I loathed the whine in my voice.

And if he pushed, which he usually did, I'd find myself clutched by fury.

I swore I would never be like Mammy and Daddy with their constant fights. Or my Aunty Kathleen, who scuttled over to stay with us after the latest 'spat' with the uncle we never saw, apart from the obligatory weddings, funerals, christenings and confirmations. He was not welcome in our home.

Aunty was a drunk. Oh, not a drunk like the men. No larger than life, shouting, roistering drunk; no swift fists; no maudlin weeping for forgiveness the morning after. Aunty Kathleen was a silent, secret drunk. Drinking herself to sleep when the broken bones and gashes were too painful. Drinking herself towards a quiet death.

Not a death where you put the rope around your neck, like my daddy.

I was to blame for that. My darling mother blamed me for that.

I blame myself for that.

I reach across my bedside cabinet for the bottle.

So hot. Summer nights. No summer loving for me. Ha ha! All alone. Sticky thoughts.

Kim

Steve comes in late. She smells weed on him more often than not. He goes straight up to the shower before giving the kids a hug. The dog can still smell it on him, sniffs his hand as he strokes her, and sneezes.

Kim hates him hanging round with Skid, so she has to say something, although she knows she'd be better leaving it.

'Where've you been?'

'The Enkel.' He ferrets inside the fridge, bringing out a lump of cheddar, extra mature, which is a fucking joke, and the dog spins for crumbs on the lino.

'Skid there?'

'Season ticket at The Enkel, my lad Skid.'

'He still doing blow?'

'Nah. Just a bit of weed now and then.'

'You sure?'

Steve lathers a couple of rounds of bread with some fake butter spread shite and shoves a huge wodge of cheese sarnie into his mouth. 'Mmm.'

Above the chomping, Kim watches his eyes avoiding hers. But, when she catches them, she sees the usual fear and pain. Nothing new.

It's time he laid off the weed. She's given up smoking.

Almost.

Then she gets a call. Adrenaline surging, she's pissed off that it's only the jumped-up manager at Darryl's Kidz Klub playgroup.

'He's been lashing out at one of the other boys – biting and kicking. If this behaviour continues, we'll have to ask you to keep him at home.'

Kim handles it well. 'You can't even spell your fucking name right, so go fuck yourself.'

To be honest, she's glad she doesn't have to send Darryl out any more. She worries when she can't watch him, panics if he's a minute late coming out of his session. She finds herself lurking outside the playgroup, although the windows are all covered over so pervs can't peek inside.

But now, with Darryl at home and the baby's groundhog-day demands, she struggles when Steve's at work. She's tired. Clumsy. She catches her hip hard against the edge of the table and there's already a bruise on her knee where she bashed it against the washing machine.

She can't call on Ayesha to help as much either, because she says she's shattered coping with Mo and Faisal when Khalid's got exams and so is even less bloody use than usual.

It's only when Steve gets in and grumbles to Kim about how knackered he feels and she says, 'Knackered? You don't know the fucking meaning of the word!' that it strikes her – she was proper mental before, wasn't she. Now she's on a more even keel, with the others playing up and acting out around her. This everyday chaos is normal.

As normal as it ever can be again.

Tonya

I count the roses from the window.

I see Elsa. I see her in the garden. I tell her, 'Run away. Run away fast.'

Mummy

The doorbell! And she's not in her room!

I panic.

Again, the door. Insistent.

I unlock the cellar, thrust the child towards the stairs. The stench punches up at me. I wrestle her onto the top step and hiss, 'Sit. Do not make a sound. Do not move. You know what will happen if you are naughty.'

Her eyes blaze in a hollow face, but she knows better than to defy me.

I quickly lock her in and head to the front door, clutching my dressing gown to my chest, bracing myself for whatever lies on the other side. Is this the end? Is this the police?

On the step, my next-door neighbour, holding a bath towel. When I can focus, I see Elsa wrapped in it, her tiny head poking out.

I get rid of the woman efficiently, perhaps rudely.

'No, it's not my cat.'

I try to close the front door but she interrupts, 'But I saw her come from your side of the wall—'

Bitch. Bitch. Bitch. I will her with all my might to leave me be.

'The cat might have come from anywhere. It's not ... mine.' I almost said 'ours'.

She dithers on the doorstep. I wish her harm. But I am commanded to love my neighbour. Even if she is an irritating, interfering cow.

The nosy old bag stares at me. So does the cat. In the chaos of this foggy morning, I have not yet arranged my hair or managed to put on my face. I must look a sight.

That night I lie in bed remembering the stench of the cellar. I still feel it on me, even after I scrubbed my skin with NARS exfoliator in the bath.

Izzy was very quiet when I let her out. I wonder if she went down the steps.

Kim's Neighbour

I saw her down the market the other day. Her face looked almost grey – that drawn look that cancer patients get? She had the other kiddies with her. One was asleep in the pushchair. He was in clean clothes, so that has to count for something, right? The baby was in a sling thing and I couldn't see his face so I didn't notice if he looked well or not.

Still, no one's got a good word about her round here. Some of them have even *given interviews* saying as much. Brian said I should tell them about the time Angie next door to us asked her to keep the noise down when they had that party last summer and how she went ballistic at her. But Angie told me that some journalist had already spoken to her and that bit had been cut out of the *feature* and there was no money in it anyway.

I wasn't following her or anything.

I was just about to pop into Greggs to get some of those doughnuts with caramel custard in, only we ended up going in the same direction. And I couldn't help overhearing her on the phone, not as I would have a conversation in the street these days, with so many of them scooter thieves about round here. Little bastards. But she didn't seem to care.

She had the phone in one hand and the pushchair in the other and she was sighing a lot in the pauses where she wasn't speaking. And at first I thought she might be talking to a fancy man? Because her voice went low and it was only that I had to hurry to get past a lorry coming up the road a bit sharpish that I was so close to her.

And I remember it clear as day because when she said, 'So, it's over then,' I thought she meant the little girl had been found and I worried that after

278

all this time, it meant her body had been found, right? And I really felt sorry for her then, because no matter what she's done and what's been said, it must be awful to lose a child.

But then I heard her say, 'I can't say I'm surprised,' which I thought was totally, like, weird. She was so . . . cold about it. And then she stopped dead in her tracks and I almost bumped into her, so the last thing I heard was, 'No, I'm not sorry and I'm not sad and I'm not going to pretend I am,' and I had to keep walking, so I didn't hear the rest. But I felt relieved for her, because it obviously wasn't anything that bad, right?

Then the next day it came out in the papers that her mother had died and I was really shocked. She seemed so hard about it. No tears. Nothing.

So, if she acts like that when she's lost her own mother, I wouldn't put anything past her.

Tonya

I want to go to sleep like Sleeping Beauty and not wake up until my mum, my real mum, comes to get me. And then we will live happy ever after and I will eat lots of cake the end.

But I got no cake to eat. I peel some wallpaper off the wall down by my bed and put it in my mouth and me and Bunny pretend it's chocolate.

Yum yum.

It tastes shit.

I don't like going to sleep because sometimes The Woman comes. I know she's there.

Sometimes I pretend I'm asleep until she goes away.

My belly aches.

Mummy

We are sitting in companionable silence, for once. She has settled down with her picture book and I am combing her hair. Usually this is an arduous process. Sometimes it's an out and out fight, but she seems calmer today.

Hair like Rapunzel. Hair I yearned for as a child.

I smooth it down, then lie back on the sofa, resting my fluffy mules on a cushion.

I close my eyes for a moment. Something drips on my forehead.

I look up and notice a dark patch on the plaster. Then another drip.

Izzy does not seem interested. I leave her where she is and dash upstairs, but I can't see anything. The bath hasn't overflown; no taps are running.

It is only when I reach for the phone to call an emergency plumber that I stall. How will I manage this?

I move the sofa, which takes some doing, and place a bucket under the drip, laying a bunch of towels around it to catch any splashes. It fills within the hour.

I worry that the weight of water in the plaster might bring down my ceiling with its lovely baroque cornicing. And I'm too afraid to switch on the lights in the chandelier (gorgeous coloured Murano glass in the shape of fruits) in case it starts an electrical fire.

I'm forced to nap on the sofa, surrounded by the soft light of candles, waking with a jump every so often to bail out.

I am tired and cranky the next morning, so I allow myself a strong coffee, which means I have to add milk to make it palatable. I resent the calories.

By the afternoon, I acknowledge that this cannot go on. The lounge begins to smell musty and I'm shaky with fatigue.

I call Pimlico Plumbers. They can be with me within the hour, but I ask for the booking to be later in the evening, even though, no doubt, the rate will be higher.

Then I make Izzy a hot chocolate, adding a couple of my old pills. She falls asleep soon enough and I wrap her tightly in one of my throws, gently applying gaffa tape across her mouth, and carry her, making slow progress so as not to jolt her awake, to the cellar.

I'm tempted to leave her at the top of the stairs, but then she could so easily topple down. And while the plumber will be upstairs, and I will have music on, I dare not risk that sound, although I could blame it on foxes.

I resolve to carry her to the bottom. It makes me breathless. I am so out of condition. Long gone are the days when I could pop out for a Pilates class or personal training session.

I have to lean my arm against the wall and reach one foot down, hoist up her body a little to get my balance, then take the next uncertain step to join it. At any moment I feel I might plunge forward. That long, single second when one foot is suspended in mid-air is terrifying.

My muscles betray me and start shaking. Each step sinks into a heavier darkness gathering at the bottom of the stairs.

But I daren't put on the light.

I try to hold my breath, but the fetid air assaults me.

The next step lunges me forward. There is no extra step. I have reached the bottom.

Izzy stirs a little as I lift her down, laying her on the cold, damp concrete floor.

I can breathe again when I'm back at the door, yet my legs still quiver.

I've avoided the cellar for such a long time. But, as Michael used to joke, 'Karma is a bitch – she'll bite you on the arse sooner or later.'

I loathed the crude saying. But it seems it's true.

I should have dealt with the body before now.

I rush to touch up my face.

Kim

Her sister can't come over for the funeral. Her kid's in hospital, after an accident on his bike. One of the twins. One of three nephews she's never met. And Kim's relieved, as much as she feels anything.

She wonders why one terrible thing happening isn't some sort of amulet against more shitty things happening.

They stay in a Travelodge with a view over a car park.

All she can remember of the day is the absurdity of the charade and the pack of photographers salivating on the edges and she's wound so tight that in the end, to diffuse violence, Steve walks across and has a go at them.

Her brother's in this graveyard.

She can't reply when random relatives say they're sorry. Doesn't recognise half the faces, not that there's many there.

She turns her head away when they lower her mother into the ground.

In the pictures of her walking next to her mother's coffin, which are published online the same day – before she's had a chance to take off the black coat, the black dress – she looks like granite.

When they get back to London and she goes next door to collect Sausage, the pup flings herself at Kim as if she's been missing in action for a thousand years.

When Kim was a kid they had a dog called, predictably, Prince. Also, predictably, an Alsatian, like every other bloody dog round their way. A gentle, dopey, unintelligent variation of the species, he'd allow Kim and her sister to dress him in one of their mum's old headscarves, or a duster.

Dave would boot the dog out of his way. That's the sort of cunt their brother was.

She loved that bloody animal. When Heather got her first boyfriend and started to spend more time with his family, Kim would crawl under the drop-leaf table and squash next to Prince, his warm bulk and regular panting soothing her, even though she knew she was too old for that sort of thing.

Her mother didn't notice, or if she did, ignored it.

Dave noticed. At all times he knew where Kim was, like radar. He sniffed her out.

When she took Prince for long walks, she could almost forget. But then he developed a limp and no one took him to the vets. Kim hated to see him hobble, so his walks got shorter and she spent more time with him under the table, their own little cave.

Sometimes she'd stay under there rather than go to bed. It worked once. She heard Dave stumble upstairs as he came in from the club, lurching about in his cartoon 'being quiet' way. Heard him open the door and go into her room. Silence. A few minutes later, a shuffle across the landing. She braced, but it was obviously too much effort for him to negotiate the stairs down, although she hoped he'd try, clinging to the rail before losing his footing, plunging and breaking his bastard neck.

But the next time, he looked downstairs before going up. His balloon-like head appeared under the table and he said, almost gently, 'Hello, honey. Let's be having you.'

The time after that she refused and he yanked at her arm and she yelped and Prince growled. As he dragged her out he kicked the dog hard in its ribs – kick, kick, kick – making him yowl, then whimper. So Kim didn't hide under the table any more because it wasn't fair on Prince.

All that floods back as Kim hugs Sausage, tumbling out in an all-together memory. Not like a story with a beginning, middle and end, but as a weight – a sickening, sad, collapsing feeling. A black star sucking joy and light out of the room, not that there's much fucking joy and light there in the first place.

After the funeral, Kim starts bringing the puppy upstairs with them, helping her little legs clamber up on the duvet, hugging her wriggling, woofly body on her side of the bed.

It doesn't help her sleep, but it soothes her to have Steve snoring on one side in his deep bass and the animal's whistle-like noises on the other.

She wonders why it's different from bringing Darryl or Nate in with them. But feelings have no logic, so she lets it be.

Perhaps it's because Sausage is a girl.

When she freezes, as she sometimes does when she changes the baby, she finds it helps if she strokes him, as if Nate's a little animal – a small, furless puppy.

One day, Kim came home from school and there was no dog. Her mother smirked as she told her, 'He's gone to some farm where he can play with all the fucking lambkins, ain't he.'

She wept for that animal. It broke her heart.

When Dave came off his motorbike, she didn't shed one tear. She clamped her mouth shut so hard at his funeral her jaw went into spasm and the pains shot up into her skull, blinding jolts, as the sparse congregation mangled hymns. And she didn't care, because if she'd unclenched her teeth even a tiny bit, she might have whooped in the church, laughing with a glorious, bitter joy.

Ayesha flutters as she bravely puts her hand out for Sausage to sniff. The dog likes her. The dog likes everyone. But any time Sausage tries to lick Ayesha's hand, she pulls it away and squeals and that sets the pup off barking because she thinks it's a game. And the barks make Ayesha jump and squeal more.

Tonya would bloody love Sausage.

Tonya would – a phrase Kim now carries with her at all times.

Steve lies on the sofa almost asleep, with the dog nestling into one meaty armpit and Nate cradled the other side. Kim stands rooted, thinking how it would be if Tonya was lying on her dad's big belly, like she used to.

Tonya

I am cold. It is dark. There is a bad, stinky smell.

I am—

Mummy

The plumber is what Michael would describe as a 'total geezer', a bear of a man who flirts and smiles and takes the tea I give him with a wink. I am pathetically grateful to learn I will not have to remove floorboards and walls. The leak is tiny – a hairline crack underneath one pipe.

It is mended soon enough. I flutter around him, tripping up and downstairs, fuelling him with several more cups of tea and numerous compliments, apologising again and again that I do not have biscuits to offer.

He hears nothing untoward. Suspects nothing.

I jump as he places his hand on my arm before he leaves, saying kindly, although it makes me want to scream, 'You know, sweetheart, you could do with getting a few bacon butties down you.'

I force a smile. I also have to lie and promise to arrange another appointment to 'sort out the drain problem'.

Still, I imagine he has smelt far worse in his line of work.

As I shut the front door behind him, I lean heavily against the frame.

Before I make that descent again, I need a drink.

Carrying her back up the stairs is much easier than the journey down, as I can focus on the square of light at the top. And she hardly weighs much now. She surprises me by clasping her skinny arms around my neck on the way.

*

The next day she is almost clingy. She lets me hug her without protest as I read her a story, although she does not exactly hug me back.

She follows me from room to room. She doesn't talk to me, yet she seems to want to be close to me.

I understand. I wouldn't want to spend any time down there in the darkness either.

Kim

Liaison Woman phones and lets something slip to Steve. They have a lead. They're not to get their hopes up and she's not supposed to say anything. (Only she's a sucker for Steve's baby blues.)

Kim does not get her hopes up, but Steve's like a little kid the night before a trip to Butlins. It hurts Kim to watch him bouncing around the flat, making it seem even smaller than it is. Somehow she just knows this isn't it.

It will come to nothing, like all the other false 'leads'. The suspicious neighbour who called in to say that a young girl seemed to be staying next door, but the old man who lived there had no children. It turns out that he did. And his daughter was in hospital, so he was looking after his grand-child. Then there was the little girl with blonde hair and a sticky-out tooth seen in Tescos. A member of the public spotted her shouting, 'I hate you! I hate you!' struggling as she was dragged along the aisles of the Peckham superstore by a man with a bald head. A small crowd gathered, preventing the pair leaving the supermarket. Police were called. Big Bob on fruit and veg stood between the bloke and the exit. The manager had the girl brought to her office and given a free carton of orange juice. When the police located the specific shaved head amongst all the others, it turned out the man was the kid's dad. The mother was called. She legged it round to the scene from a few streets away, then shouted at her husband, the kid, supermarket staff and the police, in that order. The girl was 'always playing up'. Apologies were made all round, Clubcard vouchers issued.

Kim and Steve are called again and warned that an item about the 'new lead' will be on the teatime news.

The report reveals that British police are working with their Italian counterparts, where a young girl matching Tonya's description has been found alone in a squalid flat. There is no photo accompanying the story. Liaison Woman comes round to say she's sorry they didn't tell them the details before and they don't know how the reporter got hold of the information, but yes, it is true. And no, Steve and Kim can't get on a plane right now.

She calls them later that night – after Kim's finished the best part of a packet of fags and Steve's demolished the best part of a loaf – to say the child has been identified and the mother, a drug addict known to Italian police, has also been located, brought back from a three-day bender and charged with neglect or abandonment or whatever.

Kim wonders, during the bad old days, might she have done something like that? But, no – she would never have let that happen. She would have given Tonya to her sister to bring up on the other side of the world before she let that happen.

She worries about the little Italian girl.

When she eventually sees the photo, she can't imagine anyone thinking the kids have anything in common. Apart from dirty blonde hair and crooked teeth, there's nothing similar. She also sees the crushed quality in the Italian mother's face and despairs for the kid.

She tells Liaison Woman, Jean she insists on being called, that they don't want to know about more leads. Why? Because fucking Jean doesn't seem to be on the same side as them, that's why. She's the one who brings bad news, or no news, or raises their hopes for fuck all.

Kim frequently has to stop herself from decking the bitch.

Steve takes Jean aside and has a quiet word, saying to *keep him in the loop regarding any new developments.*

But that loop – each hope kindled, then dashed – is grinding Kim down. Each disappointment another loss, another blow – a needless cruelty.

She's punch-drunk with it all.

Mummy

I first noticed it on the Wednesday afternoon, a week after the row. A stink like sewers, although there was also a different, putrid top note that caught in my gullet.

No need to call a plumber then. I knew what it was.

I gathered perfume bottles from the bathroom cabinet, laying them out on the bed, putting those I liked the least in a smaller pile. Those Michael bought me – Basil & Neroli, Lime Basil & Mandarin – the two that brought back memories of that holiday in Turks and Caicos when he spent hours on his phone 'dealing with a work crisis'. At least I thought that was what he was doing, until I discovered he had been texting *her*. Although he denied it all and made me think I was going crazy. Gaslighting me, the bastard.

Or perhaps there really was no other woman.

I opened the cellar door and flung the first bottle down the stairs. It bounced, rather than smashing. Damn Jo Malone's thick glass bottles.

The second shattered with a satisfying tinkle, releasing a shower of jasmine.

Rot and flowers. Like being in India.

The smell wafts up once more, as temperatures rise with the sunshine.

Michael still lies decomposing at the bottom of the cellar stairs.

I hate summer.

Kim

The two of them sit outside a cheap and cheerful café on Seven Sisters, taking advantage of the baking weather. The girl's sipping her frothy strawberry milkshake, bright white trainers swinging in the sunlight. Her mother's vaping and texting, sporting oversized gold sunglasses and pumped-up lips. North London glamour.

Kim doesn't envy the woman her luxe sportswear, or the designer bag (fake, naturally) propped on the table. The smart of jealousy that slaps her is triggered by seeing a mother with a daughter – a small, perfect replica, right down to the way their long, dark hair parts to fall over their left shoulders.

It's all she can do to make her feet move away.

What she wouldn't give to drink a coffee alongside her girl. If she could just have a day like that, one single hour, she would give anything.

She often makes mental lists of her 'if only' bargains.

If she made another list of what it is others have that she does not – the stuff she envies them for; actually, hates them for – it would be a bloody long one.

There were a couple of mates at primary school with normal families. She was occasionally invited round to their houses, before they worked out who she was, what her family was like: no dad, psycho brother, nasty, nasty mother.

She once made a proper friend, Alison, and kept her for a whole six months. Then Kim's mother got pissed and had a go at Alison for no particular reason. So Alison told her mum, who had a go at Kim's mum when she saw her in town. When Kim's mum got back, late that night, Kim was dragged out of bed, her mother calling her all sorts, and forced to phone Alison's mum – to lie and say stuff that Alison had never said, never done – as bad as fucking Judas.

And that night should have been a good one, because Dave was away working in Birmingham for a month.

It was the end of her and Alison. Although she'd always worried that Alison only hung around with her because she fancied Dave. All the girls in her class fancied Dave, with his jeans and his motorbike and his wicked grin. Three years older than them and a lifetime apart.

After that, she'd sit at the side of the school footie pitch, watching other girls cluster in the playground in a little gang, gossiping and braiding each other's hair. Girls who didn't dread the bell at the end of the school day.

And from then on, Kim was always the kid with her nose pressed up against the smeared glass of life. Watching families sitting down together, chatting, smiling, like they did in the adverts. When she walked home and looked in un-curtained windows, she'd want to grab a brick and hurl it through – to smash their snow globe scenes. To make those calm faces startle in shock as she screamed at them. Their cosy bubbles made her furious. That sense of entitlement they radiated – as if anyone deserved such untroubled happiness.

Even as a little kid she'd want to hurt them, or at least to bang on their door and leg it – anything to disturb their peace.

Then she'd trail about the streets for hours, the dirty dusk outside revealing more scenes of family teatimes inside, until, chilled to the bone, she'd traipse home. And as she neared their ugly flat, with the stained mattress propped outside the front door alongside the old motorcycle chassis Dave never got round to mending, her heart would settle heavy in her chest.

When she got a bit older, that same hot feeling of envy would bubble up as she flicked through magazines, sneering at the prices of the trendy skirts and shoes on the pages. She'd wait until she could get a knock-off copy from the market, although it would never look as nice or feel as good as she imagined. She and the other girls in her class (none of them actual mates) would all end up in cheapo approximations of the stuff they saw on TV. Back then, she believed the thing she felt lacking in her life was out there on a rack in some shop.

Now she knows that the thing lacking is something deep inside herself.

What is it about her that means the list of things she hasn't got now includes a mother, a father, a brother and a daughter?

It's roasting in the flat, so she sits with the doors and windows wide open and Sausage corralled by the child gate at the top of the stairs. The dog barks in outrage until she gives in and lets her downstairs. Then she has to close the doors, otherwise the bloody animal tries to escape to play with her four-legged friend next door.

She'd let her out, only she's scared she'd get lost on the estate, or run off, or someone might take her.

And she couldn't bear losing anything else.

Mummy

It is so close in her room, in the whole house, I can't breathe. I drink glass after glass of spring water to avoid dry skin and order three large fans from Amazon Prime.

When they arrive, I carry them from room to room, so now we're blasted with hot air, which is as unpleasant as the static heat and equally dehydrating.

Thanks to the child I can't open doors and windows. My nights are disturbed and sticky.

Thanks to her, I'm a prisoner.

My roses are unfurling, spilling their petals onto the weeds around them. What I wouldn't give to sit outside in the garden, but I can't relax with *her* inside.

My head's swimming as I wake. I push hair out of my face to find a sheen of sweat across my cheeks. Today I'll need to tone and spritz with Evian spray before I moisturise. This is possibly something viral, although I had thought my recent sneezing fits merely hay fever.

Or it's the drink.

My nightdress is tangled and damp. It disgusts me. I lift it, peeling the wet fabric away from my clammy skin, throwing it onto the bedroom carpet.

When I try to stand, the room reels. I slump back against the pillow. Slowly, I try to raise my legs to get back into bed, to rest a little while longer, but one falls and I haven't the energy to hoist it up again. I have to give myself a moment.

It is some time later when I open my eyes and see her. She stands gawping at me with her hard little eyes. I want to tell her to go back to her own room while Mummy rests, but I can't seem to work my mouth. My throat feels poisoned, parched, as if I have been smoking, although it's many years since I was in thrall to that particular vice.

She's like a little cat, not to be trusted. She may pounce at any moment. I note the dislike in her pinched face. I wish I'd hidden the bottles inside my bedside cabinet, but who is she to judge me?

Oh, how I had yearned for this little one. How I had ached to hold and cherish her. Yet it's like hugging a bag of sticks.

She is not an affectionate daughter.

I jolt as I realise the duvet has spilled onto the floor and I am still splayed. Nudity was frowned upon in my family, along with much else. And while I know God created us all naked, I don't want to rub it in her face, so I reach for the edge of the cover and slowly drag it up and across my body.

She continues staring, but now her eyes are on mine.

I wish she would go away.

'What is it, Izzy?'

She doesn't answer me.

Despite my exhaustion, I rouse myself, as a good parent must, making my voice bright. 'Shall we go down for breakfast, sweetheart?'

I glance at the clock to see it is somehow nearer lunchtime.

'Would you like some orange juice?'

Usually this is the perfect thing to suggest, yet she remains standing watching me, still as a small statue.

'Oh, for goodness' sake, Izzy, what is—'

I don't hear what it is she mumbles as she interrupts me.

'I beg your—'

She repeats what she's said, louder this time, 'Yucky, yucky, yuck!' She stares at the duvet, which now hides the scars wreathing my stomach – gnarled, ugly burns; a legacy from my own dear mammy.

Her scrawny little finger reaches out as if to touch the vile, warped skin and I slap her hand away.

Tonya

I hate The Woman. She breathes on me. She smells.
   She ain't my mummy.
   My mum ain't got a weird yucky belly.

Kim

Now her mother's gone, now she can't actively hate the old cow any longer, she's unable to keep out the other crap memories. It takes too much effort.

Dave comes to her, despite herself. Eating up the time she should be devoting to Tonya – time which could be better spent thinking about her, shouting at the useless coppers, or pretending to listen to Steve's latest Facebook 'updates'.

Fake fucking news.

The smell of certain smoke can bring back Kim's brother like summoning a demon from ashes. She has a visceral reaction: her bowels clench; her shoulders rise up towards her ears of their own accord; her jaw sets, sometimes cramps.

If you could see the hormones racing around her body at the very thought of Dave, there'd be a staggering tsunami of fight-or-flight responses.

She tried both.

There were times she'd punch and kick and try to bite his hand as it pressed across her mouth, but then he'd lean his forearm across her throat until she'd choke and almost black out, so in the end she'd go totally floppy and just let him get on with it.

But that could go on and on.

And there's something she hasn't even told Steve. Something that makes her shudder.

How did she discover the trick? She doesn't like to think of it at all

– spent many years actively drowning it out and anaesthetizing the memory, with sex and drugs and rock and roll and taking stupid risks combining all of the above.

She'd do something to hurry along the process.

She'd make noises. The sort of noises he liked.

Perhaps it was her classmate Glynis who told her, discovering it from her older sister who had a boyfriend and she 'did it with him' on Saturday nights, when their parents were down the Working Men's Club and she was supposed to be babysitting Glynis. Yeah, it was probably her. She might have said, 'Blokes like that sort of thing: talking dirty and groaning and stuff.'

One of the girls had asked why, and Glynis had pronounced with some authority that it 'finished them off quicker'.

Her sister was a 'dirty bitch' according to Glynis, which allowed her to share many salacious stories like this with the gaggle of girls who gathered for her illicit sex education sessions by the monkey bars in the playground, screeching with laughter because it was all so funny and *unlikely*. Kim joined in.

Only she didn't laugh inside.

Because if Glynis's sister was a dirty bitch, what did that make her?

In desperation she tried it – the noises – and it did work and it was over quicker. It also made her sick to her stomach, because then her bastard brother would wink at her as he pulled up his trousers, as if she was in on a great big juicy secret.

And when they were watching the telly, he'd look across and do the thing with his tongue and laugh.

Then no amount of scrubbing with the flannel in the bathroom made her feel any cleaner.

He creeps into her room in the darkest hours – a dense shadow against the blackness.

She can't see him, but she senses his shape and the hairs shiver up on the back of her neck. That stinking, smoky heaviness that crushes her down on the bed.

And seeping into that mattress, there's also the scalding shame of the bad thing that happened later, when he started slipping into Heather's room instead of hers.

Relief, mainly.

But, like a bruise that hasn't yet blossomed on the skin's surface, hidden deep inside, something else she can't fully admit to herself, even now. If she could, it might taste something like jealousy.

She wakes with a cry.

And Steve says, 'The dream again, babe?' and she nods.

Yet this is nothing compared with the other cry that wakes her regularly.

Worse than her brother, the noises, Heather – the whole festering heap of all that.

'Tonya!'

Mummy

Christ loves us all unconditionally. Halle-fucking-lujah!

His Father, not so much.

My mother, my father, lacked the capacity for unconditional love. But, oh, my daddy loved me in the end. Too much.

When Margaret left home, I became his favourite.

And the scales fell from my eyes.

I told my mammy, the words – stumbling, mangled words – hurting my throat.

And she grabbed the pan of boiling water from the Aga and she hurled it at me, hissing, 'Liar! Liar!' Worse.

But I wasn't. Not then.

She made me into a liar, a sinner. Forced me to tell the doctors and nurses it was 'an accident'.

And the pain was the worst.

Until the new pain, a shock, exploding like a starburst—

When you finally come home from hospital. Hurting and hunched and scarred and even *uglier*. Branded a liar by your own mammy, a wicked, dirty little whore—

And, and in, and in, and in the cowshed – the stench, the sickly warmth, the, the filth underfoot—

You see what you can't be seeing.

You find him hanging. Swaying.

He has soiled himself.

You are on your knees in the mulch and the mire. The soft eyes of the cows watch you retching as you kneel.

And Mammy screaming and screaming that you have killed him. Your lies have killed him.

But. But—

The guilt burning deeper than the scalds.

And Margaret, your perfect sister, doesn't breathe a word.

Not. One. Word.

I would be a better mother than my mammy. A good mother. A kind mother.

My leg cramps, so I get up to walk around. Inevitably that walk takes me by another bottle. I know.

I know!

My mammy blamed me.

Michael blamed me – for not giving him a child. How could he not?

'Blessed is the fruit of thy womb, Jesus.'

And yet I was denied.

Is it any wonder I drink?

Issues were taken with my weight, or lack thereof; concerns mooted regarding my eating habits. Judas Michael told them his far-fetched 'alcorexic' theory.

Months of hormonal hell. I put on so much weight! Yet not enough, apparently.

So many prayers.

Then Michael decided, persuading me, brainwashing me, not to proceed.

And the betrayal – he backed out of the adoption plan. Another cruel wrench. All I ever wanted denied by the almighty Michael, patron saint of the suffering and the sick. Bastard!

And after that final row – well, there seemed no point to anything.

I thought I was finally blessed with this child. But I have to bear witness to her spiteful judgements.

'You're not my mum. I hate you! Liar!'

It would be better if I had never taken her.

I once thought Michael could save me.

Cheers, Michael! You can't stop my 'excessive' drinking now, can you, my love. And yes, I have polished off your precious Châteauneuf-du-Pape.

So many disappointments

Promises dangling before my eyes like those of poor Tantalus.

Pictures of twins on the walls of the fertility clinic.

Blood in the toilet at home.

Tonya

The Woman snores when she's asleep on the sofa. Daddy snores. VERY
loud. We laugh at him snoring.

Daddy Pig!

I wish Daddy was here.

I can't wake The Woman.

I'm hungry.

Kim

She hoists Nate onto her hip then jiggles him up on her shoulder to burp him. Her hand cradles the soft, downy hair at the back of his head. Which is totally smooth. As it always has been. She knows that now, understands it was only her bonkersness that made the other stuff seem real. Postpartum psychosis – she looked it up, she'd heard of postnatal depression before, but never heard of that.

She read about women who'd seen ghosts, believed their own kid wasn't their own flesh and blood, felt they were in a full-on *Rosemary's Baby* land. Mums like her, who'd feared they'd do their kids harm, although in the case of the baby who looked like the spawn of Boris Johnson (all babies look a bit like bastard Bo Jo, but this one – Jesus!), Kim could see why the mother had wanted to put a pillow over its face.

Nate has rubbed a little bald patch on one side. As she shifts him round she's rewarded with a gummy, drooly smile. A forgiving baby, this one.

She carries him downstairs. Steve's sitting with the Xbox controller in his hand, but he's not playing. He stares at the black screen.

'Take him for me while I get Darryl's breakfast, yeah?'

He doesn't seem to hear her.

She recognises that look. Caught it on her own face enough times.

It's as if, now she's on the mend, on the way up, he can let himself sink down into the despair, as if they're on some kind of sick seesaw.

She has to help him upstairs. She puts him to bed like one of the kids, sits by his side and holds his hand.

He doesn't get up for the best part of a week.

*

She calls Bill, Steve's dad – the quiet, inept man who's wasting away, mirroring how his missus caved in on herself as the cancer gnawed at her body. Since Steve's mum died, Bill's neglected both his precious north London allotment (inherited from his own father – rare as hen's teeth) and himself. Blackberries are running riot there right now.

Usually, Steve goes over to his dad's in Camden for the occasional pint. Took the baby round to show him. Kim manages to get out of playing happy families with Steve's lot, mainly because none of them like her, which is a relief, really, because she's never been good at that game.

She's not expecting much from Bill, but she can't call Skid, or Kos, or Bam-Bam, or any of Steve's mates. He'd never forgive her if they saw him in this state. Plus, they're all totally fucking useless.

Tonya liked her granddad. He gave her sweets. She never seemed to mind his defeated shoulders and watery eyes. She could make him laugh. She liked gardening with him.

Bill's 'support' during the investigation has been limited to keeping his gob shut when harried by journalists. And listening to Steve over their occasional beers – that's if they ever discuss anything other than the glory days, Wenger, Čech and Welbeck, Cazorla's injuries and all things Aubameyang.

He knocks on the door in an almost apologetic way – softly, so as Kim only hears it because she's already in the kitchen.

As she makes his tea in the giant Gunners mug he got for Steve, Bill makes a meal out of taking off his jacket, revealing a stained, ancient Arsenal T-shirt underneath. Arms, which used to be beefy like his son's, withering and scrawny. Tattoos, crinkled and fading. He doesn't touch the packet of biscuits she puts in front of him.

When Steve eventually shuffles downstairs, she watches them sit across from each other. She sticks Nate on Steve's lap and leaves them to it while she tackles the pile of washing up and Darryl plays on the floor with Sausage. She can't hear what they say, but it's not much.

Then there's a bang on the front door that almost stops Kim's heart. No one ever comes to the front apart from plods. Holding back the puppy, she opens up to see Aunty Stella with her gormless teenage daughter, Shontelle, in tow.

'Bill here?' asks Stella, trooping in before she's been invited.

Some sort of family intervention with Steve must have been plotted.

Kim does another round of teas and clocks Shontelle squashed next to her mum on the sofa, gazing at Steve with her mouth open. Kim and Steve are the first celebrities the girl's ever met.

This invasion pisses off Kim big time. There's no room for her, even if she wanted to sit with them, which she doesn't. And she can't see how it'll do Steve any good to have 'family around him', which is the phrase Stella keeps repeating.

Who the bollocks is Kim supposed to be if not family?

But when she pops back in with the biscuits, she sees Bill cradling the baby. And the tenderness in that scene, the way his huge bony knuckles curl around the little one's head, that pierces her.

The next week there's another newspaper article suggesting all sorts – drugs, prostitution, violence. 'SCUMMY MUMMY!' screams another headline.

Some of it's even true.

There are a couple of quotes from Shontelle, about her 'cousin's agony'. Shontelle's thrilled to see her name in print.

Mummy

I have waited all my life to be a mummy – from the moment I held one of my sister's dolls to my breast.

And this child! She lies there feigning sleep, resisting my love, my hugs, as stiff as that plastic doll.

I tried to wrestle her into tights today. A chill in the air, promising autumn. A struggle. She is my bitter harvest.

I find I'm sitting on the floor in what was once Michael's office. I tear the old adoption brochures, the fostering leaflets, into messy confetti and throw them, hurl them, stuff them into the black bin liner.

And then I haul it, along with bag after bag of bottles, to my recycling bins, setting them out for the collection.

The injustice of it all! Some women, some mothers, are simply not good enough to deserve a child. Although, perhaps if they had a brat like this one, they too might let it wander off.

I help myself to another glass.

You would have been a wonderful father.

There's a hole in my heart, dear Michael, dear Michael. But how will you fix me now?

The next day for lunch, for we have somehow missed breakfast, I arrange the slices of carrot and pepper in a sunburst around her plate. You must eat a rainbow for the vitamins and antioxidants. Just celery for me. She demolishes the whole thing before I've finished chewing my second piece.

There are cold sores around her mouth. When she pulls her head away from me as I try and wipe her face, the cloth catches on one and makes it bleed.

Disgusting.

Tonya

In bed I squeeze my eyes shut. I want her to go away.

Kim

Steve gets up, gets on with it. No alternative.

So she determines she'll do her best to get on with it alongside him – dragging herself out of bed each morning, putting one foot in front of the other. Going through the motions of a life. Looking after her boys while she silently keens for her girl.

She might smile as she watches Nate thrash up and down like a metal fiend in his bouncer.

But that's in the daylight hours. At night, bad things happen.

She shakes Steve's shoulder, waking him. He props himself up next to her.

With a thick, sleepy voice he asks, 'Another nightmare, babe?'

The word nightmare hardly covers the horror she feels – as if something has crawled inside her soul.

And Sausage is going doolally and it freaks the hell out of Kim because the dog's not barking at a noise outside the door or window. Her little legs are set, nose pointing at the shadow in the corner of the room, seeing off something that's not even there.

Autumn slithers in. Halloween approaches. Something bad is happening. Something worse is coming.

Tonya

Where is The Woman?

I banged and banged on the door but she didn't come to let me out the room.

'PLEASE, MUMMY!'

Now I don't want her to come.

But I am so hungry.

When my mum wasn't looking I'd pinch some of Darryl's fish fingers. Yum yum! Daddy used to see and wink at me and not tell her. But then I'd laugh and she'd know I was 'up to something'. But she didn't whack me one so I don't think she minded really.

My belly is rumbling. I hold Bunny against my belly so he can hear.

Bloody, bloody hell. The Woman is coming up the stairs. I don't want her to come any more. I pull Bunny tighter. It's not my fault. I called and I called and I called. But she didn't come.

And I did a wee in the corner.

Mummy

I loathe hospitals. Even going private, as we did, it seems to me that those in nursing are often singularly lacking in aptitude for a caring profession. Like the nuns who beat my mother at the convent for the 'sin' of being left-handed. Yet when I said they must be wicked, Mammy slapped me and told me I was never to say a word against the Holy Sisters.

If my procedures had not been elective, perhaps we might have received care under Michael's corporate health insurance policy. But that was not to be, either.

So much was not to be.

All the pros and cons of IVF that I was forced to read. It is shocking to see the list of what might go wrong written down so starkly. There is no recompense. If they had shot me in theatre, no doubt I would still be at fault.

Even so, we entered a brave new world of acronyms thanks to my AN and PCOS: IVF, ICSI, FET, DOP, and the resulting PTSD, and FUBAR. (Anorexia Nervosa; Polycystic Ovary Syndrome; In Vitro Fertilisation; Intracytoplasmic Sperm Injection; Frozen Embryo Transfer; Oocyte Donation; Post-Traumatic Stress Disorder; Fucked Up Beyond All Repair – thank you, dear Michael, for that succinct damnation.)

I soak the toothbrush in bleach and scour the taps and around the plug. I have been distracted for too long by the child. The place is a disgrace. My mammy would be appalled – everything sparkled in her kitchen and her bathroom was exemplary.

So much blood on the bathroom floor.

Three times I scrubbed these tiles with bleach.

We discussed the whole plan following those 'disappointments', as if that word can contain the loss of a whole world. Michael harangued and I pretended to listen. He was emphatic – he did not want me to go ahead with more rounds of treatment. He said he couldn't bear it. An unfortunate turn of phrase.

I pour bleach down the toilet bowl, down the sink, into the bath. I have scrubbed and disinfected and consequently ruined a corner of the carpet in the girl's room where I discovered she had urinated.

Filthy animal. Worse than the kitten.

Tonya

'Catch a fallin' leaf an' put it in yer poc-ket.' Granddad sang me that. I miss
him. I miss my daddy and my mum and Mo.

I'm cold, Bunny.

She says it's falling star, not falling leaf.

Bog off, Woman.

Mummy

Now I can reward myself with a small drink. It is dark already, although hardly past teatime.

Looking down at my arm I see the marks my teeth have made. Two half-moons. I can't recall doing that.

My final row with Michael was not over a huge issue, just one small measure of wine.

Yes, I had promised, swore, perhaps, that I would stop at two glasses. But it had been a harrowing week thanks to the cul-de-sac of our debate over adoption, plus a disappointing haircut, and I was antsy and tense, so I had actually poured another before I really thought about it.

Not fair. For him a drink was no problem. But for me—

I drink, therefore I am.

And it was not the first time I had accidentally lashed out. He knew not to creep up on me. I have no control over my panic, especially if someone sneaks up from behind. It is a knee-jerk reaction.

I cannot be blamed for that.

It was simply bad luck that the bottle was still in my hand when he snuck into the kitchen as my back was turned, spying on me. A suspicious mind, Michael.

He should have moved as I whirled round. I did not raise my hand in violence, but in self-defence.

It was worse luck that he fell so awkwardly.

As I do occasionally. I stumble. I am human.

I wasn't thinking straight when I dragged him to the cellar. So heavy! I suppose it was an animal instinct to hide the terrible thing. Bury the prey.

Oh, I did pray. I did. But there was no clear answer. Nothing was clear by that point – so much blood! And then my hands slipped as I tried to lift his vast bulk to the doorway of the cellar and he fell down with a series of sickening thuds.

Thump. Thump. Thump.

Brutal.

The next few days were a blur.

I did go off the rails a little. But anyone might have done the same, suffered a psychic wobble in similar circumstances.

My nightmares were mangled.

But my fear was not that I had killed Michael with that blow. The worst fear was that I had not.

I have never been sure if I imagined the groans over the next hours. Days.

If they came from me.

Or him.

Panic hoists me upwards in my bed.

I thought I heard Michael's voice.

There is electricity in the air. Some static arcing around the sky, inside my head.

And then I hear her whining. A nasty noise from a nasty, canker-infested mouth.

At breakfast, the bruise accuses me. I hadn't thought the smack so hard. As I apply my concealer and foundation, I can't concentrate on my magnifying mirror. My eyes are drawn across the kitchen table to her face. The scabs of her cold sores make me shudder. And now it has come to this I know for certain.

I have failed.

This must end.

Tonya

Bunny and me keep looking for Elsa in the garden. But she never comes.

I hug Bunny tight cos he's cold. My breath makes the window all steamed up.

My lips hurt.

My belly hurts.

Mummy

It has been a nasty, chilly, fraught month. To every thing there is a season and this one has been a season of spite. Her behaviour has not improved. She has learned little from the scriptures I read to her. Too feral to accept God's light into her tiny, wizened heart. She has been utterly spoiled by her vile background.

The feast of Saint Michael has long passed. A destabilising time. How can I miss him more now?

Last night, when I said my prayers with her, I opened my eyes to see her sticking out her tongue at me. An altercation ensued. Bile and toads out of her mouth – shrieks and profanities and the incessant, 'You ain't my mummy!'

And so, enough.

I have decided. I cannot keep her with me. I have been too soft-hearted. Too weak. I have not been able to bring myself to do the thing I know I must do.

I must raze this episode from my life, cast out the demon, and start again.

She has threatened my moral code. Her presence not only threatens my freedom, I risk my eternal soul for her.

She has never become my Izzy, my Isaac. She never will. She is still the same old Tonya.

And I offered her so much! Her old life was a sordid shambles. I read about it in the downmarket newspapers and magazines, hastily fingering them in newsagents. That woman did not deserve a child.

But perhaps this obnoxious girl deserved that mother.

She shovels cereal into her nasty mouth. As if it's a race. It turns my stomach.

She darts a look in my direction, then carefully slips down from the chair and places her bowl and spoon in the dishwasher.

She has learned some civilised behaviour at least. But each task is completed with such insouciance. Each contains a small, hurtful rebellion. As now – her thumb disappears into her mouth.

I consider driving around the streets at night and leaving her somewhere shaded and quiet. So dark now at night. But where is free of Big Brother these days? And she knows where I live. She could identify me.

They would find me. They would find Michael.

I get up quickly to dispel that thought and notice her cower a little.

For the sin of taking her, my soft heart trying to save her, to do her a kindness, they would never believe my version of events regarding Michael's attack, especially after so long. Self-defence wouldn't enter into it. 'Murderer' along with 'kidnapper' would be my only legacy.

I would be put away for the rest of my life.

I wipe around the sink to erase the thought.

It would be better to end things now, by my own hand.

The only choice is: me, or her.

Either way is a sin.

Kim

In Morrisons, she's gripped by a terrible feeling of dread. It's so strong, overwhelming, she abandons the trolley along with her shopping and rushes away to sit on the bench outside, fearful of falling and hurting Nate.

She grabs her phone, scrolls quickly, calls and gabbles to Ayesha, 'Is Darryl there? Is he okay?'

Her friend's reassurances do little to calm her.

She can't answer when Ayesha asks, 'Are you okay? You're not going mental again?'

She waits a few minutes. Then, drawn by a feeling more than a thought, she walks round the corner like a wind-up toy, finding herself outside Peacocks.

Then she's out of the bitter winter wind and inside.

One of the shop assistants recognises her and swiftly pretends not to. The other girl may be new. After watching the pale, shaky mother trail around the store with the baby starting up crying, she wonders if she's on something and asks if she needs any help.

Oh, Kim needs help, all right. Only she has no idea what sort of help that might be, or where the fuck it might come from.

Mummy

I stand beside her bed. Her scrawny chest rises and falls. She does not have the grace to be afraid. No nightmares trouble her animal sleep.

For that is what she is: an untrained little animal. And as such, she has no soul to speak of.

We had a lovely sheepdog, Betsy, when I was young. I adored hugging her matted fur. But she was a working animal. We had no pets. Mammy's floors were not to be sullied. She wasn't allowed indoors.

Neither was I, on occasion. If I had been found wanting or wicked, Betsy and I would huddle together in the outbuilding. She did not tremble in her fur coat as I did in my thin school uniform.

When I came home from choir practice late one afternoon to discover she had died, I was heartbroken. Even more so when my mammy said that, no, she would not be waiting for me in Heaven.

'But Saint Francis—' I began.

My mammy's heavy hand stopped the sentence.

Later, I saw Daddy consoling Margaret, hugging her tight to his chest, smothering the crown of her head with kisses.

I don't know what Daddy did with Betsy's body.

When I first moved in with Michael, he suggested we get a cat, and my tender heart was persuaded. I now wonder if that proposal was to quieten me from all the baby talk, which had started even then.

The kitten we rescued we named Hercule, for he had the markings of a neat little Poirot moustache. We welcomed him into Michael's converted studio flat in London. We felt so grown up making a home together! But within eighteen months, Hercule had wandered onto the insanely busy Brecknock Road, to be crushed under the wheels of some heartless hit-and-run driver.

It was my fault. I should have looked after him better.

I wept so hard, I hiccupped and shook, and sipped a brandy, then another, and Michael said we shouldn't put ourselves through that again because it 'destabilised me', whatever that was supposed to mean. Perhaps he was referring to the brandy.

I lay with cool cucumber slices on my eyelids as I rested after the squall of grief. It all seemed so unfair. When I saw the ravages the emotions had wreaked on my face, I had to agree with Michael.

Yet I did put myself through it again. I opened myself up for more disappointment and sadness with other kittens.

As I have done with this child.

She stirs, a small sigh escaping her lips.

I never sleep well. Even when Michael was here to hold and soothe me when the disturbing dreams assailed me, I was never given the gift of this kind of sleep. The sleep of the innocent. The sleep of any base creature.

I look at the blade. And sip my drink.

Even now I am not sure I can do it. I failed in the fire pit. I do not want to fail again.

I have contemplated how and what would be the easiest method. It would be kinder to do it as she sleeps. Partly this is a practical consideration, as she fights so fiercely, sporadically, I am not sure I have the energy to contain the ball of fury I may unleash.

I don't want to see her suffer unnecessarily.

I did love her.

I'm afraid a search history of 'How to kill a six-year-old child' will flag up somewhere, precipitating a police visit. I have no contacts on the dark web and I have little idea how I would get my hands on poison otherwise.

I think of apple pips – they're supposed to contain cyanide, aren't they – but I don't know how much I'd need for her to swallow.

So many household products are dangerous. If you heed the warnings on medicine bottles, everything is potentially lethal. But there are no guarantees that it would be swift. Poison has messy consequences. She might wake – a job half done. I need something effective that will not lead to hours of wailing and, worse, sickness.

A knife seems better. Cleaner. One swift cut across her neck. I just need to reach across a little to her pillow.

I am wearing my mackintosh. And rubber gloves.

I take another sip of my drink.

Kim

On her knees, Kim is scrubbing the floor, while Sausage dances around the cloth, barking at this exciting new game. Steve lolls against the doorframe, watching this unusual display, then he reaches over to the fridge and grabs half a pork pie.

He's not sure what's got into Kim. She's manic. He's never seen her do so much housework.

'I have to clean up after other lazy bastards, but those fuckers pay me,' was her usual refrain.

She tells him she can't face going back to work now, which he gets, but Christ, they could do with the cash.

Ayesha comes round with Faisal, who joins Steve for a session of *Assassin's Creed*. She asks Kim if she can help with the cleaning, but is told, brusquely, 'No.'

So she plugs in the kettle for something to do. It's awkward when Kim's in this mood. She tries to engage her in conversation, but gets one-word answers in reply.

Darryl tears into the kitchen, clocks the look on his mum's face, pivots and bombs out again to mither his dad instead.

Then the lads press their noses against the window to watch the fireworks outside, laughing at the loud ones.

*

From the moment she wakes, carried on a sickly wave of sweat and terror, Kim keeps busy. If the lads don't need anything, she washes and wipes and tidies. The flat's the cleanest it's ever been. There's hardly a dog hair to be seen.

She daren't stop. Anything to curb the squall of dark thoughts that ebb and flow but never go away.

Anything to keep her hands moving.

Anything to stop them reaching for a needle.

Mummy

I am not sure how long I've been sitting here – my second vigil in as many weeks. Praying for guidance. Putting off the inevitable. Picking at the stitches on the side of the mattress with the tip of the knife. Picking at my thoughts. Repeating the same actions expecting a different outcome – some people might think this is madness.

My palate is jaded from Michael's stash of Waitrose Cellar wine. My mind is muddied. Muddied wine. Mulled wine. Pearls before swine.

She is not the pearl. Never was. She is Peppa Pig.

Silly thoughts.

Michael made me question my sanity on occasion. He hinted we might, after all, go ahead with my baby plans if I calmed and healed and somehow created a better version of myself.

Predictably, he encouraged me to get therapy. I resisted. He persisted. Bullying with gentle words. Iron fist. Soft, beautiful velvet gloves.

He got his way, as he so often did.

He almost broke me.

You were playing in the stone-cold outhouse at the bottom of the paddock by the broken fence. Wonky dandelions had forced their way inside, huddling in a clump. The strength of their green sap, the life force, too much for mere rock and cement.

Your sap was rising, rebelling.

And you were found doing the thing to yourself that, sinful as you were, as you are, you wished the men to do for you, to you – the postman's son; the lanky boy from the grocer's; the butcher, the baker, the fucking candlestick maker while they're at it – and your daddy caught you.

Your instinct is to cover your eyes. If you can't see him, he can't see you.

Oh, but he sees you.

You feel some primal alert – 'Run! Run!' – as he comes up behind you. Then he's on you. And he has you in a headlock, with your forehead crushed and rubbing against the rough stone wall and your throat constricted so you cannot cry out.

And he's hurting you and his hand's fumbling for his belt and you struggle and panic but you can't get away from his strength or his bulk and, and—

Awful words. 'You ugly little whore. You dirty little bitch—' Guttural noises, as he thrashes and thrashes and thrashes you.

And why did the hospital ask no questions?

Deep weals on your back which wept and wept.

There – that's a memory for you.

And no, I do not want to talk more about it and what my feelings regarding it might mean for my 'journey', thank you, doctor. And I will also thank you to use the word 'journey' only if you have bought an actual train ticket.

Come to think of it, I would be better seeking out a more practical kind of doctor to ask what I might do with these scars on my forehead, other than hiding them, as I do, with a soft, feathered fringe.

How to hide the scars on my back? The burns on my belly?

And now I am still faced with my dilemma.

Her, or me?

Perhaps it should be both of us. We could go together. Would we then be a happier family in the afterlife?

Or would we go to hell in a handcart?

Kim

She's kneeling alongside the sofa watching football. Nez lies back on the cushions. He reaches over and starts stroking her hair.

Kim really likes him touching her hair, although she's never fancied Nez Smith. But she doesn't push him away, or say, 'Leave it, Nez,' or even, 'Steve will be back soon.'

She turns to him to find he's slid his tracksuit bottoms down. He's not huge, but he's ready, abs taut, his hips arched upwards. And when he gently guides her to him, turning on his side to meet her, she doesn't flinch, like she sometimes does when Steve grabs the back of her hair because it reminds her of stuff, she just opens wide and it slides into her mouth and it's all so easy. Graceful, almost.

He doesn't even thrust, just glides in and out, so she doesn't resist, or fight back, or gag, like she can do if she panics, and she feels she's being rocked, and it's like a duet or a dream.

And the only thing that makes her sad is that she thinks of Steve. Once. But that makes her throat tighten, so she stops.

And she rocks back and forth, forward and back on her knees and they don't cramp, and she doesn't feel she has to reach to hold him back, to stop it all going in, because she's in the movement with him, like they're dancing, and then the rhythm stops and she swallows.

The sensations are still with her when she wakes. Vivid. She touches her jaw to check if it's aching, then turns to look at Steve's side of the bed, as if she might see Nez there. She reaches across. It's chilly where he's kicked back the duvet when he got up early for work.

And even when the everyday chaos starts, reruns ambush her at odd moments throughout the morning. Her arms lift Nate, but her mind's eye doesn't see him. She chats to Darryl, her mouth forming words as her body remembers her lips opening for Nez.

And the weird thing is, she never fancied Nez even when he was a teenager, glowing with hormones and the righteous certainty of being desired by most of the girls in Kim's class, the whole school. She certainly didn't fancy him when he started going downhill, so deep into the drugs all his vanity disappeared. She was shocked the last time she went up to help her sister move flat, years ago now, before Heather fled the estate and the north and finally the country. She'd never seen anyone who more embodied that phrase 'a shadow of his former self'. He'd sort of imploded – an old man hanging round the bookies, at only twenty-odd.

The most disturbing thing is that during the moments when she falls back into the dream, which feels as real to her as any memory, thoughts of Tonya recede. She can't keep the two things in her mind simultaneously.

She scrubs the dog bowl with the Poundland washing-up liquid, the kind you need four squirts more of than normal stuff to do any good, and wonders if this is what it will be like – if, some day, there will only be a pale image left; blanched plastic flowers tied to a lamppost, or a washed-out teddy bear on a grave.

More likely, there will be no grave.

Her girl will be frozen in time. The sound of her voice, the way she moves, her face – all captured on a phone, so much smaller than the real thing.

Fading.

She can't smell Tonya on the bed sheets now.

Steve's thinking of getting a tattoo of her on his arm for the anniversary. Kim doesn't need that. Tonya's her flesh and blood, she'll always be part of her, grafted to the pain, which will always be there, along with the impossible sadness. But she wonders if the essence of her girl, which wasn't at all sad – angry, furious sometimes, often arsey, but hardly ever sad – will glow bright and wild again.

When Steve comes home, bringing in a blast of the dead November air with him, she looks him right in the eye and says, 'Fancy a fuck?'

And when Nate and Darryl are settled, they do.

It's fast and fumbled and not that great. But it feels like a huge achievement. Perhaps the start of something.

And for those few, short minutes, thoughts of Tonya fade again. Just a little.

And it doesn't help one fucking bit.

More days, long weeks, pass in this limbo.

Mummy

Margaret leaves. Untethered, you unravel. You stop eating.

She leaves her job, the farm, most of her clothes behind; discarded, like you.

You borrow her clothes. You slip into her old white summer dress, as if you are taking your First Communion; imagining yourself a bride. You have now lost so much weight you can slide it up your bones. You wind a scarf around your neck: a slash of bright red; a scarlet ribbon.

You gaze on your reflection, avoiding the pitted skin of your face, wishing you could be more like your sister.

And a miracle! Your wish comes true.

You do not hear him come upstairs. But now you sense he's here.

He touches your back, gently, between the wing tips of your shoulder blades. A benediction. His hands kind.

Then, suddenly, from heaven to hell.

All in one movement, he grabs the scarf and pulls tight, then thrusts you forward so you fall across her bed, pushing your face hard into the pillow so you can't breathe. And you try to turn your head, but the scarf tightens and you fear he'll snap your neck. And, and—

'You dirty little whore. You ugly little bitch—'

You heard and you felt.

And you were amazed.

As abruptly as it started it was over and you were loosened, abandoned, tossed aside. No words. You listened to him stomp downstairs, slam the kitchen door. You lay still until you started trembling. As you reached to pull off the dress, you felt the shivery slime down the side of your thigh and you gagged.

He sways in the cowshed, a corpse on a gibbet, the soft breath of the cows gently buffeting what is left of him. You reach out to touch his hand.

And you retch into the filth beneath him.

And your mammy screams and it pierces you.

Somehow, at some point, you thrust a few things in a suitcase, took your mammy's money, hidden in the empty honey jar behind the pickled onions in the pantry, rammed the dress in the Aga fire, and walked from the kitchen, from the farm, out of your known life.

Tonya

I am tired. But my belly makes so much noise it wakes me up.
I am so bloody bloody hungry.

Mummy

I have given her Calpol. There's no brandy left. Some of it had to be forced down – not a pleasant process. At least she has not vomited it back up.

I bundle her into her new puffa jacket, ordered last week (a waste, really), pulling the hood tight and winding the scarf around her neck and head, covering most of her hollow white face. I hoist her onto my shoulder, carry her to the car and lay her inert body flat on the back seat.

I turn away from her clawed, bony fingers. I should have remembered gloves.

After all the deliberations, slowing me down, confusing me so, the preparations were simple enough. I am much calmer now.

Suicide is a sin.

Better to sacrifice the animal, which lacks an eternal soul.

I pull in as near to the entrance as I can manage, look both ways, lug her out the car. She has urinated on the seat.

I wrestle her into the pushchair I purchased on Amazon. Basic. I had wondered if it would be too tiny, but it does the job. I walk steadily towards the park's side gate, straightening her when her head lolls too far to the side.

How nice it would have been to do this in the summer, enjoying the sunshine together, mother and daughter. Rather than this final furlong. The green mile. The child, this little beast, as unresponsive as she always has been. I find my shoulders hunching upwards as I brace against the harsh winter snap.

This too shall pass.

And she might have protested, ruining a jolly outing to feed the ducks. She would probably have crammed bread into her own greedy, gaping mouth, as she is wont to do if unsupervised for a single second. But now she is still and quiet. My silent burden. A burden I can finally lay down.

Let go and let God – that is what I have decided.

I lean into the wind. It is bitter. So am I, a little.

I shouldn't make a joke at a time like this.

I am glad I too have a scarf around my face, but even so, sharp air needles against the spaces where I am not covered and harsh weather is so bad for the skin.

This whole episode has been so very . . . unfortunate.

I suddenly think I should have put her in a large bag, or suitcase, to hide her body. Always coming up with a good idea when it's too late. Or, perhaps I want her to be found?

The thought startles me, although my steps continue.

If I was serious, wouldn't I have cut her throat?

If I want to save her, I could still do it. Call someone

Might I phone the police to say I saw a person abandon a child in the park? Or perhaps I could contact an animal charity to say I thought I saw puppies left in a bag. But for either of those I would have to stand in a filthy phone box. Do they even have those any more?

The people who pick up litter might find her, but, looking around, that doesn't appear to happen too often here.

No matter. It's getting dark and it is too cold to debate any longer.

This is a kindness.

She loses a boot and one sock is almost pulled off entirely as I lift and manoeuvre and shove her into the undergrowth beneath a bush.

Earth to earth.

I check I'm unobserved, pause and bow my head for a second. Offer up a final prayer. I commit this body to you, dear Father.

And I whisper, telling her, 'I forgive you.'

For she cannot help what she is. Nature. Nurture. It would have been so different if I had brought her up from birth. But she is too far gone.

She has nothing within her that might be saved.

Yet—

The fall of a sparrow. My Lord sees all. He sees my fall from grace. I feel eyes upon me.

Stop this.

I walk swiftly away. I leave the empty pushchair by a bin.

I will treasure the memories. The Lord has blessed me with those – a few.

I will not look back.

I take a deep breath as I start the engine and drive off to my new life.

She is in God's hands now. If she is discovered, so be it. I will be long gone by then.

I squint to focus on the road. I do not look back.

Pawel

Pawel's laughing at nothing, laughing at everything, laughing at himself. He is hysterical, ribs aching, stumbling across the grass.

He wants to hug the grass. It is the greenest green – or rather, suede green dimming, smudging into the dusk and mud.

He stretches his arms wide, wide, wide and swirls as he grins up to the gloaming sky, then he hugs himself as the clouds lower like a blanket and he laughs and laughs. Pawel is pretty. Pawel is beautiful.

Pawel is off his tits.

The woman is surrounded by a rainbow aura. He sends her his heart. She is beautiful. Strange, but beautiful. She moves like an iridescent water beetle. She carries a large Minion backpack – 'Bananas! Bananas!' Pawel giggles.

The pale yellow thing is shaped like a scarecrow, a doll, a child. And it is eerily beautiful too.

When he holds his hand up to the sky, it has the same multi-coloured aura. The shine on him!

Pawel leans against a tree to light a cigarette. The woman is hiding the backpack in some bushes. The bush glows. A burning bush! A sign from God, leading Pawel – where?

The woman, a saint; the aura, the halo, surrounding her head as she walks away from the bush. Skitters away.

Perhaps he should see what she has left. A gift for him? A gift from the gods? But he can't see where she left it exactly, and his limbs can't stay still. They want to pirouette. He half wonders if he should pull back branches to search for the treasure. A pot of gold at the end of the rainbow! Finders keepers.

But his legs take him and he laughs and tastes lemon drops.

And he promptly forgets the backpack to skip out of the park, onto the Tube, on to the club, where he will dance and dance and dance and dance—

Kenny

'You stink, dude.'

Kenny knows this. He shuffles away from the lanky teen holding a skateboard. Kenny knows he's lanky too, as in 'lanky long streak of piss' – this shouted after him by the tall one's chum. All in good spirits, lads. All in good spirits, hey?

He's not been eating too much recently. Not really fancied it, No. But not eating makes him tired and he has to keep moving, he knows that. All night. Shuffle, shuffle. He's not stupid. Kenny knows the cold kills. Faster than hunger. Faster than thirst. The ice in his veins if he nods off in the wrong place. No.

He will watch his breath as he shuffles. In, out. Count the steps in time with the breaths. In – sharp cold in his throat and lungs, even through his scarf. Out – in a plume, like a dragon. One.

In. Out. Two. Shuffle. That's all he needs to do. All night. And then, finally, in the early morning, he can take his cardboard to the vent outside the Sainsbury's on Stroud Green Road. Yes! The place that smells of fresh bread. And he will lean against the warmth of the bricks as the lukewarm sun, low against the shops opposite, creeps its pale rays into his eyes, like a blessing.

If it rains, he'll huddle under the bridge by Finsbury Park Station. Yes. Although the clarinet player there drives him mad, his notes echoing through the tunnel, burrowing into Kenny's mind. Kenny finds himself humming 'Autumn Leaves', one of only six songs the bastard plays again and again.

He shouted out loud once, 'No!' and saw a clot of startled commuters give him a wider berth than usual.

The druggie kid who beds down under the bridge hates the busker as much as he does. Kenny can see it in her pained eyes, sinking week by week into her haggard face. He doesn't know where she goes when it gets dark. One day she will disappear altogether. They all do. But not Kenny. No.

Kenny has to get out of the park before it turns black, out onto the street where it's perhaps one half of a degree warmer. It surprises him he can think a whole thought like 'half a degree warmer'. Pleased with himself. In. Out. Shuffle. Thirteen.

He's not so stupid, like his father said. Like the teachers said. Like his sergeant said. No.

Kenny doesn't know how old he is. Where he was born. Although he remembers a woman who may or may not have been his mother. A female presence who brought him food.

He doesn't want to remember his father. No. But his mother – that was a warm feeling. Like bread. He wishes he could remember her properly. He knows it might be his mother because he isn't afraid when he feels her visit in his dreams.

He stops shuffling. He stops muttering to himself at the same time. Something has caught his eye in the fading light. He sees a bird of some sort rustling in a tree, which distracts him from the other thing. He shuffles on.

But he stops. He knows what he saw. A raven and—

He must investigate.

No! He has another swig. Might be dangerous. Might be a bad thing. Yes. Keep going.

Kenny thinks they might blame him. Feels like running.

In. Out. He's lost count. He watches his breath. Walks off. Comes back, shuffling faster, gearing himself up to force himself to look. Checks for enemy fire. Pulls back a branch of the bush and flinches away.

What he finds – a shocker.

He hurries away.

Kim

She's walking along that huge beach at Watergate Bay, the wind scooping up the paragliders and kids and seagulls whooping and the sun's in her face and she feels a giddy hope and she wants to run as fast as the waves.

Sausage is tearing along the beach in front of her. Steve's carrying Nate and Darryl's by his side with a bucket and spade.

And the joy! Because Tonya is somewhere just behind her.

She daren't turn her head to look in case she disappears. But she's there – close.

In her peripheral vision. Her girl.

This isn't a memory. It's too bright.

When Kim turns over she opens her eyes to darkness. She checks the digital display and sees it's not even six o'clock yet. She came back to bed as soon as she'd put the kids down, as soon as Steve left, straight after his tea, to finish the rush job over in Chigwell. It's all rush jobs these days. No one plans ahead any more.

She's been asleep for a whole twenty minutes and feels jetlagged. Or how she imagines jetlag would feel, as she's only ever flown to Spain – although they sat so long on the runway thanks to Ryan Arsehole Air, she still risked deep vein thrombosis.

The baby's quietly mithering next door.

But that's not what woke her.

Some landslip has taken place. Kim's not sure what.

Kenny

A child lies under the bush, one grimy, blueing foot poking a little ways out – that's what he saw. But he's almost at the edge of the park now, hurrying away before anyone can shout at him. No. No.

But it was so little.

Kenny had a little dog once.

'Yes.' He mutters to himself, like he's urging himself on. Sometimes, the things he says to himself are the only words he hears addressed to him all day.

He stops. He thinks of a strategy. He turns around.

He shuffles back slowly, looking in all directions, checking, afraid of snipers.

Crouching under the bush, he pulls back the branch a bit further and holds his hand out to the little thing, like you might to a dog you're not sure about.

It doesn't take it. Just lies there. Still. Frozen solid. No.

He inches forward. He puts his paw, as in 'keep those filthy paws away from me', on its little fingers. Ice cold. No!

Kenny is terrified. 'Bad Kenny. Bad Kenny,' he whispers. He should go. But the body won't let him. Something about it pulls him towards it.

It's staring into space. Kenny pokes it again. He's seen so many bodies, bits of bodies. But it was hot then. Scorching sand. Flies.

It's so cold now. Deep in the night, hypothermia kills. His training. Yes.

Then the little thing closes its eyes, and the lashes open again and it looks at him in the slowest blink he's ever seen.

What should Kenny do?

'Bad Kenny! You do this? No. Not me.'

He decides.

He grabs the child's wrist and drags the body out of the bush, looking around for anyone who might blame him for this. There's no one near, although he can see a one-man tent nearby, propped under a bush. One of the people who sometimes shout at him in a strange language stays there.

He might have shot that man's brother. His face twitches.

No one in the tent now. Too cold. The uniforms haven't taken it away yet. But it will disappear soon.

He looks closer. It's a girl. She's not rigid like the dead dog he found. That wasn't his dog. Although that too is dead. This one's all floppy. But not dead yet. No. Not yet.

He remembers what to do. His training. Kenny's not stupid. Shelter first. Water second. Establish perimeter. Establish comms.

He must warm her.

She looks up at him. Her face as pale as the moon. Her fingers white as bone.

And when he lifts her, she is light as a feather. Lighter than air.

He shoves the girl in the tent. He climbs in with her and curls around her.

Tonya

I am so – cold.
   The Woman—
   I wish—
   Cold.

The man.
   He smells.

Kenny

It is dark, but time has passed. His teeth are playing a tune like machine-gun fire, rat-a-tat-tat, rat-a-tat-tat.

It is hard to move, ice in his knees, his hips.

The child is still as a statue.

He does the only thing he can think of. He kneels on the grass and tries to prop her up so she's leaning against his leg. Yes. He attempts to give her a sip from his bottle.

The girl coughs. Then her body buckles.

She stares up at him.

He says, 'Kenny likes hot chocolate.'

In the café the smelly homeless guy pays for a hot chocolate with leathery hands, counting out small change. The girl with the blue hair behind the counter recoils, giving him the smallest, tight-lipped acknowledgement, pushing the cup towards him in such a way that she makes sure her fingers don't touch his.

Kenny warms his hands around the cardboard container and staggers across the road to where he's carried the child, leaving her wrapped in his coat near the railings where they keep the bikes. He hunches over and holds the cup to her lips. His hands wobble and some chocolate spills down her chin and onto the puffa jacket underneath.

He reaches out his ugly paw to touch her matted hair and pulls out a skeleton of a leaf. She looks at him. Sees him. Yes. Kenny feels his face widen.

They sit together, pulling the coat round them both, and share – one sip for her, one sip for him, although nothing much seems to be going in her mouth—

'You! What are you doing!?'

He jumps up, spins round, spilling more hot chocolate. He let down his guard – stupid Kenny! Didn't hear the enemy come up behind him.

The woman repeats, 'I said, what are you doing?'

She seems angry, standing too close to him, trying to see what he's hiding, shouting at him. She has a helmet on. A weapon? No. She holds a bike. He starts to back away.

'Oh, God!' She sees the crumpled child behind him. 'What have you done to her? Get away from her!'

The woman seems upset. Furious. She pushes him aside with the bike wheel, then lets the cycle fall, clattering, making Kenny tense for an explosion, and she stoops to the girl.

'Oh my God! What's happened? Jesus! She's freezing! What ... what have you done to her!' Her voice hurts Kenny. She bends and sweeps the girl up into her arms. 'Oh God, oh God—' She starts walking quickly towards the road. Kenny clasps the hot chocolate between his paws and shuffles quickly after her. The woman turns and shouts again, 'Get away from her! Now!'

She tries to push at him with her shoulder as Kenny comes closer, but she's distracted as the girl tries to whisper something. She can't articulate what the bad man has done to her because her lips are numb with cold. The poor little thing.

'Oh God! What? What is it?' The woman brings her ear next to Tonya's lips, shielding her from the man with her body.

She can barely make out the words, but it sounds like, 'Leave him alone, you.'

Kim

She gets up because the baby's noises have turned to full-on grizzling.

She felt brighter for about five whole minutes this afternoon, but now, despite the naps, after a long day with Darryl tetchy and Nate teething, Kim realises how totally knackered she feels. She misses Steve when he's on night jobs. Neither of them are keen, but the boss has done him enough favours with all the time off and night jobs pay better.

She starts changing Nate by the glow of his little illuminated toadstool light.

Her phone buzzes and she knocks over the baby lotion, jumping, as she has done every single time there's been a call over the last eleven months and nine days. Darryl's eyes open, so in a minute she'll have to deal with him too.

With one palm on Nate's chest, she reaches out to grab the phone with her sticky hand and presses it against her ear with the usual mixture of irritation and fear, dread and hope.

Darryl's head jolts up from his pillow as he hears a sound like no other.

Tonya

Lots of faces. Flashing lights.
   Where is the man?
   Where is—

Jean Hall,
Family Liaison Officer

Jean is trying to stay calm, but she's nervous. This happens so rarely – it's like a miracle. And she needs to appear in control, but people are rushing around her and asking so many questions, although there's little information at this stage. It is her job to hold steady, to be there for Kim and Steve when they arrive, but she also wants to cry with relief.

Then she sees the girl.

Kenny

The police ask him lots of questions, but Kenny doesn't mind. No. They give him hot tea with sugar.

Kim

She walks along hospital corridors, led by Liaison Woman. She does not run. She hardly hurries, although her heart races ahead. She is suddenly, inexplicably terrified. What if it's not her? What if the police are mistaken and have got the wrong kid? Could she bear that?

What if she can't recognise Tonya after so long? She has been warned to expect her to look different to how she remembers her. What if they try and pass off a stranger's kid instead of hers? A changeling.

She has been told about a lot of things. There's been a lot of talking and she's taken in very little apart from the fact that they have her.

When she's led into the room, Liaison Woman's hand on her back, Kim is too shocked to speak.

Steve

Steve is on his way back from Essex, doing his best to keep to the speed limit, gripped by shaking bouts, although the heater's on full. His face is twitching, as if it's dancing.

But he dares not hope.

It's like that Christmas when he wanted the Nikes and he saw the box under their little plastic tree and his heart skipped and he opened the present and had to fake it because his dad had got those knock-offs and then he'd had to change into the old shoes as soon as he got to school so the lads didn't take the piss during football practice and he felt sad and disappointed and embarrassed and guilty every day for months, until his giant feet outgrew the crap trainers.

He can't let himself hope.

Kim

It is Tonya.

But the child in front of her doesn't look like Tonya. She doesn't look much like a child. She's wizened, like a little old crone – both much, much older and somehow more animal than when she disappeared, as if an evil fairy spirited her away to a different realm, sucked the light out of her, and now has given back what is left of the girl to the human world.

She's wrapped in silver foil, like a Christmas present.

Kim stalls near the bed, not quite able to reach out. Liaison Woman and a nurse also stand, still as statues. Like some spell has been cast on them all.

Kim squeezes to one side as another nurse comes in and unwraps an edge of the foil to clip something onto Tonya's finger and she catches a glimpse of her daughter's knee, huge against skeletal legs. One of those doll girls from the camps.

It hurts to keep looking at her.

Her girl's cheekbones jut out. Her hair a mat, threaded with twigs and leaves. Her eyes are huge, like a starving dog's, sunken into a filthy face. She doesn't see Kim, or if she does, doesn't acknowledge her. Then her eyelids slowly close.

She's attached to a drip and other machines. Kim daren't touch her in case she does some damage.

Liaison Woman stands close to her and says, 'She's going to be okay.' Because that's what you say. What you hope.

And Kim watches herself reach out, and when her fingers touch her daughter's skin, it's so cold she flinches away.

Then a doctor arrives and bustles round the bed and they're asked to step outside. She braces, as if to fight them – all the uniforms between her and her girl – but she finds she's too wobbly to refuse, or cause a scene, or even swear.

She collapses onto a plastic chair outside the room and Liaison Woman, Jean – she keeps telling Kim her name's Jean, but Kim can't hold on to it – pats her arm and they wait together for Steve. When someone else brings her a cup of tea from the machine, her hands shake too much to hold it, let alone drink it.

She asks Liaison Woman to call Ayesha for her – to check on the boys and to tell her the news.

She hears herself say the words, 'Tell her it is her.' And she still doesn't believe them.

Steve

When he walks into the hospital room, he roars.

It takes Liaison Woman, some police kid Kim's never seen before, a nurse and eventually an orderly to hold him back and stop him punching the wall as he screams what he'll do to the bastard who did this to his girl.

It takes Kim all her strength to persuade him to come and sit with her. Liaison Woman brings him some antiseptic wipes for his knuckles.

And another waiting game begins.

Much later, they will hear a list of conditions: hypothermia, dehydration, anaemia, malnutrition, vitamin D deficiency, bacterial infection—

But Tonya will live.

They will manage to save the child's toes and fingers.

They will find no evidence of sexual assault.

No one has much to say at this stage about how they might deal with the harm no one can see.

Ayesha

As Kim and Steve keep their vigil, Ayesha checks that Kim's next-door neighbour will take the dog and she brings Nate and Darryl back to her flat. Nate sleeps scrunched in his old carrycot in their room and Darryl slips in with Faisal.

Mo seems to realise something's going on and flails enthusiastically when he wakes up.

She continues looking after them for the next few days. It means she can't get to mosque, so she offers up her thanks on the prayer mat in the living room.

Khalid is tired after studying. He admires his wife's charity. Her generosity to these poor children reflects well on her and thus on him. But he also wants his tea.

Kim

The hospital's under siege from the press. An agency nurse has been suspended for taking a picture of Tonya on her phone, which appeared in a tabloid and paid for the nurse and her family to have a lovely holiday in Tenerife.

The stories suggest all sorts. With no facts, for the child hasn't spoken yet, the police can only say 'the investigation continues' A man was held for questioning. Then released. No arrests. Theories flourish.

Steve and Kim, whatever the police tell the pack of reporters outside, are not in the clear, and while not exactly implicated, they're not exactly exonerated either.

Absolution is withheld simply because they refuse interviews.

Police are forced to put out a statement saying the man questioned had no connection to the family.

Kim pleads with a nurse to let her wash Tonya's hair. It doesn't seem to matter to Tonya. She's still in a daze. In her own world.

The child doesn't resist when Kim leans her head back, or blink when she pours warm water over her scalp, careful not to get it into her eyes.

She does everything in slow motion, using gentle pressure with the pads of her fingers as she massages in the shampoo to work up the lather. She tenses for a shout or a scream. Tonya often used to fight when she had her hair washed, hated it being brushed. Kim and Steve joked that it'd be easier to give her dreadlocks.

Only now the girl is like a rag doll. Chillingly compliant.

Kim wraps her head in a towel and scoops her back into the wheelchair. It feels like she weighs as little as Darryl.

She carefully cuts out chunks of knotted hair because Tonya's neck looks too fragile to hold up against any attempt to comb it out. By the time she's done, little hair is left.

When she lifts her daughter back into bed, just for a moment, Tonya rests her head against her mother's belly.

Nurse Linette

She's only done two shifts and still gets lost when she tries to find the canteen.

She sees the child being wheeled along a corridor – oversized head on a stick body. She can't tell if it's a boy or a girl. One of the unlucky little ones eaten up by some horrible disease. For the umpteenth time that day, she wonders if this is the right job for her

Kim

She won't look at Kim or Steve properly, although she allows herself to be hugged, brittle as a husk. Her cold sores are clearing up. She wears a little woollen hat, like an old-fashioned tea cosy. Staff who don't watch the news mistake her for a patient from the kids' cancer ward.

She hasn't said a word since she arrived in the ambulance. She jams her thumb into her mouth as if to stop speech.

Experts, who have materialised from the ether, tell them to be patient.

There are two balloons tied to the end of her bed – one from Steve's workmates and the other from Aunty Heather. There's a card from her school, signed by her classmates, although the children have mostly forgotten her.

Tonya listlessly watches the balloon shaped like a cat bobbing about when people open the door.

Darryl and Nate are brought in to see her. Neither reacts. Tonya doesn't seem to notice them and Darryl ignores his sister right back and plays with the balloons. Only when Ayesha wheels Mo's giant mobility-chair thing into the hospital room the following day does Tonya ping to alertness.

She follows his entrance, watching her dad squash against the wall to let Mo's wheels get by.

And as she hears her friend's grunts as he bounces in excitement, she takes her thumb out of her mouth and croaks, 'Mo!' and a tiny smile splits her emaciated face.

Tonya

She don't look like my mum. Her hair's all dark and she's gone all thin. And he don't look like my dad coz he's fat and my dad's not.

They pretend like I've got two brothers but I ain't. The one they say is Darryl is too big. And I've never ever seen the other.

But Mo still likes me. And he's the same.

Jean Hall,
Family Liaison Officer

They can't get anything out of the tramp or the girl. Jean would never say this to her superiors, but all that really matters is that the kid's been found.

Although if they don't find the man who did this, he could do it to another child. So enquiries continue.

Park Hero

They do a make-over on the guy who found the little girl. When they shave off his beard and cut back his hair, stick him in a suit, the shocker is that he's suddenly a half-handsome hero.

The bigger shock is he's only fifty-odd.

They paraphrase his fragmented ramblings and his story goes viral. He's set up with a place in a hostel. He's offered a job. They'd have been better offering him some counselling.

Three and a half months later, he's back on the streets.

Kim

They're finally allowed to take her home – after Christmas, so the media miss out on that tempting 'festive feel-good peg'.

Darryl and Nate will stay at Ayesha's. Tonya won't see her brothers for a few days, until she settles in. If she ever does.

Kim's nervous there'll be press outside the flat, but when she and Tonya get out of the Uber and walk through the estate, there's no one around. Then she worries that seeing her old home might upset the kid. She's not sure why – the place is no palace, but it's not that bad.

When she opens the door and they see Sausage in the kitchen with Steve crouching next to her, Tonya's face transforms and she changes from a scrawny old woman to a child, like someone's reversed the bad spell. Steve holds the dog back for a second, then she launches out to meet the girl, wildly happy – a small furry thing hurtling round a skinny feral thing, and they go off like a confetti-filled firework with hair and slobber flying and squeaks and woofles detonating and 'Oh! Oh!' and other noises and it goes on for at least ten minutes.

The best ten minutes of Kim's life.

The dog sleeps on Tonya's bed – a sentinel. A cut-price guide leading the girl up from whatever underworld she's been held in, back to N7.

And from that day forward they come as a job lot.

*

Kim scoots across to Steve's side of the bed and lays her head against his shoulder and says, 'Thanks for getting Sausage. Genius. Fucking genius.'

But she can't sleep with the knowing – Tonya's here! Just next door! That closeness itches at her so intensely, in the end she gets up, leaving Steve to his peaceful snoring, taking the throw off the top of the duvet to wrap round her shoulders as she lays on the rug next to Tonya's bed, just so she can hear the rustles and breathing noises. Sausage hops down from the girl and curls up next to Kim.

In the coming days, she and Steve watch Tonya like she's some science experiment, monitoring her reaction to everything. Look – she's picked up her toy lion. Listen – what's she saying to the dog?

Kim wonders what will happen when they eventually leave the flat. She knows people will gawk. And they'll still judge her. This will always be her fault, which doesn't bother her so much. But it means Tonya will never be allowed an unobserved childhood.

Perhaps they'll move – give her a chance of a normal life. Leave the city. Leave the fucking country.

A weird life won't matter too much anyway. It's a life.

Amy Robinson-Smith, Senior Social Worker

'Have you noticed any changes in behaviour?' asks the woman with the artfully arranged grey hair.

'Not so much, no,' says Kim. Then she actually thinks about it and says, 'Well, she tidies up her room, now. Puts things away without me asking.'

'Anything else?' says the woman, smiling at her as if she knows her. Pen poised, like she's marking her answers.

Kim wracks her brains to come up with something. 'There was the papaya.' She's thinking out loud. 'When we went to Ayesha's. She told Darryl what it was.'

'And she'd not seen one before?'

'Well, obviously she's seen them at the market and that. But we don't have them.' She doesn't state the bleeding obvious – too expensive.

'Or avocados. She knew them as well.'

Kim wonders if the social worker is wearing that cardigan to appeal to kids. It looks like it's been coloured in by one – all the bright splashes of clashing colours enough to give you a migraine.

There's a pause, so she feels she has to add something.

'She doesn't fight with her brother much either. Darryl.'

'And she used to?'

Jesus! They're fishing for bad stuff.

'Not really. She's just . . . nicer to him now.'

She's sure the woman has no idea what she means. Kim herself can't put her finger on it. The closest she could describe it would be that Tonya's grown up. But she also sounds – what is it? More polite, perhaps. She asks for a toy rather than whacking Darryl and grabbing it.

'A development in her language and social skills then?'

'Yeah, if you like.'

The woman seems satisfied, thanks Kim for her time, and goes over to interrogate Tonya. She crouches down so her face is at the same level as the child's.

'My name is Amy,' says the social worker, smiling her professional smile.

Tonya ignores her and keeps flicking through her Peppa comic, one thumb firmly in her mouth. She has seen many new adults who talk to her in hushed voices and have her play with 'special' dolls and get her to draw pictures – she often draws Elsa, but Sausage has made a few appearances lately.

Her stories are full of witches and trees made of sweets and fire-breathing dragons and rivers of chocolate and they don't make much sense, but they always feature nice things to eat.

Tonya has put on a little weight and has developed both her frown and her attitude. She now looks a little less like a baby bird.

She has given scant information about The Woman. She draws her as a wicked witch with huge hands and long, scary nails.

Police will never discover The Woman is, in fact, beautiful. They will not learn of her distinguishing scars.

Empathising with the girl's understandable reticence in this early phase of establishing a bond, the social worker ploughs on, appealing to the child's innate curiosity. 'See my colleague over there? That's Isabel.'

Nothing.

Isabel is on a work experience placement. She smiles eagerly in case the child looks her way.

Attempting to build rapport, the social worker adds, 'You can call her Izzy.'

And in a flash, Tonya is on her feet, screaming into the social worker's startled face, 'No! You fuck off! My name is Tonya. My name is TONYA! Fuck off, you!'

Kim, sitting at the side of the room picking at her nicotine patch, can't help but smirk. She doesn't know why, but she senses that, somehow, this isn't a bad thing at all.

Tonya

I don't want to talk about The Woman. But they all keep asking me loads of questions.

Me and Sausage tell them to bugger off.

Sausage is the best thing. She licks Mo's hand and we both laugh.

Kim

At night, as Kim holds her daughter's body in the narrow bed, she feels it relax a little. And that's enough for her.

She leaves Sausage alongside her and pads back to Steve, climbing under the duvet and putting her cold feet on his calves.

When Tonya's asleep, Steve often goes into rages, detailing what he'd do given half an hour alone in a room with the cunt who stole his daughter. But then, he's also taken to shouting 'yippee-ki-yay, motherfucker' for no apparent reason, to no one in particular.

Kim wonders what sort of woman would take someone else's child. She has no idea, can't picture her at all. But whoever wanted Tonya didn't want her as much as Kim does.

She's surprised that her thoughts of revenge don't seem to matter any more.

She closes her eyes as Steve's snores vibrate through her. And Kim might dream of horrors again, but now, her nightmares don't matter, because when she wakes, her girl is back.

And the trolls, the press, the police – none of them matter any more either.

They can all just fuck. Right. Off.

Mummy

I have always liked it here. I walk along the beach with my favourite Etro kaftan billowing. Of course I wear a picture hat and factor 50.

Michael brought me here on our honeymoon. The first of many visits. Blissful memories.

Dizzy with love. Dizzy with pleasure.

We sipped our drinks under a velvet sky, soft breezes caressing my face, Michael's graceful long fingers caressing my shoulder. He should have been a pianist not a banker. It was an enchanted night full of magic. I truly believed all would be well.

I felt blessed.

Our friends, mostly his friends – no family invited to my wedding on my side, naturally – had chirped their congratulations. How lucky we were!

And we were. Only—

I have rented a holiday home. Private. Secluded from the crowds who have recently discovered this area. A small villa within a walled garden scented with lavender, garlanded with hibiscus. Flamingo-pink geraniums alight against the dusky cacti.

I am still not sure what to do about the London house. I can hardly sell it.

But the day is too glorious to worry about finances.

The only teensy fly in the ointment is my ankle, still throbbing after that nasty slip last night – wedged espadrilles proving a bad choice on the gravelled drive in hindsight. Or perhaps the nightcap was the mistake. And I had been considering walking the Camino de Santiago.

No matter.

A group of older boys are bellowing, posturing in the sea, hurling a ball between them. Several toddlers are paddling or being dangled above the gentle waves. A little one sits splashing, squealing with delight, her tiny peach-coloured sun hat matching the frilled bathing costume. Her daddy stands so his shadow shields her from the sun.

The beach tilts a moment.

I lurch into all I have lost; all I am not.

And I just can't—

Times passes. An absence of awareness.

The boy is pressing shells into the sand, making a pattern. An artistic child. His fingers swift, his focus intent. Perhaps six, seven?

His shock of black hair reminds me of you, dear Michael.

I perch on a wall a little way back from him and scan the chairs, towels and windbreaks nearby. I can't make out his people.

I am about to leave when he calls out. No response. He calls again, a plaintive note tugging me.

He elicits no reply.

My heart thuds.

He shouts louder this time.

And a woman shouts back sharply, dismissing him with a lazy flick of her wrist.

Now I see her: her head lolling to one side as she turns away again to doze, oblivious to dangers; skin crepey with sun damage; long, brittle blonde hair.

I peer closer. Smoker's lines around her mouth. A roll of fat oozing over the side of the bikini waistband.

Breathe.

For long minutes I watch the child's creation, mesmerised.

When he presses the last shell into the mandala, he looks around, proud of what he's made. But there is no one to see. No one to encourage, or praise him, or—

Stop.

You cannot think of that.

'*Te gustaria un helado?*'

I am beside him. I cannot recall walking over.

My accent is by no means perfect yet, although I have been here almost six months already. But he grins and nods at the word for ice cream.

His eyes are mischievous.

I rest my vintage sunglasses on top of my hat and hold out my hand. He springs up like a jack-in-the-box and does a little dance around me. So funny, bless him.

I reach to stroke his head. He does not flinch. He looks up and beams. His hair salty, tousled, rough to the touch.

It is only an ice cream. A treat.

Yet—

My hire car is parked just around the corner, in the same direction as the ice-cream shop. No cameras on this beach.

We slowly walk off the sand, the trusting little cherub holding my hand with his small, sandy fingers, swinging my arm with glee.

Unto us a boy is born!

Something that looks like a raven is eating roadkill on the beach road.

The sun sinks, piercing the clouds. Light hurtles across sea and sand, like it's escaping from an eclipse, glances off an open window on the front, igniting the child's face into a poem, and spikes into a van driver's sleepy eyes. The Woman stands transfixed, gazing down at the child, oblivious to everything else. Startled, the driver swerves. There's a soft thud. A scrape of metal against curb. A beat of silence.

A scream.

As a flock of seagulls scatters, the light burnishes a gathering crowd. A man barks instructions, another is jabbering into a phone.

There is very little blood.

The driver stumbles from his cab.

The child looks around, startled at the noise.

She is yanking on his arm now, trying to hasten away. Jumbles of words assault her. Her hat is at an unnatural angle, her eyes too wide, her face grimacing.

He tries to prise his fingers from her grip as she jerks him along. He shouts something incomprehensible. She notes alarmed expressions, hesitates.

She stalls.

Sweating.

A woman with two little girls is staring at her. Judging her parenting skills. He is pulling away from her, scowling now, on the brink of a tantrum.

She flings his arm away, pushing past the gawkers, leaving the boy marooned in the middle of the road.

A holidaymaker asks him, 'Is that your mummy?' He doesn't understand the words. Then he hears questions in his own language, and when the phrase is repeated, '*Es esta tu madre?*' He shakes his head.

No, she is not.

She is no one's mummy.

Someone sits the driver on the tarmac and applies pressure to the deep cut on his forehead. He is the focus now. No one watches the woman hurrying away, limping, muttering, fumbling car keys.

She checks the driver's mirror before pulling away, registering the look of shock on her face. Or, possibly, rage.

She does not look back.

A flustered blonde shouts, 'Juan!' and grabs the child's shoulders, shaking him, then scolding, then hugging, then weeping and repeating it all again. He starts to sob. Silly boy. Nothing to cry about now.

The carrion bird observes. A seagull soars upwards on the warmth of the day, leaving the scene behind.

The gold light blooms brighter.

Acknowledgements

The list of people I'm grateful for and beholden to in creating my first novel – Jeez Louise, so many.

All the teachers, tutors, authors and gurus, friends and chosen family; bullies, cheaters and haters (who made me a fighter, like Christina, although I recently gave up the arseless chaps); the bakers, Bakers, and candlestick makers (for cream cakes, dysfunction and facilitating English homework by candlelight during the Three-Day Week). All those I slept with along the way. You know who you are! (I hope you do. I've forgotten.)

Thanks to the many employers who made this possible with alternative income in the worlds of journalism, broadcasting, gyms, biscuit factories and, thanks to nepotism, window cleaning.

It took me so long to claim 'being a writer' I was thrilled to be accepted into the community. Thanks to my City University novel-writing MA cohort, my wicked agent Jane Gregory at DHA, awesome editor and Viper nest momma Miranda Jewess, and my first reader, my lovely jubbly hubby Geoff, who has to wade through tons of bollocks before it's whipped into shape. (He has to. It's in our marriage contract.)

And to my furry family. I may never be called Mummy, but those little buggers know I'm theirs. It's a fair trade – love and devotion (well, a furry bum on my lap when they've nothing better to do) for a lifetime supply of Dreamies.

A thousand blessings on the houses of anyone who buys or borrows this book. Vet bills are astonishing.

And, as they say on the radio, hello to anyone else who knows me.

10% of this book's royalties are being donated to Action for Children, a charity dedicated to protecting and supporting children and young people.

https://www.actionforchildren.org.uk/

About the Author

Tina Baker was brought up in a caravan after her mother, a fairground traveller, fell pregnant by a window cleaner. After leaving the bright lights of Coalville, she came to London and worked as a journalist and broadcaster for thirty years. She's probably best known as a television critic for the BBC and GMTV, and for winning *Celebrity Fit Club*. *Call Me Mummy* is Tina's first novel, partly inspired by her own unsuccessful attempts to have a child. Despite the grief and disappointment of that, she hasn't stolen one. So far. Her second novel, *Nasty Little Cuts*, will be published by Viper in 2022.

Find her on Twitter @TinaBakerBooks